The Northern Girl's Peril

a Victorian romance saga

HOPE DAWSON

Copyright © 2025, Hope Dawson
All rights reserved.

First published worldwide
on Amazon Kindle,
in March 2025.

This paperback edition first published
in Great Britain in 2025.

ISBN: 9798314098349

This novel is a work of fiction. The characters, names, places, events and incidents in it are entirely the work of the author's imagination or used in a fictitious manner. Any resemblance or similarity to actual persons, living or dead, events or places is entirely coincidental.

No part of this work may be reproduced, stored in a retrieval system, or transmitted, in any form or by any means, without the prior permission of the author and the publisher.

www.hopedawson.com

This story is part of

The Victorian Orphans Saga

Book 1
The Courtesan's Maid

Book 2
The Ragged Slum Princess

Book 3
An English Governess in Paris

Book 4
The Young Widow's Courage

Chapter One

"What?!" Ellie slammed her fork down on her plate, causing the clatter of silverware against fine china to ring out in the dining room. "A finishing school?" she bristled, her cheeks turning red with anger.

She glanced around the table, from her mother's stern face to Pierre's concerned expression, and finally to Charlotte, who sat quietly, her usual cheerful demeanour subdued.

"You can't be serious, Mama."

Madeleine sighed, laying her own knife and fork down with more decorum. "Ellie, dear, I assure you I'm quite serious. It's a wonderful opportunity for you to–"

"To what?" Ellie interrupted, her voice rising. "To be taught how to simper and curtsy like some brainless doll?"

Pierre cleared his throat, attempting to diffuse the tension. "I'm sure your mother has perfectly good reasons, Eleanor."

Ellie was having none of it however. She turned her fiery gaze on her stepfather. "Don't tell me you're in favour of this monstrous plan as well?"

"Eleanor," Madeleine warned. "Don't speak to Pierre in that tone. He's only trying to help."

"Some help he is," Ellie muttered under her breath. She crossed her arms tightly, her chin jutting out defiantly. "It's clear whose side he's on, isn't it?"

"Perhaps we ought to discuss this at a later time," Charlotte suggested meekly. "We wouldn't want this delicious food to grow cold now, would we?"

Ignoring her cousin, Madeleine pressed on, treading softly. "Darling, a finishing school will provide you with invaluable skills and connections. It's not just about etiquette, you know."

Ellie scoffed. "Oh, please. It's nothing but a gathering of pretentious, ill-mannered girls being groomed for marriage, like… like prized cattle."

Pressing her palms down on the table, Ellie's mother closed her eyes and took a deep breath in an attempt not to lose her patience.

"Cattle," Pierre chuckled. "Most amusing, yes. I wasn't aware you had such detailed knowledge of finishing schools, Eleanor."

"I don't need to attend one to know what they're like," Ellie grumbled. "It's all so horribly old-fashioned."

"You're being unreasonable, Ellie," her mother replied. "A finishing school will teach you how to be a proper lady."

The words hung in the air for a moment before Ellie's eyes widened in hurt and disbelief. "A proper lady?" she repeated. "Are you saying I'm not a proper lady now, Mama?"

"Eleanor, *ma petite*." Pierre leaned forward, his voice calm. "That's not what your mother meant at all. We know you're a lovely young woman. But there's always room for growth, *non*?"

"Oh, of course," Ellie replied sarcastically. "Because learning how to arrange flowers and pour tea without spilling a drop is clearly essential to my personal growth. How have I ever managed to survive without such vital skills?"

"Your sharp wit is just one of the many things I like about you," Pierre smiled. "But you should consider young Mr Wainwright as well."

"Stuart?" Her ears pricked up and she sat up straight at the mention of the young man whom she had been smitten with for several years now. "What about him?"

"Wouldn't he appreciate a wife who can manage a household with grace?" Pierre asked. "Someone who can host dinner parties that impress his friends and colleagues?"

Ellie rolled her eyes. "This is Sheffield, Pierre. Not Mayfair. And Stuart isn't some pompous blowhard throwing fancy soirées at his country estate. He's an engineer at Mama's factory."

Madeleine seized the opening. "Stuart may be an engineer now, darling. But he's incredibly talented. I predict he'll go far. Given enough time, he'll become an important figure in the company one day, I'm sure. Perhaps even a partner."

"Exactly," Pierre nodded. "And when that day comes, he'll need a wife who can help him navigate those higher social circles."

Ellie's mouth opened and closed, searching for a rebuttal. "Stuart isn't like that," she said finally. "He doesn't care about any of that frivolous nonsense."

"It's not frivolous, Ellie," Madeleine insisted. "It's an important part of business and society. You'll understand once you–"

"No," Ellie slammed her hands on the table, making the cutlery jump. "You don't understand. Neither of you do."

Before anyone could respond, Ellie shoved her chair back with a screech. She stood, trembling with frustration, tears threatening to spill from her eyes.

"I won't go," she declared. "You can't make me."

"Eleanor, darling–," her mother began.

But Ellie couldn't bear to hear another word. She whirled around and stormed out of the dining room. Ignoring her family's pleading calls to come back, she took the stairs two steps at a time and fled to her bedroom.

After slamming the door shut, she leaned against it with her back as she fought to catch her breath.

How could they do this to her? Didn't they see how perfect her life was here? With Stuart, and with everyone else she knew and loved? How dare they make decisions about her life without even considering her feelings?

Exhausted by her own emotions, Ellie flung herself onto the bed. Tears came streaming down her cheeks as she hugged her pillow tightly. She felt so alone, so misunderstood.

Was this what it meant to become a grown woman? Having your dreams and wishes disregarded by those who were supposed to love you?

The gentle knock at the door barely registered through her misery. "Ellie, dearest?" Charlotte's soft voice called. "May I come in?"

When Ellie didn't respond, the door creaked open cautiously. The bed dipped as Charlotte sat down beside her, a comforting hand coming to rest on Ellie's back.

"I thought I'd come up to see how you were," Charlotte whispered. "You took the news much worse than I had anticipated."

Ellie rolled over, her face tear-stained and flushed. "You knew about this, too?"

"Your mother told me, yes."

"What is this? A family-wide conspiracy? Is everyone that eager to get rid of me then?"

"That's not fair, duck. Your mother loves you dearly. We all do. And you know it."

"But then why is she doing this? Why is she sending me away?"

Charlotte smoothed Ellie's hair back from her forehead. "Because she wants what's best for you, love. Just as she always has."

Ellie sniffled, avoiding Charlotte's gaze.

"What's really troubling you, duck?" Charlotte prodded gently. "Is it just the thought of finishing school?"

"N–not really." Ellie hesitated and her lower lip trembled. "I'm... I'm afraid, Charlotte. I've never been away from home before. Not like this."

"Ah, there it is," Charlotte smiled. She gathered Ellie into her arms, just as she used to do when Ellie was little.

"It's only natural to be nervous, love," she went on. "This reminds me of our first trip to the seaside when you were a wee little girl. Do you recall how frightened you were of the waves?"

"I was?" Ellie frowned, trying to remember.

"Oh yes," Charlotte chuckled. "You wouldn't go near the water for the first two days. You were convinced the waves would sweep you away."

"What changed?"

"We coaxed you to just dip your toes in. You were so nervous, but oh so brave. And once you felt that cool water on your feet, your eyes lit up with delight."

A smile appeared on Ellie's face. "I remember loving the feel of the sand between my toes as well."

"So you did," Charlotte nodded. "By the end of the holiday, we could hardly get you out of the water. You were splashing about like a little fish, laughing and having the time of your life."

Charlotte gave Ellie a gentle squeeze. "You see, dear, sometimes the things that frighten us the most end up bringing us the greatest joy. This finishing school might seem scary now, but who knows what wonderful experiences await you there?"

Ellie sighed, pulling away slightly to look up at Charlotte. "But why can't I just stay here with you? You've always been the perfect nurse and governess. What could I possibly learn at a finishing school that you can't teach me?"

"Oh, my sweet girl," Charlotte laughed quietly. "An old spinster like me is hardly the right person to teach you how to be a good wife and mistress of the house."

"That's not true," Ellie protested. "You've been running our household for years. And rather brilliantly too, I might add."

"That's very kind of you to say, duck. But while I may know a thing or two about managing a household, there's so much more for you to learn. It's important that you broaden your horizons. You should meet new people, and experience different ways of doing things."

"I suppose," Ellie said reluctantly.

"Besides, it's only for a year. A year that will fly by before you know it. And just think of all the exciting things you'll see and do in London. The museums, the parks, places like Westminster Abbey and the Tower. Oh, and let's not forget the shops." Her eyes twinkled. "It will be quite the adventure, you'll see."

"I guess it does sound rather thrilling when you put it that way," Ellie admitted, a small smile tugging at her lips.

"That's the spirit, duck. And remember, home will always be here waiting for you."

"Stuart as well, you think?" Ellie asked, a slight blush colouring her cheeks. "He won't forget me, will he?"

"My dear girl, how could he possibly? That young man's devotion to you is as steady as the

North Star. A mere year apart won't dim it in the slightest."

Ellie's cheeks flushed an even deeper shade of pink. But she knew Charlotte was right.

"Now, shall we go downstairs again and have a nice cup of tea?" Charlotte smiled. "I saw Mrs Dobbs putting the finishing touches to a scrumptious Victoria sponge earlier today."

Ellie nodded, allowing Charlotte to help her get off the bed. As they left the room, her heart felt lighter already. Perhaps this finishing school wouldn't be so terrible after all.

Chapter Two

Two weeks later, Ellie stood before her mirror, fussing with the lace collar of her pale blue dress. Her fingers trembled slightly as she adjusted the fabric, smoothing out imaginary wrinkles.

"You look lovely, dear," Charlotte said, watching from her perch on the edge of Ellie's bed. "Although a wonderful girl like you would probably look just as fetching if you wore an old potato sack."

"Oh, Charlotte, don't tease," Ellie begged as she turned away from the mirror. "This is important."

"And why is that?" Charlotte's eyes continued to twinkle with amusement. "It's only a walk with Mr Wainwright, after all. And not the first one either. We've been on so many strolls with that young man, I must have worn through two pairs of boots already."

"But this isn't just any walk," Ellie protested. "This one is goodbye."

The word hung heavy in the air. Charlotte's smile faded, replaced by a look of gentle understanding. "Come here, duck," she said, patting the space beside her on the bed.

Ellie crossed the room and sank down next to her mother's cousin. Charlotte wrapped an arm around her shoulders, drawing her close.

"They say absence makes the heart grow fonder," Charlotte said. "But I guess that's not much comfort to you right now, is it?"

Ellie shook her head.

"What if he forgets me, Charlotte? What if I go away to this horrible finishing school and... Stuart falls in love with someone else?"

"Nonsense. That young man positively adores you. Being apart for a while won't change that."

"But what if it does?" Ellie insisted. "What if I come back and everything's different?"

Charlotte took Ellie's hands in her own, her touch warm and comforting. "My dear girl, if your bond with Stuart is as strong as I believe it to be, then distance will only make it stronger."

Ellie managed a weak smile. "Do you really think so?"

"An old spinster I may be, but I'm no stranger to matters of the heart," Charlotte chuckled. "Now, chin up. And then put your hat on. We don't want to keep Mr Wainwright waiting, do we?"

With a deep breath, Ellie stood and returned to the mirror. She carefully pinned her hat in place, adjusting the angle until it sat just right.

"There," Charlotte said, coming to stand behind her. "Perfect. Looking like that, Stuart won't be able to get you out of his mind, even if he tried."

Ellie smiled. She did look rather pretty, she thought.

"Right, off we go then," Charlotte said after giving Ellie's shoulder an affectionate squeeze. "And remember, I'll be right behind you the whole time. Although I doubt that either of you will even notice I'm there."

They shared an innocent giggle and then made their way outside, where their coachman Bill was waiting for them by the side of the family carriage.

The ride to the park was a short one, but Ellie's nerves made it feel like an eternity. Fortunately, deliverance came quickly when Bill halted the carriage at the park entrance and Ellie spotted Stuart standing by the iron gate.

"He's here already," she babbled breathlessly at Charlotte. "And he's brought flowers. Did you see how dapper he looks?"

"Yes, I do see, duck." Charlotte chuckled and gave Ellie a gentle nudge. "Now, why don't you go greet the poor lad before he and those beautiful flowers of his begin to wilt?"

Ellie stumbled slightly as she descended from the carriage, her cheeks flushing red. Stuart stepped forward, a bouquet of wildflowers clutched in his hand.

"Good afternoon, Eleanor," he said. "You look– That is... I hope you're well."

"Thank you, Stuart," she replied, shyly casting down her eyes. "I'm quite well. And you're very kind to bring flowers."

Their hands brushed as Stuart passed her the bouquet, causing both of them to start and blush even deeper.

"Shall we?" Stuart gestured towards the path, offering his arm.

Ellie nodded, carefully looping her arm through his. As they began to walk, a heavy silence fell between them. The gravel crunched beneath their feet, punctuating the quiet afternoon.

Behind them, Charlotte followed at a discreet distance, her presence barely noticeable as the young couple grappled with the weight of their impending separation.

Ellie's eyes darted nervously to Stuart's face, then away again. There were so many things she longed to say. Fears and doubts that she wanted to pour out, instead of letting them press so heavily on her heart. But her head seemed incapable of coming up with the right words.

Stuart cleared his throat. "It's, umm... It's a fine day for a walk, isn't it?"

"Oh. Yes, quite," she replied, wincing at the clumsiness of their exchange.

This wasn't at all how she had imagined their farewell. She frowned and then glanced at Stuart again, trying to read his face. Why was he so quiet? Was he just as nervous as she felt?

Or was he looking for a way to end things now that she was going away? Maybe he was glad she was leaving?

No, she told herself firmly. Stuart wasn't like that. He was kind, honest and devoted.

But as they continued their stroll, the awkward silence stretched on, broken only by the sound of their footsteps on the path.

Finally, unable to bear it any longer, Ellie spoke up. "Stuart, you're awfully quiet today. Is something wrong?"

He blinked, as if startled from a daydream. "Oh no, not at all," he said quickly. "I was just thinking about the time we first met. Do you remember that day?"

"How could I ever forget? It was when that steam engine exploded in the factory, just as Mama was going to sign an agreement with the new investors."

What an odd topic for a conversation, she thought. *But still, better than nothing, I suppose.*

"You were so brave that day," he said. "The way you volunteered to help Mrs Pemberton-Thorpe with treating the wounded."

"I was terrified," Ellie admitted. "But I knew I had to do something to help."

"And what a cracking job you did. Mine was probably the first wound you'd ever cleaned and dressed in your whole life."

"Goodness, yes. I was worried I'd hurt you. My hands were trembling. And there was so much blood."

"But you didn't waver. If anyone had told me that you were an experienced nurse, I would have believed them."

"I was simply following Mrs Pemberton-Thorpe's instructions."

"You did much more than that," Stuart replied. "You put your heart and soul into it, too. Looking back, I think that's the moment I knew."

"Knew what?"

He stopped and half-turned to gaze into her eyes. "That you were special," he said softly.

Ellie felt a blush creeping up her cheeks. "Oh, I don't know about that," she replied modestly. She glanced over her shoulder at Charlotte. But their chaperone had paused as well and was now pretending to look at a cluster of trees somewhere in the distance.

"Stuart, I'm frightened," Ellie blurted out. "I'm frightened about going to this finishing school in London."

"Why, my love?"

"For various reasons. What if I hate it there? I'll be so far away from home. And for so long."

He took her hands in his and smiled at her. "We'll write to each other often, I promise. And your friend Phoebe is going as well, isn't she? So you won't be alone."

"Yes, but..." She dropped her gaze and stared at the ground. "There's something else I'm worried about."

She looked up again, straight into those tender eyes of his. "I'm worried about us, Stuart. Will this separation change things between us?"

"Eleanor," he said, his tone serious. "My feelings for you are not some passing fancy. Why, they are as solid and dependable as... as the engines we build at the factory."

She laughed. "Spoken like a true engineer."

"I'm sorry," he blushed. "That wasn't the most romantic comparison, I know. But I hope you understand my meaning."

"I do," she smiled. "And I feel the same way. Although sometimes part of me wonders..."

"What, my love? If we're going to be apart for so long, let's not have any more fears or doubts between us."

"Stuart, you're not courting me simply because my mother owns the factory, are you? In hopes of securing a promotion or advancing your career?"

"Heavens, no," he gasped, taking a half step back in shock. "Ellie, how could you even think such a thing?"

"Just a foolish notion of mine," she said quickly, already regretting her words.

"If that's truly what you believe, Ellie, then I'll hand in my resignation first thing tomorrow morning. And I'll look for employment elsewhere. I'd rather give up my position than have you doubt the sincerity of my affections."

"Oh Stuart, no! Please don't do that." She closed the distance between them and grabbed his hands. "Mama would never forgive me if you resigned because of me."

"Is everything all right over there?" Charlotte's voice suddenly rang out, startling them both.

Ellie and Stuart sprang apart, their hands dropping to their sides. "Yes, quite all right," Ellie answered, her voice a touch too high.

"I just wanted to let you know," Charlotte said as she came ambling over with a knowing smile on her face, "I've been studying all these trees and shrubs with great interest. But now I'm getting rather cold standing still. So what do you say we go for a slice of cake and a nice cup of tea instead? My treat, of course."

"That sounds lovely, Miss Kimble" Stuart replied. "Thank you."

"Yes, thank you, Charlotte," Ellie added, grateful for the distraction.

"Before we leave though," Stuart said while patting his pocket, "I have something for you,

Ellie." He pulled out a small velvet box and held it out to her. "A little something to remember me by while you're away."

Ellie's eyes widened as she opened the box: inside lay a delicate silver locket. Its shiny surface was etched with intricate swirls and flowers.

"Oh, Stuart," she breathed. "It's beautiful."

"Open it," he urged her gently.

Carefully, she pried open the locket to find a tiny picture of Stuart on one side, and on the other, an inscription: *'My heart is yours, always'*.

Ellie looked up at him, close to tears. "Thank you," she whispered. "I shall treasure it forever."

Taking the locket from her hands, he lovingly fastened it around her neck. As he did so, he leaned in close.

"Let this be a promise, Ellie," he murmured. "A promise that no matter the distance between us, my heart belongs to you."

"And mine to you, Stuart," she said, her voice cracking slightly. "I'm going to miss you terribly."

He raised a hand to cup Ellie's cheek, tenderly brushing away a tear that had run down her face. Their eyes locked.

"I wish–" she began. But the words escaped her.

"I know," he replied. "I wish too."

His face was so close to hers. How easy it would be to bridge that short distance, she thought, and then–

"Time for cake and tea, I do think," Charlotte interrupted strategically.

Blushing furiously, Ellie and Stuart pulled back from each other.

"Follow me, you lovebirds," Charlotte laughed as she led the way. "I happen to know there's a splendid tea room at the edge of this park."

The earlier tension between them had melted away as they walked together. Moments later, they were settled inside the cosy tea room, surrounded by the sounds of polite chatter and the smell of delicious cake.

Ellie savoured every moment, every stolen glance, and every silent smile she and Stuart exchanged.

All too soon though, it was time to go.

Time to say their farewells.

Outside, Stuart first helped Charlotte into the waiting carriage. Then it was Ellie's turn. Their hands lingered together for a moment, neither wanting to let go.

"Goodbye, Ellie," he said, his eyes never leaving her face.

"Goodbye, Stuart."

Quickly, she pressed a chaste kiss to his cheek before hurrying into the carriage. Charlotte pretended not to have seen the little parting gift.

As their carriage set off, Ellie looked back one last time. She saw Stuart standing on the pavement, waving at her with one hand while touching his cheek with the other.

Ellie's fingers brushed against her lips, still tingling from that fleeting farewell, then drifted down to clasp the locket resting close to her heart.

She smiled as she remembered the inscription.

'My heart is yours, always'.

Chapter Three

"This way," Pierre called over his shoulder, clearing a path through the crowd at the busy railway station. Walking arm in arm, Ellie and her mother followed him closely. Behind them, Charlotte kept dabbing at her eyes with a handkerchief.

"Your train is on platform number 3," Pierre said as he gestured towards one of the platforms, where a gleaming locomotive waited, venting steam and belching smoke.

Ellie stared with wide open eyes at the swirling sea of people around them. Her heart seemed to thump more heavily with each step that brought them closer to her train.

This was it. The moment she had been dreading.

"Oh, my darling girl," Madeleine said, squeezing Ellie's arm. "Are you ready for your grand adventure?"

"To be perfectly honest, my heart says no. But my head knows I must."

Pierre set down Ellie's travel bag and turned to face them, pride shining in his eyes. "You'll do splendidly, *ma petite*. I have no doubt."

"Thank you," Ellie said, forcing a small smile onto her lips. She wished she shared his confidence. But she could barely manage to keep her legs from trembling.

A loud sob from behind made them all turn. Charlotte stood there, handkerchief pressed to her mouth, tears streaming down her cheeks.

"Oh, Ellie," she wailed, throwing her arms around the girl. "How I'll miss you, my dear."

Ellie rubbed Charlotte's back, feeling her own eyes well up. "I'll miss you too, Charlotte. So very, very much."

"Lottie," Madeleine said gently, prying her cousin away. "You'll get Ellie all wrinkled before she even boards the train."

Charlotte sniffled, nodding as she stepped back. "You're right. Forgive me. I'm being silly."

A shrill whistle pierced the air.

"That's the five-minute warning," Pierre said, checking his pocket watch.

Madeleine cupped her daughter's face in her hands. "We've given you roots, my precious darling," she said. "Now it's time for you to grow and spread your wings."

Ellie nodded, unable to speak because of the lump in her throat. She hugged her mother fiercely, then turned to embrace Charlotte one last time.

"Be brave, duck," Charlotte said. "And do let me know what the cakes in London are like."

With a watery chuckle, Ellie pulled away. She looked at the train, then back at her family. She still couldn't quite get her mind around it: she wouldn't be able to see their faces or hear their voices for a whole year. Despite their occasional differences and squabbles, Ellie wondered if perhaps this was the part that she found the most upsetting.

You don't know what you've got until it's gone, she thought.

"There you all are," a powerful female voice rang out above the din of the station.

They turned to see Mrs Pemberton-Thorpe striding towards them, her radiant silver hair peeking out from underneath a fashionable hat. Right behind her, Ellie's best friend Phoebe was scurrying to keep up with her great-aunt's long strides.

"I was beginning to think we'd missed you entirely," the sturdy widow said.

"Constance, how lovely to see you," Madeleine greeted her friend warmly.

Ellie's eyes met Phoebe's, and she was surprised to see her friend looking even more anxious than she felt. Phoebe's hands twisted the handle of her travel bag, her face pale beneath her colourful bonnet.

"Well, girls. What's this?" Mrs Pemberton-Thorpe asked, eyeing them both critically. "You look as though you're about to face a firing squad. It's merely a train ride to London, you know."

"It's not the train journey that worries me, Aunt Constance," Phoebe protested weakly. "It's the idea of being away from home for so long."

"The youth of today," Mrs Pemberton-Thorpe said before clucking her tongue. "I spent years living in India when my Hubert was stationed there. Now that was a challenge, let me tell you."

"Yes, Aunt Constance," Phoebe sighed, rolling her eyes. "We've heard those stories before."

"Snakes in the garden," Mrs Pemberton-Thorpe continued, ignoring her grand-niece, "monsoon rains of biblical proportions, and all manner of nasty insects whose sting could leave you delirious with fever for days on end. Going to London for a year? That's a jolly jaunt by comparison."

Another whistle blew, more insistent this time.

"Time to board, girls," Pierre said.

A flurry of final hugs and kisses ensued. Ellie embraced her mother tightly, breathing in the familiar scent of lavender. Charlotte dabbed at fresh tears, and even Pierre's eyes looked suspiciously moist as he patted Ellie's shoulder.

"Do the North proud, girls," Mrs Pemberton-Thorpe said as Ellie and Phoebe climbed aboard. "And for heaven's sake, try to have a bit of fun as well."

Ellie and Phoebe found their compartment and opened the window to wave at their families. As the train began to move, the platform slowly disappeared from view, taking with it the familiar faces of home.

The girls flopped down in their seats, and Ellie sighed. With nothing else to do, she reached for her bag and pulled out a small package wrapped in brown paper.

"Charlotte packed us some refreshments," she said, untying the piece of string around the parcel. Inside, she found a selection of treats: a few slices of gingerbread cake, some shortbread biscuits, a small bag of sweetened almonds, and two apples.

"How thoughtful," Phoebe smiled, accepting a biscuit. "Your mother's cousin is so considerate."

Ellie chuckled. "Dear Charlotte wouldn't dream of sending anyone off on a trip without a snack."

She took a few almonds and started munching on them without much enthusiasm. She wasn't particularly hungry, but focusing on the food would stop her from dwelling on what lay ahead. Or so she hoped.

"I can't believe Mama actually went through with this," she grumbled. "A finishing school, of all things. As if I'm some sort of rowdy little child that needs taming."

"At least your family came to see you off," Phoebe replied with a sad frown. "My parents couldn't even be bothered. Father's too busy with that wretched old house he's just bought in the countryside."

"Oh, Phoebe, I'm sorry. I didn't mean—"

"It's all right," Phoebe shrugged, attempting a smile. "I'm glad Aunt Constance was there. I don't know what I'd do without her."

"Your great-aunt is quite... formidable," Ellie chuckled.

"That's one word for her," Phoebe giggled, relaxing a bit. "What do you suppose this school will be like?"

"Dreadful, I expect. Full of stupid girls, and strict matrons who'll rap our knuckles if we so much as breathe wrong."

"Oh, surely it won't be that bad," Phoebe said, though she didn't sound entirely convinced. "Perhaps the teachers will be kind. And we might find some new friends."

"Friends?" Ellie scoffed. "More like a flock of chattering magpies, I'll wager. All obsessed with frills and lace and catching wealthy husbands."

Phoebe bit her lip. "Do you really think so? I was rather hoping—"

"I wouldn't get my hopes up if I were you. Less risk of being disappointed that way."

"Oh," Phoebe merely said, with an unhappy pout to her lower lip. "Catching a wealthy husband would have been nice though.

"Why, Phoebe Greenwood," Ellie teased. "I didn't know you were that shallow."

"Well, it's all right for you, Miss Dubois," Phoebe giggled. "You've got Stuart Wainwright to look forward to. Last thing I heard, Father was scheming to marry me off to that dreadful Edmund Sinclair."

"Oh, Phoebe, that'd be awful," Ellie gasped, feeling instantly sorry for her friend. "Listen, I'm sure that not everything about this school will be terrible. And no matter how it turns out, we'll face it together, won't we?"

"Promise?" Phoebe asked, looking at her with sad and fearful eyes.

"Cross my heart," Ellie replied, reaching out to squeeze her friend's hand. "We'll show those birdbrained ninnies what Sheffield girls are made of."

When Phoebe smiled, Ellie offered her another biscuit. They spent the rest of their journey chatting about happier things and gazing out the window at the changing landscapes.

Many hours later, the train finally pulled into St Pancras Station in London. Exhausted and rumpled, the two girls pressed through the bustling crowd to make their way outside, where they needed to find a hansom cab that would take them to the school.

After several increasingly brash attempts, Ellie managed to get a driver's attention. She gave the man the school's address and then they settled on the well-worn seat.

"Traffic in London is mad," Phoebe winced anxiously as the carriage navigated the busy city streets. She took hold of Ellie's hand and didn't let go until the driver stopped in front of an imposing Georgian townhouse.

"Here we are, my lovelies," the man called out from his high seat at the back of the carriage. "The Bloomsbury Academy for the Refined Education of Young Ladies, as it's called."

"Refined, indeed," Ellie snorted. "What a ridiculous name. 'Finishing School for Cocky Little Upstarts' would have been too honest, I suppose."

Phoebe nudged her, trying to suppress a giggle. "Hush, Ellie. We've only just arrived."

They paid the driver and stepped out of the hansom. As soon as they set foot inside the foyer of the house, scenes of utter chaos greeted them.

Girls of all ages pushed and jostled, filling the air with a cacophony of excited chatter. Luggage was piled everywhere, and a maid was attempting to navigate through the crowd with a precarious stack of hat boxes.

In one corner, a trio of older girls held court, eyeing every new arrival with a mixture of curiosity and disdain. When they caught sight of Ellie and Phoebe, the dark-haired girl in the middle whispered something to her friends, who duly sniggered.

A tall, angular woman came into the foyer, shouting instructions and directing the flood of girls with military precision.

"Newcomers, this way," she commanded. "Returning senior students, proceed to the sitting room at the rear, please."

Still standing on the doorstep, Ellie and Phoebe exchanged glances before being swept along in a fresh tide of girls that came surging through the front door.

"Discipline, ladies. Discipline," the woman ordered. "And mind where you put those trunks." Her sharp eyes landed on Ellie and Phoebe. "Ah, new blood. Names?"

"Eleanor Dubois and Phoebe Greenwood, ma'am," Ellie replied politely.

"The Northern girls," the woman nodded. "I am Mrs Bennett, owner and headmistress of this fine institute."

"How do you do, Mrs Bennett," Ellie and Phoebe said in perfect unison.

Mrs Bennett straightened her back even further, to better look down her nose at them.

"Welcome to the Bloomsbury Academy. Let me warn you straight away that we have exacting standards here," she began. "Our rules are strict, our expectations high. Our reputation is built on producing refined, marriageable young women. And I will not have it tarnished by provincial manners or uncouth behaviour."

She paused briefly – for dramatic effect, no doubt, Ellie thought – and then continued with her lecture.

"You will attend to your studies with diligence, and you are expected to conduct yourselves with the utmost decorum at all times. And never, under any circumstances, will you engage in unladylike pursuits or conversations. Failure to abide by these rules will not be tolerated. Is that clear?"

Ellie bit back a snarky response, already disliking Mrs Bennett's haughty demeanour. But Phoebe simply nodded and replied, "Perfectly clear, ma'am."

"Third floor, room twelve," Mrs Bennett said, consulting a ledger. "Off you go."

The two girls squeezed through the crowded foyer and up the stairs, dodging elbows and travel bags. The hallways were a sea of pastel dresses and high-pitched voices.

"Did you see her hat?"

"I heard they make you eat all your vegetables here."

"Do you think we'll have dancing lessons?"

Finally reaching their room, Ellie and Phoebe stumbled inside, shutting the door on the chaos. The small chamber held two narrow beds, a shared desk, and a wardrobe that had seen better days.

Ellie dropped her bag and flung herself onto the nearest bed, wincing at its unyielding surface. She stared at the ceiling, feeling the weight of homesickness settle over her like a heavy blanket.

"A whole year," she groaned. "A whole year in this madhouse."

Taking hold of her silver locket, she rubbed a finger over the swirls and flowers etched into its surface. With her eyes closed, she pressed the cool silver to her lips while she imagined Stuart's warm smile.

"Give me strength," she murmured.

Chapter Four

Ellie stifled a yawn as she pushed her half-eaten porridge around in her bowl. The breakfast room buzzed with the chatter of the other girls, their shrill laughter and gossip stabbing at Ellie's throbbing head like tiny needles.

"Did you sleep at all?" Phoebe asked, looking concerned.

Ellie shook her head. "Barely. My bed feels like it's stuffed with rocks."

"Ladies," Mrs Bennett's crisp voice rang out over the long breakfast table. "If you would all proceed to the sitting room for your first class, please. I shall join you there shortly."

A flurry of movement ensued as chairs scraped against the floor and girls rose, talking excitedly. Ellie and Phoebe followed the crowd out of the breakfast room and down the hallway.

When they entered the sitting room, the interior seemed to assault Ellie's tired eyes. Plush sofas and ornate chairs, upholstered in clashing patterns, were arranged in a semicircle. Sunlight streamed through tall windows, illuminating gaudy wallpaper and an excess of gilt-framed portraits. The room was trying hard to impress its visitors... and failing spectacularly at it.

Ellie and Phoebe claimed spots on one of the sofas, sinking into the soft cushions. Phoebe's eyes darted left and right, taking in every detail.

"This isn't too bad, is it?" she said to Ellie. "I was expecting hard wooden desks and blackboards, but this is... Well, it's much lovelier than a classroom anyway. Perhaps finishing school won't be so terrible after all?"

"We'll see," Ellie shrugged.

A girl with mousy brown hair and a nervous air about her perched on the edge of the sofa beside them. She latched onto Phoebe's remark like a lifeline.

"Oh, I know exactly what you mean," the girl prattled. "I was ever so anxious about coming here. Mama said it would be good for me, but I was terrified. Truly I was. But now that I'm here, well, it doesn't seem quite so dreadful, does it?"

The words tumbled out in a rush, as the girl barely paused for breath. Ellie and Phoebe blinked, momentarily stunned by the torrent of speech.

"I'm Agnes, by the way," the girl continued. "From Sutton. Where are you two from?"

"Sheffield," Ellie replied.

A sharp, mocking laugh sounded from behind them. "Northern girls, eh?"

Ellie's head snapped round. She recognised the dark-haired girl from the foyer. Lounging in an armchair with her two friends by her side, a smirk played on the girl's lips.

"It's a small miracle you managed to find your way to the railway station," the girl said. "Or did someone help you to read the signs?"

Ellie opened her mouth to reply, but at that moment, the door swung open and Mrs Bennett swept into the room.

"That's Lydia Price," Agnes whispered to Ellie and Phoebe. "You'll want to be careful with her."

Standing at the front of the room, Mrs Bennett clapped her hands to get everyone's attention.

"Ladies, welcome to your first lesson on etiquette," she announced most formally. "Over the course of this year, we shall mould you into proper young women, fit for society's most discerning circles."

Ellie fought the urge to roll her eyes. This was exactly the sort of pompous nonsense she had been dreading.

"We shall begin with how to talk," Mrs Bennett said. "Proper forms of address and introductions are crucial. One must never assume familiarity where it hasn't been granted."

"Mrs Bennett?" Lydia asked.

"Yes, Miss Price?"

"Will those lessons include guidance on correct enunciation as well, please?"

"But of course, Miss Price."

"Oh dear," Lydia said with more than a hint of sarcasm. "That might present a challenge to one or two people in this room then."

Her friends let out a mean little snigger. Ellie knew Lydia's remark had been directed at her and Phoebe, but she kept her eyes forward.

Mrs Bennett decided to ignore the matter. "The art of conversation is a vital one," she said. "A lady must be well-versed in suitable topics. Politics and business for instance are best left to the gentlemen."

A derisive snort escaped Ellie before she could stop it. Mrs Bennett's gaze snapped to her. "Do you find something amusing, Miss Dubois?"

"No, Mrs Bennett," Ellie replied. "My apologies, ma'am."

As the academy's headmistress turned away, Ellie caught the worried look on Phoebe's face.

"Equally important for a lady is deportment," Mrs Bennett declared. "How one holds oneself speaks volumes. We'll practise correct posture for walking, sitting, and standing."

Ellie sighed quietly. Hours of practising how to sit, with a back so straight and stiff it hurt, no doubt. What a thrilling prospect, she thought.

"Of course, a lady must be prepared for life's major occasions," Mrs Bennett went on. "We'll discuss the intricacies of mourning etiquette and appropriate behaviour during times of loss."

The room grew sombre for a moment before Mrs Bennett added, "And naturally, we'll also cover the delicate matter of courtship and engagement."

A wave of giggles swept through the class. Girls grasped each other's arms and erupted into nervous cackling.

Heaven help me, Ellie grumbled inwardly.

Mrs Bennett smiled patiently until the excitement had died down. "Day-to-day life requires its own set of skills," she then continued. "Household management and directing servants are essential for any future mistress of a home. Just remember, the lower classes are not your friends. They exist to serve."

Ellie couldn't suppress a groan. Mama and Charlotte had always taught her that just because someone was a servant, this didn't give their master or mistress the right to be mean or cruel to them.

"Miss Dubois," Mrs Bennett said, fixing Ellie with an ice cold stare. "If our curriculum doesn't meet with your approval, perhaps you'd prefer to spend the year in the kitchen instead?"

"No, ma'am," Ellie mumbled.

"Then kindly hold your peace." Her nostrils flared and she made a show of taking a deep breath, before calmly addressing the class again.

"Finally, we'll cover social events. You'll learn the nuances of paying and receiving social calls, as well as dining etiquette: proper use of cutlery, napkin placement, and impeccable table manners."

"Do you hear that, Sheffield?" Lydia whispered, loud enough for Ellie and Phoebe to hear. "That means no gathering round the communal trough, and no eating with your hands."

Unable to control herself, Ellie twisted round to face Lydia. "At least my hands are clean," she snapped. "Unlike that forked tongue of yours."

A collective gasp rose up from the other girls.

"Miss Dubois," Mrs Bennett hissed. "A lady never stoops to such vulgar retorts. One must learn to either grin and bear it, or to master the art of the polite riposte."

Ellie's face turned red. Partly out of embarrassment, but mostly because of the anger she was bottling up.

Stupid Lydia.

Clenching her jaw, she exhaled through her nose with a short, indignant huff.

"Let us move on to our first practical lesson," Mrs Bennett said, clasping her hands together. "The proper form of curtsying."

Her eyes swept the room, coming to rest on Ellie with a glint of satisfaction. "Miss Dubois, since you seem to adore being the centre of attention, perhaps you would like to assist with our demonstration?"

Ellie's stomach lurched. She glanced at Phoebe, who gave her an encouraging nod, before reluctantly rising to her feet.

"Come now. Please stand here in the middle of the room," Mrs Bennett instructed, gesturing impatiently.

Ellie made her way forward, acutely aware of the eyes following her every move. She stood awkwardly, hands fidgeting at her sides.

"Now, Miss Dubois, show us how you would curtsy."

Taking a deep breath, Ellie bent her knees slightly and bobbed down in a quick, perfunctory movement.

Mrs Bennett's lips thinned. "I see we have our work cut out for us," she said, addressing the class. "That, dear ladies, was not a curtsy. It was barely a twitch."

She turned back to Ellie. "Now, let us try again. This time, Miss Dubois, I want you to perform a full curtsy. As though you were being presented to Her Majesty the Queen."

Ellie wavered. She had never formally curtsied to anyone in her life, let alone royalty. Charlotte had shown her a picture book about it once, many years ago. They had done a few curtsies together, but it had mainly been a bit of silly fun. Certainly not serious practice.

"Miss Dubois?" Mrs Bennett said. "We're waiting."

Ellie hurriedly placed one foot behind the other.

"That's the wrong foot, Miss Dubois. The right foot should go behind the left leg. Never the other way around."

"Perhaps they don't know their left from their right up North," Lydia suggested. "All that factory soot must cloud their vision."

"That'll do, Miss Price," Mrs Bennett said. "Please proceed, Miss Dubois."

Ellie bit her lip, even as she felt an angry heat rising up from her neck to her cheeks. Desperately trying to recall the illustrations from Charlotte's book, she began to lower herself.

She tried to make the movement look graceful, but then she lost her balance. She stumbled slightly, her arms flailing as she fought to stay upright.

Laughter rippled through the room. Lydia's voice rose above the giggles, "Is this how they dance at Northern balls? No wonder London gentlemen never venture up there."

Mrs Bennett silenced everyone with a sharp look.

"Miss Dubois, I'm afraid that was utterly abysmal. You looked like a newborn foal attempting to stand for the first time."

Something snapped inside Ellie. Before she could stop herself, the words tumbled out. "I'd rather be a newborn foal than a preening peacock, strutting about and showing off feathers I didn't even grow myself."

The room fell dead silent as every girl seemed to hold her breath. Mrs Bennett's eyes widened in shock before narrowing dangerously.

"Miss Dubois," she said slowly. "Your behaviour is completely unacceptable. Report to my office after this lesson. Furthermore, you are to read the chapter on polite behaviour and good habits in 'The Lady's Guide to Proper Etiquette and Decorum'. And then you will prepare a full report about it, to be presented to the class tomorrow morning."

Ellie opened her mouth to protest, but thought better of it. She nodded stiffly and returned to her seat, ignoring Lydia's triumphant smirk.

Her legs felt like jelly beneath her as she dropped back down on the sofa. The room seemed to spin, and the dull ache in her head had returned with a vengeance. She thrust her trembling hands in her lap, willing them to be still.

Beside her, Phoebe's eyes were wide with horror. Her friend reached out, taking one of Ellie's shaking hands in her own.

"Are you all right?" the girl whispered.

Ellie shook her head. Even with Phoebe sitting next to her, she felt alone. Drifting in an icy sea of hostile faces and cruel laughter.

A lump formed in Ellie's throat as an intense wave of homesickness hit her. She longed for the peace of her own room, for Charlotte's reassuring presence, for the familiar sound of her mother's voice, and for the comforting smells of Mrs Dobbs' cooking.

Tears began to prick at her eyes.

No, she grumbled to herself. She refused to give Lydia and her cronies the satisfaction of seeing her cry. She had already suffered enough humiliation for one day. Swallowing hard, she blinked rapidly, forcing back the tears.

Her free hand moved to her chest, fingers brushing against the slight bulge where Stuart's locket lay hidden beneath her dress.

Would every day be like this, she thought while Mrs Bennett's voice droned on, continuing the lesson as if nothing had happened.

Would this entire year turn into an endless parade of mockery, humiliation, and loneliness? How could anyone possibly hope to withstand that sort of torment?

She lowered her hand again and balled her fist. She would endure. She had to. And if anyone wanted to break her, then they'd have to try much harder.

Chapter Five

"Miss Dubois, as I told you earlier, your behaviour today was utterly unacceptable. I have never in all my years witnessed such a disgraceful display of insolence and vulgarity."

Mrs Bennett sat behind her large and cluttered desk, eyeing Ellie sternly. Ellie stood in the middle of the office, trying hard not to appear nervous or frightened. But her hands, clasped together in front of her at waist level, felt hot and damp.

"But Mrs Bennett," she protested, "Lydia was deliberately provoking me. She–"

"Silence! A true lady does not make excuses for her shortcomings. Nor does she allow herself to be provoked by mere words."

"But it's fine for a 'true lady' to wilfully offend others then, is it? What Lydia did–"

"What Miss Price did is of no consequence," Mrs Bennett interrupted. "Her behaviour is not the issue here. You on the other hand must learn to rise above such trifles. Your reaction was completely disproportionate and unbecoming of a young lady."

"But why should I have to endure her insults?" Ellie blurted out. "Is it because I'm from up

North? Are we expected to simply accept being mocked and ridiculed?"

"Your background is irrelevant, Miss Dubois. What matters is your conduct. I've seen girls like you before: headstrong and resistant to gentle, well-meaning guidance. Do you know where such behaviour leads to?"

Ellie remained silent, staring hard at a point on the wall somewhere behind Mrs Bennett.

"Nowhere good, I assure you," the headmistress continued. "Think of your future, child. And of your marriage prospects. No gentleman of quality would consider a wife who cannot control her temper or hold her tongue."

Ellie's mind went to Stuart. He seemed to like her strong character just fine. And she couldn't imagine him ever being ashamed of her just for standing up for herself.

But then again, he was from Sheffield, too. So perhaps that made it impossible for him to be a 'gentleman of quality' in Mrs Bennett's view.

"I appreciate your concern for my future, ma'am," Ellie said. "But surely, there must be a way to address unkindness without resorting to... grinning and bearing it, as you called it?"

Mrs Bennett sighed. "It depends, Miss Dubois, on how one chooses to define unkindness. The problem, I'm afraid, lies not with Miss Price or anyone else, but with your own rebellious spirit. It clouds your judgement.

And it leads you to perceive slights where there are none."

"But–"

"You're being rebellious again, Miss Dubois."

Ellie suppressed the urge to stamp her foot on the ground in frustration. "Yes, ma'am," she merely said instead. "Sorry, ma'am."

Knowing it was useless to argue with Mrs Bennett, her eyes drifted off to the wall behind the headmistress again. She spotted framed certificates and flowery letters of recommendation, designed to impress the visitor.

It seemed the owner of the Bloomsbury Academy was as skilled in self-promotion as she was in etiquette.

"Let's put all this behind us now," Mrs Bennett said, mistaking Ellie's silence for compliance. "Your class is scheduled for piano lessons this afternoon. I have assigned you and Miss Greenwood to Mrs Novak. She lives close by, so you'll be walking to her home."

"Yes, ma'am," Ellie repeated, relieved at the change of subject.

"After lunch, I will give you her address and directions on how to get there. But it's an easy walk, really."

"Thank you, Mrs Bennett. Will that be all, ma'am?"

"Not quite." The headmistress picked up a book from her desk and held it out to Ellie. "The Lady's Guide to Proper Etiquette and Decorum, remember? For that report you are due to give to the class tomorrow."

"Of course, ma'am." As Ellie accepted the book, she had a vision of hitting Mrs Bennett over the head with it. But she wisely resisted acting out that particular fantasy.

"The chapter on polite behaviour and good habits, was it?" she asked.

"That's precisely the one, Miss Dubois. May it inform you and serve you well."

"I'm sure it will, ma'am."

Old hag.

"Splendid. You may leave now."

"Thank you, ma'am."

As soon as Ellie had left the office and closed the door, she shuddered in disgust. Oh, how she loathed conversations like this. People pretending to be nice and civilised while they both knew they despised each other.

But who knew, she thought with a snigger as she looked down at the heavy book in her arms. Maybe the Lady's Guide would help her to see the light.

After lunchtime, Ellie and Phoebe stepped out of the academy's front door and started heading for Mrs Novak's. The sun was shining, which helped to instantly lift their mood.

"That was quite an eventful morning, wasn't it?" Phoebe said, eager for a chat away from the other students.

"I'll say," Ellie replied. "How am I going to survive a whole year in that place if I can't even make it through the first day without landing myself in trouble?"

They turned down a tree-lined street. A pair of sparrows flitted overhead, their cheerful chirping at odds with Ellie's worries.

"What did Mrs Bennett say to you?" Phoebe asked, quietly and after casting a quick glance over her shoulder. As if the headmistress might have been following them.

"The sort of nonsense you'd expect," Ellie said, rolling her eyes. "I'm unladylike, I'll never find a husband, I'm bringing shame upon the entire female sex. You know, nothing too dramatic."

Phoebe giggled, then covered her mouth. "I shouldn't laugh, sorry. I'm sure it was nowhere near as funny as you made it sound."

"Laughing about it makes it more bearable," Ellie shrugged. "I just wish I understood why Lydia decided to have it in for me."

"Oh, I don't think it's anything personal, strange as it may sound."

"What makes you say that?"

"Something Agnes told me while you were in Mrs Bennett's office." Phoebe leaned in closer and dropped her voice to a whisper. "Apparently, Lydia's father is desperate to land some sort of title, either for himself or for his future grandchildren. So he's been trying to find a nobleman for his darling daughter."

Phoebe sniggered with glee. "But our dear Lydia's reputation for being difficult has already scared off more than a few potential suitors."

"Ha," Ellie scoffed. "No wonder she's so bitter. Imagine being shipped off to finishing school because you're too disagreeable to land a husband."

Around them, the grand façades gave way to more humble homes. Ellie's smile slipped as their talk about Lydia reminded her of Mrs Bennett's criticism of her own so-called rebellious behaviour.

"Phoebe," she said softly. "What if I can't do this? What if I'm simply not cut out for all this proper lady nonsense?"

Phoebe stopped walking, turning to face her friend. "Now you listen to me, Eleanor Dubois," she said, her usually gentle voice firm. "You are by far the cleverest girl I know."

"Is that a blessing or a curse though, I wonder? Some would argue I'm too clever for my own good."

"Rubbish. Your cleverness is what makes you special. And don't forget, I'm right here with you. We promised each other we would face this together, remember?"

"Yes, we did," Ellie smiled. "What would I do without you, Phoebe Greenwood?"

"Probably get into twice as much trouble," Phoebe teased. They both laughed and then resumed their walk.

A few moments later, they arrived at their destination. Or so they hoped. Because the house that rose up before them certainly had seen better days. Most of the paint on the window frames had peeled off years ago, the brickwork was crumbling, and the stone steps leading to the front door were cracked and worn, with tufts of weeds growing between them.

"Are you sure this is the right address?" Phoebe asked.

Ellie checked the slip of paper Mrs Bennett had given her, and nodded. "According to these directions, this is where Mrs Novak lives."

She went up the cracked steps and knocked. They waited, but nobody came to answer the door. Phoebe shifted from foot to foot as Ellie knocked again, harder this time. Still nothing seemed to stir inside the house.

"Maybe she's not in," Phoebe suggested.

Ellie shrugged and raised her hand to knock a third time. But then the door swung open with a dramatic creak. A cloud of tobacco smoke billowed out, enveloping the girls in its smelly embrace.

"You must be my new students," a husky voice with a heavy Central European accent sounded from within the haze. As the smoke cleared, a woman materialised before them. She was tall and as thin as a rake, with wild silver hair escaping from a careless knot that was meant to look like a chignon.

"Mrs Novak, I presume?" Ellie asked.

The woman proudly raised her chin. "Madame Irina Novak," she introduced herself, peering down at them. Her bright green eyes were heavily lined with kohl.

"How do you do, Mrs Novak," Ellie said politely. "I'm Ellie Dubois and this is Phoebe Greenwood."

Mrs Novak gave a vague wave with her hand. "I'll have forgotten your names by the end of the lesson, more than likely."

She turned around and strode back into the house, leaving a bewildered Ellie and Phoebe outside on the doorstep.

"Well, don't just stand there gawking like peasants at the opera," she called from inside the dim hallway. "Come in, come in."

The girls hesitated for a moment before Ellie shrugged and entered. With Phoebe close on her heels, she followed Mrs Novak's retreating figure.

The parlour was a cluttered maze of mismatched furniture and scattered piles of sheet music. Faded wallpaper was peeling off the walls in several places. A grand piano, its ivory keys yellowed with age, dominated the room.

"Welcome to my domain," Mrs Novak proclaimed, floating across the parlour. "Where art is worshipped, and music reigns supreme."

She collapsed onto a worn *chaise longue*, a cigarette holder dangling from her bejewelled fingers.

"I know what you're thinking," she said. "Who is this mad lady? But let me assure you, Madame Novak used to play for the crowned heads of Europe."

"You played for royalty?" Ellie blurted out.

"Many times. And with great success. Why, the old king of Prussia himself wept when I performed Chopin for him. And once, I had to turn down an invitation from the Emperor of Austria because I was already booked for a performance at the Winter Palace in St Petersburg."

"I had no idea," Ellie said. She found the notion somewhat hard to believe, glancing around at the chaotic and rundown state of Mrs Novak's home.

"Oh, the stories I could tell you," the piano teacher said. "And look at me now. Reduced to teaching spoiled little English girls how to mangle Beethoven."

She reached for a glass that held a clear liquid and drained it. Ellie doubted it was water that Mrs Novak was drinking.

"Let's see what Mrs Bennett has sent me this time. Which one of you will go first in your assault on my poor piano?"

When neither of them volunteered, Mrs Novak pointed at Phoebe and then at the piano. "You. Sit. Show me how good, or how bad, you are."

As Phoebe settled nervously at the piano, Mrs Novak reclined on her chaise, eyes closed, one arm flung theatrically across her forehead. Ellie perched on the edge of an overstuffed armchair, unsure whether to watch her friend or their eccentric teacher.

Phoebe began to play, her fingers moving hesitantly over the keys. She had barely made it through the first page when Mrs Novak let out a painful groan.

"Stop, stop," she cried. "My dear girl, you play as though you're afraid of that instrument. There's no passion. No fire."

She got up and waved her empty glass around. "It must be the English affliction. This tepid approach to everything."

Mrs Novak stumbled over to a small side table cluttered with bottles. With a practised hand, she poured a generous measure of that same clear liquid into her glass. She lifted it to her lips and took a long swig, draining half of the contents in one go.

"Bah," she shrugged. "It's not that you're awful, child," she said to Phoebe. "There's potential, yes, buried underneath that English reserve. But it will take work. Now you," she pointed at Ellie. "Your turn."

With a dramatic flourish, she flung herself back onto the chaise longue, her limbs sprawling across the worn fabric. She raised her glass once more, tilting her head back to drain the other half.

Heart pounding, Ellie sat down at the piano. She took a deep breath and began to play. All the emotions of the day – the anger, the frustration, the homesickness – she poured it all out through her fingers and into the music.

When she finished, there was nothing but silence. Ellie turned to find Mrs Novak apparently fast asleep, her chest rising and falling.

"Should we wake her up?" Phoebe whispered.

"I don't know," Ellie said. "I wouldn't want to offend her."

"Nothing offends Mrs Novak if you ask me," Phoebe giggled.

Suddenly, the piano teacher's eyes snapped open. "Brava," she exclaimed, leaping to her feet with surprising agility. "That was so magnificent you mesmerised me. Such fire, such passion. You have the heart of a true Bohemian, my dear."

She bustled over to her collection of bottles again. "This calls for a celebration. A toast. To life, and music."

She refilled her glass and paused. "I'd offer you one as well," she said, looking at the girls. "But it's probably against one of Mrs Bennett's precious rules."

With a shrug, she downed her drink. "Well, never mind. Let's get to work."

For the next two hours, Mrs Novak alternated between brutally honest critiques and nostalgic tales of her glory days, while she smoked, drank and had the occasional snooze.

When it was all over, Ellie and Phoebe took their leave and headed back to the academy, with a wide grin on their faces.

"That was... different," Phoebe said.

"I'm not entirely sure what it was," Ellie chuckled. "But I think I liked it."

They burst out laughing, the strangeness of their encounter making them forget the day's earlier troubles.

With a smile, Ellie realised that, despite the woman's eccentricities, Mrs Novak had given her an unexpected gift: a spark of joy, and a glimmer of hope.

Chapter Six

Ellie stood before her classmates, clutching 'The Lady's Guide to Proper Etiquette and Decorum' to her chest like a shield. Her cheeks burned as she delivered her third report on ladylike behaviour in as many weeks.

"And so," she concluded, "a true lady always maintains her composure, even in the face of provocation."

"Very good, Miss Dubois," Mrs Bennett nodded approvingly. "What a commendable effort. Your insights were most illuminating."

"Yes, do keep up the good work," Lydia sniggered from the back. "It's ever so convenient having you read the book for us, chapter by chapter."

Ellie's fingers tightened on the book. She drew a deep breath, forcing herself to remember the words she had just recited. With effort, she relaxed her grip and offered a tight smile.

"I'm happy to be of service, Miss Price," she replied evenly. "And I shall gladly lend you my copy of the Lady's Guide should you ever feel the need for it."

The scowling look that Lydia threw her made it worth it.

"I see you've been taking the lessons to heart, Miss Dubois," Mrs Bennett gushed. "Wonderful, simply wonderful."

When Ellie returned to her seat, Phoebe gave her hand a quick, supportive squeeze. "Well done," her friend whispered.

Ellie sank into her chair, exhausted. How much more of this could she take?

But at least they had their piano lessons with Mrs Novak to look forward to three times a week. Because notwithstanding their tutor's bizarre quirks and exotic behaviour, Ellie welcomed the opportunity to get away from the school for a few hours.

Mrs Bennett cleared her throat, drawing everyone's attention. "Young ladies, I have an announcement to make. Tomorrow, we will be embarking on a very special guided tour."

A ripple of excitement ran through the classroom. Girls straightened in their seats, eyes bright with anticipation.

"How fabulous," Susan Harris chirped. She was one of the two girls who were always by Lydia's side. "Are we going to Bond Street? To look at all the fashion boutiques?"

Emily Baker, Lydia's other lackey, shook her head. "Oxford Street is so much nicer. And shopping at Whitely's in Park Street would be grand, too."

"Perhaps we're going for a stroll through St James or Grosvenor Square," Lydia suggested, a sly smile playing on her lips. "You never know, we might catch a wealthy gentleman's eye."

But Mrs Bennett held up a hand, silencing the chatter. "I'm afraid you're all rather wide off the mark, girls. Our expedition tomorrow will take us to an area where the lower classes reside."

A shocked collective gasp filled the room, followed by a stunned silence.

"A rookery?" Lydia asked, audibly disgusted by the very idea.

"That's such a harsh word for it, Miss Price," Mrs Bennett replied. "But yes, Spitalfields is a neighbourhood considerably less affluent than what you're accustomed to. The purpose of our visit is to instil in you all the virtue of charity."

Agnes, the nervous girl Ellie and Phoebe had met on their first day, raised a trembling hand. "But Mrs Bennett, isn't that terribly dangerous? I've heard there are all sorts of thieves and cutthroats in such places."

A murmur of agreement swept through the room as other girls nodded, their faces pale with fear.

"Now, now," Mrs Bennett said soothingly. "I assure you, it's perfectly safe. People go on these tours quite frequently. We'll have an experienced guide, and as long as we all stay together as a group and don't wander off, we'll have nothing to fear."

The girls exchanged uneasy glances, clearly unconvinced.

"Oh, and one more thing," Mrs Bennett added. "It is advisable for you to dress in the plainest garments you have for this. We don't want to draw undue attention to ourselves."

The class broke up, with girls huddling together in worried whispers. When Lydia brushed past, she looked down at Ellie and Phoebe.

"I imagine you two will feel right at home tomorrow. After all, it can't be much different from that grimy home town of yours up North, can it?"

Ellie wanted to reply something about hoping that their visit would be an eyeopener for a spoiled little pretend-princess like her. But Lydia had already flounced off, leaving behind the lingering scent of her expensive perfume and the sound of her friends' malicious giggles.

The following day, a small fleet of hired carriages rattled through London's streets, carrying the Bloomsbury Academy girls towards their destination.

In Ellie's carriage, the atmosphere was gloomy. She could almost smell the fear coming from her classmates.

"I heard they eat rats," someone murmured.

"They steal babies, too," another girl said. "Just for the thrill of it."

"Don't be ridiculous," Ellie snapped. "They're poor, not savages."

The other girls fell silent, eyeing her warily. Ellie turned to stare out of the window. At last she'd have the chance to see a very different side of London.

Maybe among these less fortunate souls, she would see some of the authenticity and warmth that was so lacking in the world of Lydia Price and Mrs Bennett.

After they had entered a narrow, cobbled street, the carriages slowed to a stop. Mrs Bennett gathered everyone around her, while a stern-faced woman in a plain dress stood next to her and waited.

"Good morning, ladies," the woman said primly. "Welcome to Spitalfields. I'm Mrs Fitch, and I shall be your guide today. Please stay close and follow my instructions at all times."

She turned and led them into the warren of streets that made up the slum. The change was immediate and stark. Gone were the wide, clean avenues. Here, the buildings loomed close on either side, their walls grimy and blackened with a layer of soot from the city's factory chimneys.

The stench of sewage and all manner of rotting waste hung heavily in the air, making several of the girls want to gag.

Barefoot children with hollow cheeks whooped and shouted as they chased a pair of mangy dogs that had been sniffing at a pile of refuse in the open gutter running down the middle of the street.

Gaunt women hung laundry from windows, while their ragged husbands slouched in the doorways, watching the group of students as they passed.

Ellie heard gasps and mutters of disgust from her classmates. Phoebe clung to her arm, eyes darting around nervously.

"At our first stop," Mrs Fitch announced, "you will witness how some of these women earn their keep."

They rounded a corner to find a group of women bent over large washtubs, scrubbing furiously at piles of laundry. Steam rose from the hot water, and the women's hands were red and raw.

"Oh, how dreadful," Agnes whimpered. "I can't imagine having to do such menial work all day long."

Lydia sniffed haughtily. "Someone has to clean our dirty laundry. And they can always use the waste water to wash their own filthy rags in."

Ellie shot her an irritated look. Then she watched the women, noting their tired faces and stooped shoulders. When one of the washerwomen glanced up, Ellie was shocked to see the emptiness in her eyes.

Almost as if her soul has already left her body, she thought. But maybe that was for the best, given their dire circumstances.

"This way, please," Mrs Fitch said. "Our next point of interest showcases another common occupation in these parts."

A quiet snigger sounded at the back of the group. "I wonder what that might be. Girls lifting their skirts in some dirty alley for a penny?"

The voice was unmistakably Lydia's.

Ellie clenched her fists, itching to give Miss Price a piece of her mind. But Mrs Fitch walked on, either because she was oblivious to the vulgar comment, or because she chose to ignore it.

They entered a house where a stuffy room was buzzing with the whir of sewing machines. In this cramped space, a dozen women and girls laboured tirelessly, their eyes straining in the dim light as they pieced together shirts and dresses that none of them would ever be able to afford for themselves.

"Many women find employment as seamstresses," their guide explained. "They work long hours for very little pay."

"Ghastly," Emily said with a turned-up nose. "And I thought our needlework lessons were tiresome. How do they bear it?"

"Why don't they simply find better work?" Susan asked. "Surely, there must be more pleasant occupations available?"

"Or better yet," Lydia chuckled, "they should land themselves a rich husband who can take care of them."

Ellie gritted her teeth. Didn't they understand? These women didn't have the luxury of choice. They were doing what they had to in order to survive.

As they moved on, Ellie lingered for a moment, watching a young girl struggle with a tangled thread. Their eyes met briefly, and Ellie saw a flash of resentment in the girl's gaze before she ducked her head back to her work.

Ellie hurried to catch up with the group. How could her classmates be so blind to the hardships these people faced? And more importantly, what could be done to help them?

They stopped before a crumbling tenement building. Most of the window panes were missing and had been replaced with dirty pieces of discarded sackcloth. Looking at them, Ellie doubted they did much to keep out the elements.

Mrs Fitch knocked on a worn wooden door. After a moment, a woman answered. Her skin was an unhealthy shade of grey, with deep lines etched into her face that made her appear far older than she likely was.

"This is Mrs Higgins," Mrs Fitch said. "She has kindly agreed to share her experiences of living in this neighbourhood."

Mrs Higgins nodded and began to speak in a hoarse voice. "Life 'ere ain't easy, young ladies. Work's hard to come by. And when you do find it, the pay's barely enough to keep you alive. We're packed in 'ere like sardines, whole families in one room. The damp gets in your bones, and there's always some sickness going 'round."

As Mrs Higgins continued her tale of hardship, Ellie noticed several of her classmates fidgeting uncomfortably.

"I'm sure it can't be as bad as all that," Lydia muttered under her breath. "She's probably exaggerating to get more sympathy from us. And more coins."

When Mrs Higgins finished speaking, Mrs Fitch turned to the group with a practised smile. "If any of you feel moved to offer a small token of charity, now would be the time."

A few girls reluctantly fished out a coin or two from their purses, dropping them into Mrs Higgins' outstretched hand. Ellie's contribution was by far the most generous of them all.

"Don't get too close," Lydia warned. "You might get lice. Or worse."

When they began to move on again, Ellie approached Mrs Fitch. "Excuse me, ma'am, but how can we help these poor people? There must be more we can do than just gawk at their misery and toss them a few pennies."

Mrs Fitch's eyebrows shot up as if Ellie had suddenly sprouted a second head. "My dear girl, I'm afraid most of these people are beyond salvation. Their poverty is often the result of their own ignorant choices, don't you see? A punishment for their wickedness and their sins."

"But surely that can't be true of all of them? Shouldn't we–"

"The best one can do for these poor wretches," Mrs Fitch interrupted, "is to pray for their souls. And to give money to charitable causes, if one is so inclined. But make no mistake, dear: interfering directly in their lives rarely ends well for anyone involved."

Ellie fell silent, struggling to understand how anyone could entertain such a heartless opinion. She glanced back at Mrs Higgins, who was already retreating into her squalid lodgings again.

There had to be a better way to make a difference here, she thought. There must be.

As they neared their final stop, Ellie's frustration continued to simmer. The group arrived at a modest building with a sign that read 'St Mary's Charity Mission'.

"Our last visit of the day, ladies," Mrs Fitch announced. "This is where many of the area's unfortunates come for a hot meal and a kind word."

A stout, middle-aged woman emerged from the building, wiping her hands on a stained apron. "Welcome," she said warmly. "I'm Mrs Collins, and I run this mission."

The group followed her inside, where the aroma of mutton stew greeted them. Men, women and children crowded the long wooden tables that lined the room. They ate in muted silence and with mechanical movements.

"We serve hundreds of people a day," Mrs Collins explained. "For many, it's their only proper meal."

Ellie watched a young mother who was spoon-feeding her toddler from her own bowl. The sight nearly made her want to cry.

"I suppose it's good they have a place to go," Agnes murmured, clearly torn between compassion and the desire to be elsewhere.

Lydia sniffed arrogantly. "Yes, although it makes you wonder if such charity only encourages idleness. After all, why would they look for work if they can fill their bellies for free here?"

Ellie stepped forward. "Mrs Collins, I think it's wonderful what you're doing. Are there any opportunities for us to contribute? Could we lend a hand in the kitchen perhaps, or help serve meals?"

A stunned hush fell over the group. Mrs Bennett's eyes widened in horror, while some of the girls giggled nervously.

"That's a generous offer, dear," Mrs Collins smiled. "We're always in need of volunteers."

"I'm afraid that won't be possible," Mrs Bennett cut in sharply. "Our students' schedules are quite full, and their welfare is our primary concern."

"Of course," Mrs Collins nodded, though Ellie noticed a flicker of disappointment in her eyes.

"Not even a few hours a week?" Ellie pleaded to Mrs Bennett.

"I think this concludes our tour, don't you, Mrs Fitch?" the headmistress said, a little too hastily.

As the girls began to file out of the mission, Ellie overheard Lydia sniggering to her friends. "How utterly adorable. Our little Northern savage wants to play saviour to the unwashed masses."

Laugh all you want, Ellie thought, clenching her jaw. A fire burned in her chest, fuelled by indignation and resolve. Mrs Bennett and Mrs Fitch might dismiss these people as lost causes, but Ellie knew better. There had to be a way to make a difference, to offer more than fleeting charity or condescending pity.

After they had climbed back into the carriage, Phoebe touched her friend's arm. "Were you serious about volunteering?" she whispered.

Ellie merely nodded, then turned to stare out the window. As the carriages set off to the academy again, the streets of London rolled by, a blur of brick and stone. But Ellie's mind was elsewhere.

Her fingers absently traced the outline of Stuart's locket beneath her dress.

I have to make my way back to St Mary's Mission, she silently vowed to herself. *Rules or no rules.*

Chapter Seven

"You look dreadful," Phoebe said as they walked to Mrs Novak's for their piano lesson the next day. "Did you sleep at all last night?"

Ellie trudged along with tired eyes and heavy feet.

"Hardly," she replied, stifling a yawn. "No matter how much I tried, I just couldn't get my mind to go to sleep."

"I know exactly what you mean," Phoebe nodded sympathetically. "That visit to Spitalfields... It left quite an impression, I have to say. All that poverty and misery. I tossed and turned for hours, thinking about those poor souls."

"Actually, that's not what kept me awake."

"No? Then what was it?"

"I kept asking myself how I could help."

"Ah, your idea of volunteering at St Mary's. Which, in case you had forgotten, Mrs Bennett turned down."

"I hadn't forgotten," Ellie replied. Then she grinned and added, "But I believe I've come up with a plan."

Phoebe sighed. "Why do I have a feeling this plan of yours is going to land us both in trouble?"

"It won't, I promise," Ellie insisted. "At least, not if we're cautious."

"Let's hear it then."

"What if I used our piano lesson time to volunteer at Mrs Collins' mission instead?"

"Mrs Bennett would never allow it," Phoebe replied, shaking her head. "She's dead against the whole idea, don't you see? All that talk yesterday about busy schedules and the welfare of her students: that was just an excuse."

"I know that," Ellie said. "And it's why we simply won't tell her."

"What?!" Phoebe stopped walking and placed a hand on her friend's arm. "Ellie, you can't be serious?"

"Oh, but I am. And I need you to cover for me, Phoebe. Tell Mrs Novak that I've been assigned to a different teacher, and that you'll be taking both hours."

"Two hours on my own with Mrs Novak?" Phoebe groaned. "One hour is already more than enough for me, thank you very much. You know how I struggle with the piano, Ellie."

"Please, Phoebe," Ellie begged, taking her friend's hands in hers. "It's for a good cause. Think of all those people we saw yesterday.

They need help, real help. Not just a few coins tossed their way during a guided tour."

"I don't know, Ellie. It's an awful risk we're taking. What if Mrs Bennett finds out?"

"She won't," Ellie assured her. "I'll be ever so careful. And just think of the difference we could make."

"The difference *you* could make, you mean. I'd just be your accomplice in this crazy scheme."

"But your contribution will be a vital one. Your help is what would allow me to offer hope and support to those poor, struggling families."

"And if you get caught, we'll both be in serious trouble."

"If that happens – and it won't, trust me – but if it happens, then I'll take full responsibility. I'll tell Mrs Bennett it was all my idea, and that I forced you into it."

"Ellie–"

"Remember that young mother we saw at the mission? The one feeding her baby? We could help people like her, Phoebe. We could actually do something that matters."

"Oh, very well," Phoebe conceded with a sigh. "But promise me you won't take any unnecessary risks. And if there's even a whisper of suspicion from Mrs Bennett or anyone else, you'll put an end to it at once."

"Thank you," Ellie cooed as she threw her arms around Phoebe. "You're a true friend. I knew I could count on you."

"I just hope I don't end up regretting my decision."

"You won't. I promise I'll be the very soul of discretion."

"You'll have to be if you want to make this work." They let go of each other, and Phoebe shook her head. "Two whole hours with Mrs Novak, dearie me."

"You never know," Ellie teased. "Perhaps all that extra practice will turn you into a piano virtuoso."

"I very much doubt it," Phoebe laughed. "But with any luck, Mrs Novak might just sleep through most of the lesson." Her expression turned more serious as she stared in the direction they had been heading. "When do you want to start doing this?"

"Straight away," Ellie replied confidently. The memory of those haunted faces at the rookery spurred her on. "If that's all right with you?"

"There's no time like the present, they say." Phoebe took hold of Ellie and hugged her again. "But please do be careful."

"I will." When Ellie took a step back, she thought she saw a shimmer of tears in her friend's eyes. "It's for a greater cause, Phoebe," she smiled encouragingly.

"I know," the girl sniffled. "But that doesn't mean I have to like it."

"We'll meet each other here in two hours," Ellie said. "So we can walk back to the academy together."

After one final quick embrace, they said their goodbyes and then Ellie hurried down the street. On the corner she stopped and hailed a passing hansom cab.

"St Mary's Mission in Spitalfields, please," she told the driver as she climbed in. "As quickly as you can."

"Spitalfields?" the driver asked incredulously. "Are ya' sure, Miss? A young lady like yerselves ain't safe in them rookeries, y'know?"

"Quite sure, sir. It's for charity, so I'll be perfectly fine."

"Have it your way, Miss," the driver replied before setting off.

As the carriage began to make its way through traffic, Ellie's fingers toyed nervously with the coins in her purse. The hansom was a luxury, she knew, far more expensive than walking or taking the omnibus. But speed was of the essence if she was to make the most of her stolen hours.

"It's an investment," she muttered to herself, trying to quell the guilty flutter in her stomach. Her mother had been generous with her allowance, but it wouldn't last very long this way.

Not to worry though, she told herself. When the money ran out, she could always write home to ask for more. She would claim that everything was so much more expensive in London. Which wasn't that far from the truth, she reasoned.

The trip from Spitalfields was a fairly short one. Just as well, Ellie thought. Because it meant there was less time for her to grow even more nervous than she already felt.

When the driver stopped at St Mary's Mission, she paid the man and stepped out. *This is it,* she murmured to herself. *No turning back now.*

With her heart pounding in her chest, she marched to the door of the mission and went inside. The dining space was already busy, but Ellie spotted Mrs Collins near the serving area. Mustering her courage, she went over.

"Mrs Collins?" she said. "Do you remember me? I'm Eleanor Dubois. I visited with my class yesterday."

"Yes, of course," the woman smiled kindly. "The young lady who wanted to volunteer, wasn't it?"

"That's right," Ellie nodded eagerly. "And that's why I'm here today. I'd like to help, if you'll have me."

Mrs Collins raised an eyebrow and looked over Ellie's shoulder. "You've come alone? And didn't your headmistress object to your idea yesterday?"

"I managed to change her mind," Ellie lied without blushing. "Mrs Bennett can be quite reasonable when you approach her the right way."

"I see. Well, in that case, we can certainly use an extra pair of hands. But I must warn you, Miss Dubois. This isn't a gentle world you're stepping into."

Ellie glanced at the sad and tired looking people who sat eating their stew at the long tables. It was clear to see that life had been hard on them.

"Not everyone in the rookery is what they seem," Mrs Collins said, catching the direction of Ellie's gaze. "There are dangerous folk about, criminals even. They're not all helpless victims, you understand?"

"I understand, Mrs Collins," Ellie replied solemnly. "Rest assured, I won't do anything foolish."

"Good. Now let's put you to work. You can start by serving meals. The big kettle here is full of stew. Just ladle it out as people come through the queue."

She gave Ellie a clean apron and then busied herself with clearing tables and carrying stacks of used bowls to the kitchen.

After putting on the apron, Ellie positioned herself by the kettle, ladle in hand and a smile on her face. She was ready, determined to dish out a measure of kindness with every meal she served.

A ragtag parade of hollow cheeks and weary eyes passed by her station. "Enjoy," she said warmly to each patron. But most avoided her friendly gaze, and fixed their eyes instead on the steaming bowl that she handed them.

As the queue advanced, a man came shuffling forward who seemed to carry the weight of the world on his shoulders. He walked with a pronounced limp and leaned heavily on a gnarled walking stick. His face was a map of deep furrows and scars, the marks of a past filled with countless hardships.

Yet something in his eyes – a spark of vigour and intensity – suggested that he wasn't nearly as old as he appeared.

"Good day to you, sir," Ellie said, making an effort to put extra cheer into her voice. "Would you like some stew?"

He fixed her with a hard stare. "Wouldn't be here if I didn't, would I?" he growled.

"Of course," she blushed. "How silly of me. Here you go then, sir," she said as she ladled a generous portion into his bowl. "Shall I see if I can get you a little bit of butter for your bread as well?"

"Don't waste your pity on me, girl," he sneered. "I've had my fill of people offering me their false sympathy."

"I wasn't–" Ellie began, but he cut her off with a harsh laugh.

"Course you were. You're all the same, you do-gooders. Think a smile and a kind word will make up for the nightmares I've been through."

"My apologies if I've upset you, sir," Ellie said sincerely. "That wasn't my intention at all."

"Oh, never mind me," he replied, his tone turning softer. "I'm just a bitter old man. You're young. You probably still believe in the goodness and decency of others, don't you?"

"Has the world been that unkind to you, sir?"

"Unkind? Ha! That's putting it mildly. Betrayed by those I trusted. Chewed up, spat out and left to rot by the powers that be. Makes a man rather wary of kindness, let me tell you."

"I'm so sorry," Ellie said softly. "That must have been terrible for you."

He snorted and wanted to say something, but he was interrupted by Mrs Collins, who appeared by Ellie's side with a fresh kettle.

"More stew, Miss Dubois," the woman said. "How are you coping so far?"

"Very well, thank you, Mrs Collins," Ellie smiled. Together, they emptied the rest of the old kettle into the fresh one, and then Mrs Collins went back to the kitchen.

"Dubois, eh?" the man asked. "Isn't that a French name?"

"It is," Ellie nodded as she started ladling out stew to the other people in the queue.

"But you sound like you're from the North," the man said.

"I am. From Sheffield, actually. My name was Fletcher originally, but my mother remarried after my father passed away. My stepfather is a Frenchman from Paris: Pierre Dubois."

The old man went very still, his eyes boring into Ellie with an intensity that made her want to take a step back. For a long moment, he said nothing, just stared.

"Is everything all right, sir?" Ellie asked, unnerved by his scrutiny.

He seemed to shake himself out of whatever thoughts had gripped him. "Fine, fine," he muttered.

Then, with a hint of amusement he asked, "What's a Northern lass with a French stepfather doing serving sloppy stew to a bunch of misfits and vagrants?"

"I'm attending a finishing school here in London," Ellie explained. "We visited Spitalfields yesterday on a guided tour, and I wanted to help."

"Slumming, eh?" he grinned, revealing yellowed teeth. "Tell me, did they take you to see old Mrs Higgins?"

"Why, yes. How did you know?"

He chuckled, a raspy sound that devolved into a cough. "Everyone knows Mrs Higgins. She's part of the show, love. Tells you all about the harsh life here, makes your hearts bleed so you'll give generously." He leaned in closer. "Did you know she has to give a cut of those donations to the tour guide?"

"What?" Ellie gasped. "But that's awful."

The man laughed again. "Oh, there's so much you don't know about life in the rookery, dear girl. But don't worry that pretty head of yours over it. You're young and innocent. Better to keep it that way."

He straightened, wincing slightly. "Well, I'd best be off. Have to eat this before it gets cold. Be a shame to waste my only real meal of the day."

"Would you like me to give you a fresh bowl, sir? It would still be hot from the kettle."

He waved her off. "Nah, cold stew's good enough for the likes of me. There were times – not that long ago even – when a bowl of cold stew would have seemed like a meal fit for a king to me."

Ellie felt for him as he began to shuffle away. "You can always come back for more bread if you want, Mr..."

She realised he had never told her his name.

He stopped, but didn't turn around.

"Yates," he called back over his shoulder. "Percy Yates. It's been a pleasure to meet you, Miss Dubois. A real pleasure."

She watched him move slowly to an empty corner seat at one of the tables. Her mind was troubled by their encounter, and by the bitter truths he had hinted at.

There were so many things she didn't know yet about this world. So much injustice she was completely ignorant of.

And if she truly wanted to help these people, the vulnerable outcasts of society, then she simply had to learn more about their troubles.

Chapter Eight

"You're late," Phoebe said, her voice tight with anxiety as Ellie hurried up to the street corner where they had agreed to meet.

Ellie pressed a hand to her chest, trying to catch her breath. "I'm so sorry," she panted. "I had trouble finding a hansom cab near Spitalfields. And then I asked the driver to let me off a few streets away. To avoid the risk of anyone seeing me stepping out of a carriage this close to Mrs Novak's house and the academy."

Phoebe glanced around nervously. "We should go. If we dawdle too long, someone might notice."

They set off towards the Academy again, Ellie's legs and lungs still protesting after her mad dash. But as they walked, she smiled, thinking of the people she had helped at St Mary's Mission.

"How did Mrs Novak take the news?" she asked, in order to break the tense silence that seemed to hang between her and Phoebe.

"She was disappointed when I told her you wouldn't be coming any more. She said you had shown promise."

"Did she?" Ellie's smile faded. "Oh dear, now I feel even worse about lying to her."

"Well, it was your idea," Phoebe shrugged.

"I know, I know," Ellie sighed. "But at least my first day of volunteering went well. You should have seen the gratitude in their eyes, Phoebe. It made me feel like I was doing something that actually mattered."

"That's wonderful, Ellie. But you have to be more mindful of the time. Please? You can't keep coming back late like this."

"You're right, of course. It's just that – with the time it takes me to get there and to come back afterwards – two hours isn't an awful lot. I wish I had more..."

She fell silent, frowning as her mind wrestled with the problem.

"If I knew how to create time out of thin air, I would tell you," Phoebe sympathised.

"Hmm, funny you should say that," Ellie replied. "But there just might be a way to do it."

"Oh, dear. Another idea of yours?"

"What if I told Mrs Bennett that Mrs Novak thinks I'm so talented, she wants to give me an additional hour of tuition? Free of charge, of course. That would give me more time to volunteer. Surely, Mrs Bennett wouldn't object to more piano lessons when she hears they're free?"

"Ellie, no," Phoebe said. "You can't keep piling one lie on top of another. Don't you see how dangerous this is becoming?"

"But think of the good I could do with that extra time," Ellie insisted. "In for a penny, in for a pound, they say. I'm going to tell Mrs Bennett the good news the moment we get back to the Academy. I'm certain she won't refuse."

"I'm worried about you, Ellie. You're becoming entangled in a web of your own making. What happens when you can't keep all these stories straight?"

"I promise you, I have everything under control. This is important, Phoebe. Those people at the mission, they need our help."

Phoebe sighed. "I hope you know what you're doing."

"Trust me," Ellie said, giving her friend a confident smile.

Two days later, she found herself back at St Mary's Mission, with an additional hour to spare. Just as she had predicted, Mrs Bennett hadn't had any objections to the 'arrangement'. The headmistress had even seemed pleased when Ellie told her.

She wondered if that was because Mrs Bennett thought that having a talented pianist among her students would be good for the Academy's prestige, or if the woman was simply glad to be rid of her for a few extra hours each week.

"Well, well, look who's back," a familiar gruff voice said.

Ellie looked up to see Percy Yates shuffling towards her, his cane tapping a slow rhythm on the worn floorboards.

"Hello, Mr Yates," Ellie greeted him with a warm smile. "How are you today?"

Percy's lips twitched in what might have been an attempt at a grin. "Missed you yesterday, girl. Thought maybe you'd had enough of us lowly folk already."

Ellie shook her head. "Oh no, nothing like that, sir. I'm afraid I can't be here every day. My schedule at school keeps me quite busy."

"Ah yes, your finishing school," Percy said with a sarcastic smirk. "Learning all sorts of useful things there, I'm sure. How to pour tea without spilling a drop? The proper way to faint into a gentleman's arms?"

"Sounds about right," Ellie laughed. "I admit, there are many times when I question the value of what they teach us. It feels so... disconnected from the real world."

"Ha," he scoffed. "That's because it is, my dear. No amount of embroidery or etiquette will prepare you for the harsh realities of life."

"Isn't that the truth," she sighed sadly. "And the worst thing is, I didn't even want to come to this stupid finishing school. It was my mother's idea."

He paused, seeming to consider something. "You know, I have some friends: a brother and sister about your age. They kindly share their room with this old cripple. Now there's a pair who could teach you about real life."

Ellie's eyes lit up with interest. "Really? What are they like?"

Percy waved a dismissive hand. "Oh, never mind. I shouldn't have mentioned it. Better if you stick to your world of tea parties and dancing lessons. The rookeries are no place for a young lady like yourself."

"But Mr Yates," Ellie protested, her curiosity piqued, "I want to understand. How can I truly help if I don't know what life is really like for people here?"

Percy regarded her for a long moment, his eyes unreadable. Finally, he sighed. "Well, if you're sure... Perhaps you'd like to meet them? See the real world of the rookery with your own eyes?"

"I would like that very much, Mr Yates," she nodded eagerly.

"Very well then," Percy said, sounding almost reluctant. "Meet me outside after you've finished here."

"That's wonderful," she chirped gratefully. "It just so happens I have a bit more time today. So

I'll leave here at my usual hour and then we can go and meet these friends of yours."

"As if it was meant to be," he said with a short grunt of approval. "But remember, girl: you asked for this. Don't go blaming me if you don't like what you see."

An hour later, Ellie rushed off and found Percy waiting for her outside. He gave her a short nod and then set off.

As she followed him through the winding streets of the rookery, her senses became overwhelmed by the sights and smells of poverty. The narrow alleys were choked with refuse, and the air was thick with a foul stench, making Ellie wish she could hold her breath indefinitely. Children with dirty faces and ragged clothes darted between buildings, their shouts and laughter a stark contrast to their gritty surroundings.

"Not quite what you're used to, eh?" Percy called over his shoulder. Despite his limp, Ellie was surprised by his speed and she had to quicken her pace to keep up with him.

"I had no idea it was this dire," she replied. "It's a different world entirely. Far worse than what we glimpsed on our guided tour."

"Course it is," he scoffed. "Those tours show you just enough misery to make you feel charitable, but not enough to disturb your delicate sensibilities. Welcome to the real Spitalfields, girl."

They turned down a particularly narrow street, where the buildings on either side seemed to be leaning towards each other. As if they were ancient, crumbling monsters blocking out the sunlight and draining all hope and joy from anyone who passed through their shadows.

Percy stopped at a door that hung crookedly on its hinges and pushed it open with a creak. "Home sweet home," he said, gesturing for Ellie to follow him up a set of rickety stairs.

The room they entered was small and draughty. A single, grimy window let in a weak shaft of daylight. A young man sat on a threadbare chair, cutting slices out of a wrinkled apple with his penknife. Across from him, a girl about Ellie's age was bent over a piece of fabric, her needle flashing in and out with practised precision.

"Jack, Lucy," Percy announced, "we have a visitor."

The girl glanced up only briefly to look at Ellie, and then turned back to her sewing. But her brother took in Ellie's appearance from head to toe.

"Not just any visitor from the looks of it," he said as a lopsided grin spread across his face.

"You've brought the Queen herself to grace our humble abode, Percy."

Ellie giggled. "Hardly," she replied. But as she glanced down at her modest dress, she realised with a start how out of place she must seem. Compared to the tattered and patched hand-me-downs of the others, her clothes felt extravagant.

"This is Miss Eleanor Dubois," Percy said. "She's been volunteering at St Mary's Mission, and she wanted to see for herself where the people of the rookeries live."

"So we're a zoo now, are we?" Jack quipped. "For the viewing pleasure of the rich and curious?"

Percy shook his head and turned to Ellie. "As you can tell, young Jack here has quite the sense of humour."

From her seat at the table, Lucy muttered without looking up from her sewing, "That's a nice way of saying he's a clown and a fool."

Ellie smiled. She was beginning to warm to these two siblings: even in the middle of so much poverty, they had pluck and spirit.

"Don't let their words deceive you, girl," Percy said. "Angels in disguise is what they are. Letting a useless old cripple like me share their space."

Jack popped the last piece of apple into his mouth and folded up his penknife. "You're volunteering at St Mary's? A rich blighter with a heart: we don't get those around here very often. Never, actually."

Ellie shifted uncomfortably. "I'm not that rich, really. There are many people far wealthier than my family."

"Maybe so. But I bet even the privy at your house looks ten times nicer than this place," Jack said, gesturing at their pitiful room with a sweep of his arm.

Ellie felt a wave of shame wash over her as she studied the sparse surroundings once more. The contrast with her own comfortable world was stark and unsettling.

"But it's home," Jack continued, with a hint of pride in his voice. "And that's good enough for Lucy and me. Ain't that right, sis?"

His sister didn't answer and continued with her sewing instead.

"I'd offer you something nice," Jack said to Ellie. "Like a piece of cake and a cup of tea. But unfortunately, we don't have those sorts of luxurious treats. The only thing you'll find in our cupboards is dust and mice droppings."

He paused and then grinned. "Not the mice themselves, mind you. They've long since moved off to better places, where there's actually something to eat."

Ellie's feelings of guilt intensified. She thought of the abundant meals served at Mrs Bennett's Academy, and the amounts of uneaten food that were cleared from the table afterwards.

"I'm so sorry," she said softly. "I had never imagined things were so difficult for you."

"Now you know, girl," Percy said. "It's what you wanted, wasn't it? To see the ugly truth?"

Ellie nodded, keeping her eyes to the ground, too ashamed to look directly at any of them.

"Did you say your name was Dubois?" Jack asked.

"Yes, it's a French name," Ellie explained.

"Sounds very posh to me," he joked to lighten the mood.

"Actually, it's a fairly common one," she smiled. "In English, it would be Woods."

"Ah, so at least your name is common as muck then," he laughed. "Does that mean you're French?"

"Her stepfather's French," Percy put in.

"That's right," Ellie said. "I'm just from Sheffield. Nothing special."

"Sheffield?" Jack asked. "You're a long way from home then. What brings you to London? Surely, it's not just to see glorious Spitalfields?"

"I'm attending a finishing school here in London. My mother's idea, not mine."

"What's a finishing school?"

Percy chuckled. "That's where they teach girls how to become a proper lady."

"Hear that, Lucy?" Jack said to his sister. "That must be why you're not a lady: we never sent you to finishing school."

Lucy made a short snorting sound to acknowledge his joke.

"It's not nearly as glamorous or useful as you might think," Ellie hastened to say. "Being a lady takes more than a few silly lessons on manners and how to run a household. Or it does in my view anyway."

She thought of Lydia. That one would never be a lady, no matter how many finishing schools she went to.

"Nevertheless," Jack said. "You'll have to teach me some of those fancy manners. I've always wanted to walk around town like a dandy."

He stood up, pranced around for a few steps and then pretended to tip an imaginary hat as he addressed Percy with an exaggerated posh accent. "Good day to you, fine sir. Might I trouble you for the time? I seem to have left my gold watch at home."

Ellie giggled and even Lucy's lips twitched in what appeared to be a smile.

"I'm not sure I'd be the best teacher," Ellie said. "Half the time, I feel like I'm doing everything wrong."

"So what?" Jack winked. "Down here, we're all doing everything wrong. The difference is, we can't afford to care."

Chapter Nine

A rap at the door jolted Ellie from her fitful slumber.

"Time to rise, young ladies," the voice of one of Mrs Bennett's maids called out from the landing as she went round knocking on everyone's door. "Breakfast is in half an hour."

Ellie groaned, pulling her blanket tighter around her shoulders. The chill of the early morning air nipped at her nose, making her long for just a few more minutes of warmth.

"Phoebe," she whispered urgently. "Time to wake up. The maid is making her rounds."

"Already?" her friend moaned, her voice thick with sleep. "It can't be morning yet, surely?"

"I'm afraid it is," Ellie sighed, swinging her legs over the side of the bed. The floorboards creaked beneath her feet as she padded over to the washstand, splashing cold water on her face to chase away the last traces of sleep.

As she dried her face with a rough towel, vivid images from the nightmare she had been having came rushing back. Her hands began to tremble, and she gripped the edge of the washstand to steady herself.

"Ellie, what's wrong?" Phoebe asked as she got out of bed and came over to the washstand as well.

"Nothing. Just this dream I had."

"It must have been a pretty nasty one: you look as pale as a ghost."

With a heavy sigh, Ellie crossed the small room and settled back onto her bed, drawing her knees up to her chest.

"Want to tell me about it?" Phoebe asked as she began to wash her face.

"It was about Jack and Lucy," Ellie said, her eyes distant. "They were starving, Phoebe. Wasting away before my very eyes. And Lydia was there, too: laughing at their misery." She shook her head, as if trying to dispel the memory.

"Oh, Ellie." Phoebe finished washing her face and came to sit beside her. She took Ellie's hand, squeezing it gently.

"And do you know what Lydia did?" Ellie continued. "She looked down at them and said, 'Let them eat cake.' Can you believe it? As if their suffering was nothing but a joke to her."

Phoebe sighed, her thumb tracing soothing circles on the back of Ellie's hand. "It was just a dream, Ellie. You know Lydia's never even met Jack and Lucy."

"But that's not the point, is it?" Ellie said, pulling her hand away and standing up. She began to pace the small room. "My dream might not have been real, but Jack and Lucy's suffering is. And Lydia – well, she might as well have said those words, given how little she cares about the plight of the poor."

"I understand how you feel," Phoebe said gently. "But Ellie, you're already doing so much to help. You volunteer at St Mary's whenever you can. You've befriended Jack and Lucy. You've shown them kindness. That's more than most people in our position would ever do."

Ellie stopped her pacing and sighed. Phoebe was right of course. But that didn't make the injustice of it all any easier to bear.

"We'd better get dressed," her friend said. "You know how Mrs Bennett feels about tardiness."

At the breakfast table, Ellie sat stirring her porridge listlessly, her spoon tracing slow and random patterns in the creamy oats. The chatter of her fellow students washed over her, a meaningless babble that only served to highlight her sense of isolation.

"I simply cannot fathom why anyone would choose such heavy fare for breakfast," Lydia's voice cut through Ellie's brooding. "It's as if some people have no regard for their figures or their digestive health."

To emphasise her point, she delicately picked at the few slices of fruit that lay on her plate, next to a single piece of sparsely buttered toast.

Nibbling on a morsel of pineapple, her eyes flicked dismissively over the other girls' choices before landing on Ellie's bowl of porridge.

A smirk played on Lydia's lips as she continued, "But I suppose when one is accustomed to shovelling coal, one develops rather primitive tastes."

Susan, seated to Lydia's right, nodded in agreement. "Porridge is so terribly common, don't you think? It's what labourers eat, for goodness' sake."

"Or savages from the North," Lydia added with a snigger.

Emily chimed in, pushing away her barely-touched plate of kedgeree. "It's no wonder some girls here look rather robust. I'd sooner fast than risk eating such vulgarity. One must maintain standards, after all."

Lydia sighed dramatically, setting down her fork. "This pineapple is frightfully tart. I don't know why I bothered."

Susan, following Lydia's lead, pushed her own plate away, despite the fact that she had clearly been in the midst of eating her eggs and toast.

"Oh, I simply can't stomach another bite," she declared with affected weariness. "Let the maid take it away and feed it to the pigs. I'm sure the filthy beasts will be glad of the scraps."

"Now, now, Susan," Lydia said. "That would be terribly cruel to the pigs. Even they deserve better than this poor slop."

As the mean trio burst out in a fit of nasty giggles, Ellie's knuckles turned white and she clenched her jaw, trying to contain the angry words that threatened to spill out.

How could anyone be so blind to their own good fortune?

Her gaze swept across the table, taking in the abundance before them. So much food, destined to be discarded simply because it didn't meet the exacting standards of these pampered girls.

The nightmare faces of Jack and Lucy flashed in her mind, their hollow cheeks and weary eyes a painful contrast to the pettiness she witnessed here.

Ellie's heart ached at the unfairness. Here at this table, people turned their noses up at perfectly good food. While just a few miles away, others were slowly starving.

It made her angry to think about how much of this abundance before her would be wasted, while Jack and Lucy struggled to fill their bellies.

But as her eyes darted around the table, an idea began to form in Ellie's head. Making sure no one was watching, she reached for her napkin.

Quickly, she placed a plump bread roll upon it, followed by a small wedge of hard cheese. Her hand hovered over the fruit bowl before selecting a perfect peach.

"Ellie," Phoebe whispered, leaning in close. "What on earth are you doing?"

"I can't stand to see all this food go to waste," she replied quietly. "Not when I know how desperately Jack and Lucy need it. Please, Phoebe. Help me."

For a moment, Phoebe hesitated. Then, with a small nod, she reached for her own napkin. Ellie watched as her friend carefully wrapped up a bun, two hard-boiled eggs and a crisp apple.

"Are you two still that hungry?"

Ellie started at the sound of Agnes' voice. The girl was peering curiously at the small pile of food on their napkins.

"Oh, we..." Ellie fumbled for a plausible explanation. "We always get rather peckish during Mrs Novak's piano lessons. So we thought we'd take a little snack with us."

Agnes' face lit up with understanding. "I know exactly what you mean. I'm always famished during dancing class. Although," she giggled, "I don't think Mrs Bennett would approve of me nibbling on a scone while we're practising the waltz."

Ellie forced a laugh, relief flooding through her. "No, I don't imagine she would."

"Here," Agnes said, pushing a fruit scone towards Ellie. "You might as well take this too. I'm sure Mrs Novak won't mind if you have a little extra sustenance."

"Thank you, Agnes," Ellie said, blushing furiously. She added the scone to her already full napkin, and then carefully folded the corners to conceal its contents.

As breakfast came to an end, Ellie and Phoebe rose from their seats, their precious bundles hidden within the folds of their dresses. Ellie's heart pounded as they made their way out of the morning room, half-expecting Mrs Bennett's sharp voice to halt them at any moment.

But no one stopped them. And no one questioned the slight bulge in their garments or the careful way they held themselves.

As they stepped into the hallway, Ellie allowed herself a small smile of triumph. It wasn't much perhaps, but it was a start.

"And what do we do now?" Phoebe whispered nervously.

"We go to our room and get ready to go to Mrs Novak's, of course," Ellie replied, wary of being overheard in the busy hallway.

They hurried up the stairs and entered their room. Phoebe quickly shut the door and locked it, before letting out a long breath in relief.

"This isn't stealing, is it?" she asked timidly.

"Of course not," Ellie replied while she unwrapped her napkin and placed the food in a small basket. "These scraps and leftovers would only end up being thrown away. We're not stealing, we're... redistributing. Jack and Lucy will be so grateful for this food, Phoebe."

Phoebe nodded slowly, but she still looked worried. "I'm sure they will be. It's just... Well, it feels a bit like we're going behind Mrs Bennett's back."

"I suppose we are, in a sense." Ellie took Phoebe's napkin and added its contents to the basket. "But think of it this way: we're not really breaking the rules, we're merely bending them a little. In the interest of charity."

"Charity," Phoebe repeated, not quite sounding convinced. "I just hope my father will see it in that light as well. If he ever finds out I've been smuggling food out of the morning room..."

"He won't find out," Ellie said, trying to put a reassuring tone in her voice. "And even if he did, surely he would understand? This is a good deed we're doing here, Phoebe."

She picked up the basket, its weight a comforting reminder of her mission. "Now, let's go before we're late for Mrs Novak."

Chapter Ten

Ellie stood behind the serving table at St Mary's Mission, ladling steaming stew into the chipped bowls that passed before her. The small basket at her feet seemed to tug at her attention like an impatient child. She could hardly wait to deliver its precious cargo to Jack and Lucy.

"Here you are, sir," she said warmly to the gaunt man before her. "Steaming hot and plenty of meat in it: it'll do you a world of good."

The man merely grunted, his eyes fixed on the floor as he shuffled away. Ellie's smile faded slightly. No matter how hard she tried, most of the mission's visitors seemed determined to avoid any genuine conversation.

As she watched them file past, each face a canvas of despair, her heart ached. What terrible hardships had these poor souls endured to make them appear so empty? So devoid of even the smallest spark of joy?

"Well, well," a familiar sardonic voice sounded. "If it isn't our newest angel of mercy, spreading light and happiness among us wretched sinners."

Ellie looked up to find Percy Yates standing before her, leaning on his gnarled walking stick.

"Mr Yates," she beamed. "I was beginning to worry you wouldn't come today."

"Miss me, did you?" he asked with his usual gruffness. But Ellie caught the ghost of a smile playing at the corners of his mouth.

"As a matter of fact, I did." She glanced around to make sure Mrs Collins wasn't within earshot, then lowered her voice. "I have something for Jack and Lucy."

Percy raised an eyebrow. "Oh?"

Ellie subtly nudged the basket with her foot. "Just a few things from breakfast. Nothing much, but..."

"Ah," Percy's eyes gleamed with understanding. "Been playing Robin Hood, have we?"

"Not exactly," Ellie blushed. "It would have gone to waste otherwise."

"Well then," Percy said. "Why don't you come along with me when you're done here? Give them your bounty yourself?"

"Could I?" Ellie's face lit up. "I'd love to see them again."

"They seemed quite taken with you after your last visit," Percy remarked casually. "Though heaven knows why. Must be going soft, those two."

Ellie laughed, recognising the gruff affection beneath his prickly exterior. "In that case, I'd better not keep them waiting too long."

She quickly ladled out a generous portion of stew for him, then glanced towards the kitchen where Mrs Collins was busy directing other volunteers.

"Mrs Collins?" she called out. "I'm terribly sorry, but I'm afraid I need to leave a bit early today. My piano teacher has requested an extra lesson this afternoon."

"Of course, dear," Mrs Collins replied without looking up from her work. "Thank you for all your help."

Ellie's stomach twisted with guilt at the lie, but she pushed the feeling aside. After all, she told herself, she was only trying to help those in need. Surely that counted for something?

She continued serving for a little while longer, so that Percy could eat his stew. Then she untied her apron, collected her basket, and followed him out into the streets of Spitalfields.

Making their way through the twisting alleyways, Percy set that same brisk pace as on her first visit. Ellie stayed close behind him, already imagining Jack and Lucy's happy faces when they saw what she had brought them.

"You know," Percy said over his shoulder, "Jack and Lucy were talking about you the other day."

"They were?" Ellie nearly stumbled over an uneven cobblestone in her eagerness to hear more.

"Oh, yes. Jack said it was refreshing to meet someone from your world who didn't look down their nose at the common folk. And Lucy... Well, you must have made quite an impression."

"I did? How so?" Ellie couldn't hide her surprise. The girl had barely spoken two words to her.

"Full of praise, she was," Percy assured her. "And believe me, that's quite something. Lucy's not exactly known for sharing her thoughts and feelings."

"Really?" Ellie's heart soared at this revelation. "What did she say?"

"That you seemed genuine. Different from the usual do-gooders who come to gawk at our misery." He paused, then added, "Mind you, Lucy's not one to trust easily. Been hurt too many times before, she has."

Ellie's joy dimmed slightly at these words. "I would never want to hurt either of them."

Percy stopped so abruptly that Ellie nearly walked into him. He turned to face her, his eyes boring into hers.

"Are you certain about that?" he asked, his voice low and serious.

"I... Of course I am," Ellie stammered, confused by the sudden change in his demeanour.

"Because you see, Miss Dubois, Jack and Lucy have had their fair share of well-meaning ladies swooping in to save them." Percy's grip tightened on his walking stick. "Women who come here full of grand ideas about helping the poor. They hang around for a week or two, and then they disappear back to their comfortable lives after the novelty has worn off."

"But I'm not–"

"Oh, I'm sure you mean well," Percy cut her off. "But what happens when the excitement fades? When the reality of our dreary existence becomes too much for your delicate sensibilities?" His voice grew harder. "I won't have Jack and Lucy getting attached only to be abandoned again. I won't have their hearts broken by another fleeting act of charity."

Ellie clutched her basket closer, as if it might shield her from Percy's harsh words. "Mr Yates, I assure you, my intentions are sincere. I'm not here for excitement or novelty."

"No?" He raised an eyebrow. "Then why are you here?"

"Because..." Ellie paused, searching for words that would convey the depth of her feelings. "Because it isn't right. The way people live here, the suffering they go through while others waste so much. Now that I've seen it, I can't possibly ignore it."

Percy studied her face for a long moment. Finally, his stern expression softened slightly. "Well, perhaps you are different," he conceded. "Time will tell, I suppose."

He turned and resumed walking, leaving Ellie to hurry after him. Her mind whirled with what he had said, and she felt a fierce determination growing in her chest. She would prove herself worthy of Jack and Lucy's trust.

She would show Percy, and everyone else, that not all charity came with strings attached. Some people, she told herself, simply wanted to help because it was the right thing to do.

They turned down a narrow street that Ellie still recognised from her previous visit. Entering the familiar tenement building, they climbed the creaking staircase where a musty smell hung in the air.

When they reached the right floor, Percy paused to catch his breath and then he used his stick to push open the crooked door to the room.

Jack's face broke into a broad grin at the sight of their visitors.

"Why look, it's our favourite lady from finishing school," he said cheerfully.

Lucy glanced up from her sewing, and though she didn't speak, the corners of her mouth lifted in what Ellie was certain was a smile.

"I've brought you something," Ellie said, stepping forward and setting her basket on the rickety table. Her fingers trembled slightly with nervous excitement as she unwrapped the napkins to reveal their contents.

Jack's eyes widened when he saw the food. "Would you look at that, Lucy? We've got ourselves a proper feast here."

He picked up the peach, turning it over in his hands with an expression of wonder. "I've never tasted one of these before," he mused.

Holding the peach underneath his nose, he closed his eyes and took in its delicate fragrance. Then, without hesitation, he handed it to his sister.

"Here, you have it, Lucy. Smells like it's perfectly ripe, too."

Lucy accepted the fruit carefully, as if she were being given a precious jewel.

Jack began to pull out chairs for everyone. "We're all going to sit down and share this bounty properly. Like civilised folk at a fancy tea party."

He winked at Ellie, and with a playful flourish, he invited her to take a seat. "That's what they teach you at finishing school, isn't it? How to host elegant gatherings?"

Blushing, Ellie let out a nervous little giggle as she sat down with the two siblings.

"Nothing for me, thank you," Percy said, holding up his hands. "I've had my stew at the mission, so I'll gladly leave these delicacies to you young people. You need it more than I do. And besides," he added with a pointed look at the modest spread, "there's little enough as it is."

Ellie's face fell as she glanced at the meagre offering she had brought. "I'm so sorry. I know it isn't much. Just a tiny drop in the ocean, really."

She twisted her hands in her lap, then added hesitantly, "But I could try to bring more next time?" She paused, her cheeks flushing. "That is... If you want there to be a next time?"

"Want?" Jack laughed, already breaking the bread into equal portions. "My dear Miss Dubois, you're welcome here anytime you please. With or without these delicious treats." He gave her a warm smile. "Though I won't pretend we don't appreciate them."

Ellie felt as if her heart might burst. Her breath caught in a small gasp: they actually wanted her to come back. Did this mean they had accepted her?

Blinking back tears of joy, she busied herself helping Jack divide the cheese.

"Right then," Jack announced, rubbing his hands together. "Let's tuck in. Lucy, why don't you put the kettle on? Nothing like a cup of tea to go with a splendid little meal like this."

"Oh, please, let me," Ellie said, jumping up eagerly. "It's the least I can–"

A sharp ripping sound cut through her words, followed by a horrified gasp. In her haste to rise, her dress had caught on a jagged edge of the wooden chair. A sizeable tear now gaped along her skirt.

"Oh no," she whispered, her face draining of colour as she fingered the torn fabric. "Oh no, no, no..."

"It's just a little tear," Jack said soothingly. "Nothing to fret about."

"But how am I going to explain this at the academy?" Ellie's voice rose in panic. "Mrs Bennett notices everything. She'll want to know exactly how it happened, and then what will I say? I can't tell her I was here because I'm supposed to be at my piano lesson and–"

She clapped a hand over her mouth, realising too late what she had just revealed.

Percy lifted an eyebrow. "Piano lesson, eh? So that's your cover story for these charitable expeditions of yours?"

Ellie nodded miserably. "Please don't tell anyone. If Mrs Bennett found out I've been lying about where I go..."

"Your secret's safe with us," Percy assured her, his voice unusually gentle. "We're not in the habit of betraying friends. Are we, Jack?"

"Certainly not," Jack agreed firmly. Then he brightened. "Besides, you're in luck. Our Lucy here happens to be the finest seamstress in all of Spitalfields."

His sister got up from her seat and came over to Ellie's side, examining the tear with expert eyes. Without a word, she retrieved her sewing basket and selected a needle and thread that matched Ellie's dress perfectly.

"Do you think you can fix it?" Ellie asked, biting her lip anxiously. "I'd be ever so grateful."

Lucy's only response was to gesture for Ellie to stand still. Her fingers moved with incredible speed and precision, the needle weaving in and out of the fabric in tiny, even stitches. Within minutes, she tied off the thread and stepped back.

Ellie twisted around, trying to spot the repair. "Why, I can hardly see where it was torn. Lucy, you're absolutely magical with that needle."

A faint blush coloured Lucy's cheeks at the praise, and she ducked her head, returning to the task of making tea.

"See?" Jack grinned. "Everything works out in the end. Now, let's raise our teacups to new friendships and Lucy's skills with a needle and thread."

As Ellie sank back into her chair – more carefully this time – she felt a warm glow of happiness spread through her chest. Here she was, sharing tea and companionship with people who accepted her, who would keep her secrets.

For the first time since coming to London, she felt truly at home. In ragged old Spitalfields of all places.

Chapter Eleven

"Quick, quick," Phoebe giggled as she and Ellie raced up the stairs, their skirts rustling with hidden treasures. "Before anyone sees us."

They burst into their room, and Ellie swiftly locked the door behind them. Both girls were flushed and breathless, their eyes sparkling with excitement.

"I can't believe how much we managed to save this time," Ellie whispered triumphantly as she began to empty her napkin. "Look: three fresh rolls, and that lovely little apple tart that Lydia turned her nose up at."

"And these," Phoebe added, carefully unwrapping her own bundle. "Two perfectly good hard-boiled eggs, and a thick slice of ham that Emily declared 'thoroughly unpalatable' just because it wasn't cut thin enough for her delicate taste."

They worked quickly, transferring their morning's spoils to Ellie's basket. The sight of so much rescued food made Ellie's heart soar.

"Just imagine Jack and Lucy's faces when they see all this," she said softly. "Oh, Phoebe, doesn't it feel wonderful? To know that instead of being thrown away, this food will actually help someone?"

"It does," Phoebe agreed, though her voice held a touch of anxiety. "But Ellie, we must be more careful. I saw Mrs Bennett watching us rather closely this morning."

"Did she? I was too busy trying to catch that wedge of cheese before Susan sent it back to the kitchen."

"Well, she was. And Agnes kept glancing our way too."

"Agnes wouldn't say anything even if she did suspect something," Ellie said confidently. "She's too timid to cause trouble. Besides," she added with a grin, "who would believe that two respectable young ladies from the Bloomsbury Academy would resort to smuggling breakfast scraps in their napkins?"

Phoebe laughed. "When you put it that way, it does sound rather absurd, doesn't it?"

"Precisely." Ellie stepped back to admire their well-stocked basket. "And speaking of gifts for our friends in Spitalfields..."

She moved to their shared wardrobe and reached into the far corner, behind her neatly folded clothes. "I have something special for Lucy."

"Oh?" Phoebe's eyes widened with curiosity. "What is it?"

Ellie withdrew a small cloth-wrapped package. Opening it carefully, she revealed several lengths of thread in various colours, two gleaming needles, and an assortment of fabric scraps: some in silk, others in fine cotton and wool.

"Ellie," Phoebe gasped. "Are those from our sewing class?"

"They are," Ellie admitted, running her fingers over a particularly lovely piece of lavender silk. "But they're only leftover bits and pieces. Miss Thompson would have thrown them away anyway."

"But still..." Phoebe bit her lip. "Taking food that would be wasted is one thing, but this..."

"Oh, Phoebe, you should see what Lucy can do with just a needle and thread," Ellie insisted. "The way she mended my dress the other day. You couldn't even tell where the tear had been. Just think what she might create with proper materials."

"I suppose..." Phoebe's voice trailed off uncertainly.

"She has such talent, Phoebe. Such skill. It seems cruel that she should be denied the tools to use her gift properly, just because she was born poor."

"You're right, of course," Phoebe said quietly. "It's just..."

She didn't finish her thought, but Ellie noticed that her friend's earlier enthusiasm had faded. The giddy excitement that had carried them up the stairs now felt distant, replaced by something heavier and more sobering.

Ellie carefully wrapped the sewing supplies back up and tucked them into her basket alongside the food. Neither girl spoke for a moment, both troubled by the growing weight of their deceptions, no matter how well-intentioned they might be.

And this sense of unease hadn't faded yet by the time Ellie sat in the hansom cab that carried her towards the rookery. She was in two minds about what to do: go to St Mary's first, or head straight to Jack and Lucy's?

The idea of skipping her duties at St Mary's – even just this once – felt wrong. Volunteering at the mission was the whole reason why she had spun this complicated web of lies and excuses.

But her basket was so full today, and she couldn't bear the thought of making Jack and Lucy wait for their much-needed provisions.

Besides, she reasoned with herself, her true goal was to learn more about the poor people of Spitalfields. And Jack and Lucy were infinitely more open and friendly with her than any of the regulars at the mission.

"You can let me off here," she called to the driver, making an impulsive decision. "I know my way."

The familiar maze of narrow streets soon welcomed her with their usual bleak sights and appalling smells. A group of barefoot children scattered as she approached, like twittering birds taking flight. One small boy paused to stare at her fine dress before darting away after his companions.

When she reached the tenement where Jack and Lucy lived, she climbed the creaking stairs with practised steps, careful to avoid the loose boards she had learned to recognise.

She knocked at their door. "Lucy? Jack?" she spoke up softly. "It's me, Eleanor Dubois."

"Our guardian angel returns," Jack smiled as he opened the door. "And she comes bearing gifts again, from the looks of it."

Ellie giggled and nodded as she held up her basket for him to see.

"Please, do come in," he said with an exaggerated bow. "Lucy, we have esteemed company."

Lucy glanced up from her work – she appeared to be mending a torn shirt – and offered Ellie one of her rare, slight smiles.

"I brought a few things," Ellie said, setting her basket on their table. "A bit more than last time."

Jack's eyes widened as she began to unpack. "Would you look at that, Lucy? Real ham. And is that an apple tart I spy?"

"The ham is perfectly good," Ellie assured them. "It was only rejected because the cook sliced it too thick for some of the girls' liking."

"Their loss is our gain," Jack replied cheerfully. Then, noticing Ellie was still holding something back, he raised an eyebrow. "What else have you got hidden in there, Miss Dubois?"

"Please, call me Ellie," she said warmly. "After all, we're friends now, aren't we?"

Jack's face lit up. "That we are... Ellie." He tried out her name, as if testing how it felt. "Though I have to say, calling you 'Miss Dubois' made me feel like a proper gentleman."

"We can't have that now, can we?" Ellie giggled. "You're much more charming when you're being yourself."

Suddenly shy about her own forwardness, she quickly turned her attention back to her basket. "Actually, I brought something special for Lucy. Just a small token of thanks, really. For mending my dress the other day."

She withdrew the small package and held it out to Lucy, who set aside her sewing and accepted it with questioning eyes. Then the girl's long, sensitive fingers began to unwrap it.

"I know it isn't much," Ellie said hurriedly. "Just some odds and ends from our sewing class.

But I thought perhaps you might be able to use them?"

Lucy's breath caught as she touched the silk scraps, her fingertips barely grazing their surface as if she feared they might dissolve at her touch. When she came to the needles, gleaming and straight, Ellie saw her blink rapidly.

"What our Lucy means to say," Jack stepped in, "is thank you. She's not used to... Well, people don't generally..."

He cleared his throat and tried again. "Thing is, Ellie, most folk don't show us this sort of kindness. Not without wanting something in return, if you take my meaning."

"Oh, but I don't want anything," Ellie protested. "Except perhaps..."

"Yes?" Jack prompted, a hint of his usual mischief returning to his eyes.

"I would love to see more of Lucy's work." She turned to the girl and added, "You're so talented."

Lucy ducked her head, but not before Ellie caught the gleam of a tear on her cheek.

"Gifted is what our Lucy is," Jack declared proudly. "Why, I always say she could've been the Queen's seamstress if only we'd been born in better circles."

He scratched the back of his head. "Listen, Ellie, I feel like we ought to do something in return for you. How about we give you a taste of the real London?"

"The real London?"

"Not the fancy streets and shops. I'm sure you've already seen those. I'm talking about the real heart of the city: the markets, the taverns, the places where ordinary folk go to enjoy themselves."

Ellie's eyes lit up at the prospect, but then reality intruded. "Oh, I wish I could. But the academy... Mrs Bennett would never allow it."

"Who says Mrs Bennett needs to know?" Jack's eyes sparkled with conspiracy. "Surely, a clever girl like you could think of some excuse? Some way to slip out for an evening?"

"I suppose I might," Ellie said slowly, her mind already working on possibilities.

"Excellent," Jack exclaimed. "How about tomorrow evening? Lucy and I could meet you outside St Mary's."

Ellie hesitated, torn between excitement and apprehension. "You're sure it would be safe?"

"Safe as houses," Jack assured her. "Lucy will be with us the whole time. And I know every street and alley in this part of London. No harm will come to you, I promise."

Looking at their eager faces – even Lucy seemed animated by the idea – Ellie felt her resistance crumbling. "Well... perhaps..."

"That's the spirit," Jack grinned. "Trust me, it'll be an evening you won't soon forget."

Ellie managed an awkward smile. This was what she wanted, she told herself: a taste of real life.

But then why did the prospect make her so nervous?

Chapter Twelve

"They invited you to do what?" Phoebe stopped walking, her mouth falling open in shock.

"To see the real London," Ellie repeated. "Jack says he knows all sorts of interesting places. Markets and taverns and such."

Ellie had told Phoebe all about Jack's invitation on their way back to the Academy. She had hoped that Phoebe might have some useful advice on the matter. But now it seemed her friend wasn't on board with the idea at all.

"Surely you're not thinking of accepting?" Phoebe's voice rose slightly. "Ellie, that's... that's completely mad."

"Is it though?" Ellie resumed walking, forcing Phoebe to hurry after her. "Think about it, Phoebe. We don't know anything about Spitalfields apart from what we saw during that guided tour and on my brief visits to Jack and Lucy's. There must be so much more to understand about how these people live."

"But at night? In taverns?" Phoebe shook her head. "It sounds terribly dangerous."

"Jack promised me it would be perfectly safe. Lucy will be with us too."

"Oh, well, if Lucy will be there," Phoebe said sarcastically. But then her expression softened. "How did she like her gift, by the way?"

"She nearly cried," Ellie replied. "Can you imagine that, Phoebe? Nearly brought to tears by a few scraps of fabric and some needles. It really makes you think about how fortunate we are."

Her friend nodded and sighed. "I suppose I can see why you want to go," Phoebe said. "You've always been curious about... well, everything really. And you're clever. You'll figure out some way to pull it off."

"That's just it though," Ellie said. "I haven't the faintest idea how to get permission for an evening out. Mrs Bennett is never going to allow it."

"Not likely, no."

Ellie let out an exasperated sigh. "But enough about my problems. How was your lesson with Mrs Novak today?"

"Oh, the usual," Phoebe replied. "She dozed through most of it. Though she did wake up long enough to tell me about some grand concert she said she once gave at the Royal Opera House. She does love to reminisce about her glory days as a concert pianist."

"That's it," Ellie blurted out suddenly. "Oh, Phoebe, you're brilliant."

"I am? What did I say?"

"When you talked about concerts at grand places. Don't you see? I could tell Mrs Bennett that Mrs Novak wants to take me to a piano recital. Since I'm Mrs Novak's best and brightest student – supposedly anyway – it would make perfect sense for her to want to expose me to professional performances."

"Ellie, no," Phoebe protested. "That's going too far. It's one thing to bend the truth about extra lessons, but this..."

"Why not? Mrs Bennett already believes I'm some sort of musical prodigy. This would only reinforce her idea."

"But what if she asks Mrs Novak about it?"

"She won't," Ellie said confidently. "She never has before. And you know how much she loves to brag about her students' accomplishments. Having one attending special recitals with a former concert pianist? She'll be delighted."

Phoebe still looked troubled. "I don't know, Ellie."

"You could come too, you know," Ellie suggested brightly. "I could easily tell Mrs Bennett that Mrs Novak invited both of us. Then you could see the real London as well."

"Me?" Phoebe's eyes widened in alarm. "Oh no, I couldn't possibly. I mean, I appreciate the offer, but–" She shook her head firmly. "No, I simply couldn't. But please be careful, Ellie. Promise me you'll be careful?"

"Of course I will," Ellie assured her, giving her friend's arm a gentle squeeze. "Everything will be fine. You'll see."

By the time they reached the academy, Ellie had made up her mind. "I'm going to see Mrs Bennett straight away," she announced as they climbed the front steps. "There's no point in delaying."

"Now?" Phoebe's eyes widened. "But shouldn't you take some time to think this through properly?"

"If I wait, I'll only lose my nerve." Ellie squeezed her friend's hand. "Wish me luck?"

"You'll need it," Phoebe sighed. "Try not to talk yourself into an even bigger mess than you're already in. Please?"

Ellie nodded and headed for the stairs that led to Mrs Bennett's office on the first floor. Her heart began to beat faster with each step she climbed.

Outside the headmistress's door, she paused to collect her thoughts. She had rehearsed her story during their walk back. But now that the moment had arrived, the words seemed to scatter like autumn leaves in a strong wind.

"Mrs Novak wants to take me to a piano recital," she whispered to herself, running through the key points. "A wonderful educational opportunity... Exposure to professional musicians."

Her fingers found Stuart's locket beneath her dress. The familiar touch of the cool silver against her skin helped to calm her racing pulse.

Taking a deep breath, she knocked on the door.

"Enter," Mrs Bennett's crisp voice called out.

Ellie stepped into the office, where she found the headmistress seated behind her large mahogany desk.

"Miss Dubois?" Mrs Bennett's eyebrows lifted slightly. "I don't recall having an appointment with you this afternoon."

"No, ma'am," Ellie replied, forcing herself to meet the older woman's stern gaze. "But I needed to speak with you about a rather urgent matter. If you could spare a few minutes?"

Mrs Bennett's lips pursed as she considered the request. "Very well," she said at last. "Take a seat."

But as soon as Ellie had settled into one of the straight-backed chairs, Mrs Bennett picked up her pen and returned her attention to the stack of papers before her.

"You won't mind if I finish this correspondence first?" she asked, though it wasn't really a question. "Since you've arrived without an appointment."

"Of course not, ma'am."

Ellie sat perfectly still, trying not to fidget as the scratching of Mrs Bennett's pen filled the silence. The minutes stretched out like hours. She could feel perspiration beginning to dampen her palms.

At last, Mrs Bennett set down her pen and folded her hands on the desk. "Now then, Miss Dubois. What is this urgent matter you wish to discuss?"

"It's about Mrs Novak, ma'am," Ellie began, willing her voice to remain steady. "She has very kindly invited me to attend a piano recital with her."

"A piano recital?" Mrs Bennett's eyes narrowed. "In the evening, I presume?"

"Yes, ma'am."

"Miss Dubois, surely you're aware that evening outings are highly irregular and strictly against school policy?"

"I understand that, ma'am," Ellie said quickly. "But Mrs Novak felt it would be tremendously educational for me to observe professional musicians perform. She says there's only so much one can learn from practice. And that watching true masters at work is essential for artistic development."

Mrs Bennett tilted her head, considering this. "An interesting perspective," she conceded. "However, I cannot allow a student to be out alone after dark. It simply wouldn't be proper."

"Oh, but I wouldn't be alone, ma'am," Ellie said. "Mrs Novak would be chaperoning me the entire time."

"I see." Mrs Bennett drummed her fingers on the desk. "Tell me, Miss Dubois, why hasn't Mrs Novak approached me about this directly?"

Ellie's heart skipped a beat, but she maintained her composure. "She felt it would be more convenient if I made the request, ma'am. Given that you're so busy with running the academy."

"Hmm." Mrs Bennett's expression grew thoughtful. "Perhaps I should discuss this with her first. I could send her a note–"

"Oh, but the recital is tomorrow night," Ellie blurted out. "And Mrs Novak has already purchased the tickets."

"Tomorrow night?" Mrs Bennett's voice sharpened. "Such short notice is completely unacceptable."

"I do apologise, ma'am," Ellie said, thinking quickly. "But you know what Mrs Novak is like: always doing everything with great passion and spontaneity. Must be her Slavic nature."

A ghost of a smile touched Mrs Bennett's lips. "Yes, these artistic Continental types. They certainly can be rather peculiar in their ways. Which begs the question: where exactly is this recital to be held? Not in one of those seedy music halls, I trust?"

"At St James's Hall, ma'am."

The headmistress sat up straighter, her interest visibly piqued. "St James's Hall, you say? Most prestigious."

"Yes, ma'am. Mrs Novak mentioned it's quite an important performance." Ellie leaned forward slightly. "Several distinguished musicians from Vienna will be attending."

"Indeed?" Mrs Bennett's eyes took on a calculating gleam, just as Ellie had hoped. "Foreign performers of note?"

"Oh yes, ma'am. Mrs Novak was particularly excited about introducing me to them after the concert." Ellie paused, then added carefully, "She said they're always eager to meet promising young talents."

"Did she now?" Mrs Bennett rose from her desk and walked to the window, clasping her hands behind her back. "And these Viennese guests: they move in influential circles, I assume?"

"Mrs Novak certainly implied as much, ma'am. She mentioned something about wealthy patrons of the arts being in attendance."

A moment of silence followed as Mrs Bennett gazed out at the academy's front garden. Ellie held her breath, hardly daring to hope.

"I suppose," Mrs Bennett said at last, turning back to face her, "that it would reflect rather well on the academy to have one of our students mixing in such elevated musical circles."

"I would certainly do my best to represent the school with dignity, ma'am."

"Yes, well." Mrs Bennett returned to her desk and sat down. "If I were to permit this highly irregular outing, there would need to be certain conditions."

"Of course, ma'am. Anything you say."

"You must be back at the academy no later than eleven o'clock. Not a minute later, is that clear?"

"Perfectly clear, ma'am."

"You will wear your best evening dress, obviously. Something suitable for such a distinguished venue. And do try not to slouch, Miss Dubois. Your posture does nothing to elevate your appearance."

"Yes, ma'am. Thank you, ma'am."

"Most importantly," Mrs Bennett fixed Ellie with a stern look. "Should you have the opportunity to converse with any persons of consequence, you will be sure to mention the Bloomsbury Academy."

"I understand completely, ma'am."

"Very well then." Mrs Bennett picked up her pen again. "You may go. But I shall expect a full report about the performance and any notable personages you encounter."

"Of course, ma'am. Thank you so much."

Ellie rose from her chair, willing herself to move at a dignified pace despite her urgent desire to flee the office. Her hand was on the doorknob when Mrs Bennett spoke again.

"Oh, and Miss Dubois?"

"Yes, ma'am?"

"Do try to pay attention to the musical program. I should be most interested to hear which pieces were performed."

"I'll be sure to remember every detail, ma'am."

Once safely outside in the corridor, Ellie sagged against the wall, her knees weak with relief. She had done it. She had actually done it.

But as her racing heart began to slow down, the reality of her situation sank in.

Now she would need to fabricate an entire evening of classical music, complete with names of performers and pieces she had never heard. And she would have to make Mrs Bennett believe every word of it.

Touching Stuart's locket once more, she couldn't help but wonder: how many more lies would she need to tell before this adventure was over?

Chapter Thirteen

A sharp wind whistled through the darkening streets of Spitalfields, playing with Ellie's skirts and making them rustle like whispered secrets. She pressed one gloved hand against Stuart's locket beneath her bodice, while the other gripped her reticule so tightly her knuckles ached. Every shadow seemed to hold watching eyes, every footstep behind her made her heart leap.

"You're being ridiculous," she told herself firmly, though her voice trembled. Jack and Lucy lived their lives here, and they walked these streets every day without fear.

But knowing that didn't stop her from flinching when a drunken laugh echoed from a nearby alley, or from quickening her step when she passed a cluster of ragged children who stared at her fine clothes with hungry eyes.

Good thing Mother didn't know about this little escapade, she thought. Her caring, sensible mother, who had sent her to finishing school to become a lady.

Yet here she was, sneaking through London's most notorious slum in her best evening dress, about to spend the night with a pair of street-wise siblings she barely knew.

The thought made her want to laugh and cry all at once. Instead, she lifted her chin and walked on, the thrill of rebellion warming her blood despite the chill air.

As St Mary's Mission came into view, she spotted two familiar figures lurking in the shadows.

"Over here," Jack's voice called softly.

Ellie hurried towards them, lifting her skirts clear of the filthy cobblestones. As she drew closer, Jack stepped into the dim light of a gas lamp and performed an elaborate bow.

"Well, strike me down," he declared with theatrical flair. "If it isn't an angel descended from heaven itself. Lucy, look at this vision of loveliness."

"Oh, stop it," Ellie giggled, though she couldn't help feeling pleased. She had spent nearly an hour choosing this dress, knowing Mrs Bennett would inspect her appearance before letting her leave the academy.

Lucy emerged from the shadows and circled Ellie slowly, her expert seamstress's eyes taking in every detail of the gown. Her fingers reached out to touch the fabric, then withdrew quickly, as if remembering her place.

"No, please," Ellie said. "Go ahead and look. I'd love to hear what you think of it."

Lucy's hand returned to the dress, this time with more confidence. She examined the intricate pleating at the waist, then moved to study the delicate lace trim at the collar.

"The pintucks are perfect," she murmured, speaking more words at once than Ellie had ever heard from her before. "And these tiny French knots: absolutely exquisite."

"Not nearly as nice as the ones you make though," Jack teased his sister. "Put this fancy dress to shame, they do."

Lucy shook her head, but Ellie caught the glimmer of a proud smile on the girl's face.

"Right then," Jack said, rubbing his hands together. "Before we begin our grand evening of adventure, we need to earn ourselves a bit of spending money. Can't show a fine lady like yourself a proper good time without a few pennies in our pockets, now can we?"

"Oh, but I brought some money," Ellie protested, reaching for her reticule.

"Now, now," Jack wagged his finger. "None of that. Tonight you're going to see how we common folk make our way in the world. Follow me."

He led them through a maze of narrow streets until they reached a small park surrounded by iron railings. Without hesitation, Jack vaulted over the low fence and began gathering flowers from the carefully tended beds.

"Jack," Ellie gasped. "You can't just take those."

"Course I can," he grinned, plucking another handful of blooms. "The park keeper's gone home hours ago. Besides, these flowers belong to everyone, don't they? Shame to let them waste away here when they could bring a smile to someone's face, don't you think?"

Before Ellie could argue further, he had assembled several small posies and climbed back over the fence. He handed one bunch to Lucy, keeping the rest for himself.

"Now watch and learn," he said with a wink. Then, spotting a well-dressed couple approaching, he stepped into their path.

"Fresh flowers for the lady, sir?" he called out cheerfully. "Picked at sunset to capture the day's last warmth. Just look how they glow, like your lovely wife's smile."

The gentleman started to wave him away, but his companion touched his arm. "Oh, Charles, aren't they lovely? And such a charming young man."

Jack's grin widened. "A penny a bunch, madam. And if I may say so, these pale yellow ones would complement your dress beautifully."

The lady blushed with pleasure, and her husband grudgingly produced a penny. Jack presented the flowers with a flourish worthy of a duke presenting a bouquet to the Queen.

"Quite the silver tongue you have, lad," the gentleman remarked, not unkindly.

"Why thank you, sir," Jack replied. "My dear mother always said it would either make me a fortune or get me into trouble. So far, it's done a fair bit of both."

The couple chuckled and moved on, the lady already arranging her flowers. Jack turned to Ellie with a triumphant smile, holding up his penny.

"And that, my dear Miss Dubois, is how it's done. Though I must say, having such a fine lady in our company certainly helps. Makes us look more respectable-like."

Jack's charm worked its magic on several more passersby, his quick wit and flattery earning them a handful of pennies.

When he declared they had enough for refreshments, he led them to a shabby public house tucked away in a narrow side street.

"Wait," Lucy said as they approached the entrance. "You can't go in there looking like that, Ellie."

She reached into the bundle she was carrying and pulled out a worn grey shawl, which she draped over Ellie's shoulders, carefully arranging it to hide the fine silk of her dress.

"We'll make a real street girl out of you yet," Jack quipped. "Bit less fancy, eh? Though we can't do much about that face of yours. Far too pretty to pass for a local."

Ellie blushed at the compliment as Lucy adjusted the shawl one final time. "Keep your head down," the girl advised quietly. "And stay close to us."

They entered the pub together, with Jack leading the way through the press of people while Lucy kept close to Ellie's side. The smell hit her first: a thick mixture of tobacco smoke, unwashed bodies, and spilled beer.

Jack shouldered his way through the crowd to an empty table in the corner, gesturing for the girls to follow. Once they were settled, he grinned at Ellie.

"Time for your first proper taste of London refreshment." He went to the bar and returned with three mugs of dark beer, sliding one towards her. "Nothing like what they serve at your fancy finishing school, I'll wager."

Ellie lifted the mug carefully, trying not to grimace at its sticky handle. The liquid inside was a deep amber colour, crowned with a foamy head. She took a tentative sip and nearly choked at the bitter taste.

"Good, isn't it?" Jack grinned, already halfway through his own drink.

"It's... different," Ellie managed, not wanting to seem ungrateful. She took another sip, finding it slightly less shocking this time. A peculiar warmth began to spread through her chest.

By the time she had finished half her mug, her cheeks felt flushed and the room had taken on a pleasantly fuzzy quality. Everything seemed funnier somehow, especially Jack's outrageous stories about his adventures in the streets of London.

"Time for some real fun," he declared when they had finished their drinks. He led them back into the night air, which seemed to make Ellie's head spin even more.

They wandered the darkened streets until Jack stopped them in front of a respectable-looking house.

"Watch this," he whispered, creeping up to the front door. He reached for the bell pull, gave it a firm yank, then turned and fled.

"Run," he yelled, laughing.

Ellie gathered up her skirts and ran after them, her shoes clattering on the cobblestones. Behind them, she heard the door open as an irritated voice called out "Who's there?"

They didn't stop running until they reached the end of the street, where they collapsed against a wall, breathless with laughter.

"I wish I could've seen his face," Jack wheezed, wiping tears from his eyes. "All proper and annoyed, he sounded."

"Shhh," Lucy hissed, but she was giggling too.

"I haven't run like that since I was a little girl," Ellie gasped, her sides aching. The beer had left her feeling wonderfully reckless.

"I'm starving," Jack announced suddenly. "Lucky for us, I know just the place."

He led them around the corner to where a grand hotel rose up into the night sky. At the service entrance, a loaded cart stood unattended, sacks of potatoes piled high.

"You ladies wait here," Jack said as he hefted one of the sacks onto his shoulder. "Won't be a minute."

Before Ellie or Lucy could protest, he was already strolling through the entrance as if he belonged there, whistling a cheerful tune. Ellie gave Lucy an incredulous look, but the girl merely shrugged: she was obviously used to her brother's antics.

Moments later, Jack reappeared, walking quickly but carefully. Once they were safely around the corner, he produced several fresh bread rolls and a wedge of cheese from inside his jacket.

"Courtesy of the hotel kitchen," he said proudly. "The cook was too busy shouting at some poor scullery maid to notice me. Though I did have to abandon the potatoes," he added with an exaggerated sigh. "Bit too heavy for a quick getaway."

"But Jack," Ellie started, her conscience pricking through the beer-induced haze. "That's–"

"Dinner," he finished firmly, breaking the bread into three portions. "And a fine one at that. Now, tuck in. Before anyone spots us."

After they had eaten the food, they wandered back into the rookery's narrow streets, where washing lines criss-crossed overhead between the crowded buildings, white linens fluttering like ghosts in the evening breeze.

"Perfect," Jack declared, reaching up to unhook a sheet. "These good people won't mind if we just rearrange things a bit."

"What do you mean?" Ellie asked, but Jack was already gathering an armful of washing.

"Think of it as a puzzle," he explained, moving to another line further down the street. "We're simply giving them something interesting to sort out tomorrow morning."

He began hanging the borrowed items in a completely different order, mixing pieces from different households.

"Like this tablecloth, for instance. Looks much better over here, don't you think? Adds a bit of variety to the neighbourhood."

Despite her misgivings, Ellie found herself giggling as she watched him work. The beer had left her feeling delightfully bold, as if anything were possible.

The evening wore on with more mischief and laughter, until Jack declared, "Let's pay a visit to our wealthy neighbours."

He guided them out of Spitalfields and into the respectable streets beyond, where they soon discovered a small square with a fountain splashing quietly in the darkness.

"Just the thing," Jack said, already pulling off his jacket. "Nothing like a late-night swim to end a perfect evening."

"You can't be serious," Ellie protested, but he was already stripping down to his underclothes.

"Look away if you must, ladies," he called out cheerfully, clambering onto the fountain's edge. "But I promise you won't see anything shocking."

With that, he dropped into the water with a splash that made both girls shriek with laughter.

"Jack," Lucy said, glancing at his discarded coat. "This white shirt poking out of your pocket... Isn't that from the washing line?"

"Oh, that old thing?" He followed her gaze to where the fine linen was visible beneath his crumpled jacket. "Must have got mixed up somehow. Don't worry, I'll return it. Eventually."

He grinned at them through the spray of water, then ducked under the surface again.

Lucy shook her head in fond exasperation while Ellie settled beside her on the fountain's wide stone rim, careful to keep her dress clear of the spray.

"Does he always get into such mischief?" she asked softly.

"Always," Lucy replied, but there was warmth in her voice. "Though tonight he's showing off a bit more than usual. Because of you, I expect."

They sat in comfortable silence for a moment, watching Jack splash about like a cheerful otter.

"Tell me about Sheffield," Lucy said suddenly. "What's it like there?"

"Oh, it's... different from London. Smaller, but busy in its own way. Full of factories and workshops." Ellie fingered Stuart's locket as she spoke. "That's where I met Stuart, actually. He's an engineer at my mother's steam engine factory."

"Stuart?" Lucy's eyes sparkled with interest. "Is he your sweetheart?"

Ellie blushed. "Well... yes. More than that, really. We're not officially engaged yet, but we both know it's only a matter of time before he asks."

"How romantic," Lucy sighed. "To marry for love... That must be wonderful."

"What about you?" Ellie asked. "What are your dreams for the future?"

Lucy's face grew serious. "I'd love to have my own shop someday. Nothing fancy, just a little dressmaking business. But..." She shrugged. "Dreams don't put food on the table, do they?"

"But you're so talented," Ellie insisted. "With your skills, surely–"

"Skills aren't enough," Lucy cut in gently. "You need money to start a business. Connections. Respectability. Things Jack and I will never have."

Ellie sat up straighter. Touching Stuart's locket, she thought of her mother's thriving factory. And of Mrs Pemberton-Thorpe and the many connections that the wealthy widow had. Perhaps...

"Time to head back, ladies," Jack announced, hauling himself out of the fountain. "Can't have our finishing school student missing her curfew."

As they walked back towards St Mary's Mission, Ellie's head spun from more than just the beer. The evening had shown her a different side of London, a world of freedom and adventure she had never known existed. And it had shown her how much more she could do to help her friends.

Jack and Lucy had so little, yet they had shown her such kindness. They had trusted her with their friendship, their dreams. Surely she owed them more than just scraps of food and stolen moments of companionship?

"I'll see you soon," she promised as they parted. Searching for a hansom cab, the streetlights of respectable London beckoned ahead. But Ellie found herself glancing back one last time, at the shadowy streets that were beginning to feel more and more like home.

Chapter Fourteen

"Weren't you frightened?" Phoebe whispered, her needle pausing mid-stitch. "Walking those dreadful streets in the dark?"

"Not with Jack and Lucy there," Ellie replied, her own work lying forgotten in her lap. "Though I must admit, that first sip of beer was rather shocking."

"Ellie," Phoebe's scandalised gasp drew a sharp look from Miss Thompson at the front of the sewing room. Both girls quickly bent their heads over their work, threading needles with exaggerated concentration until the teacher's attention moved elsewhere.

"I can't believe you actually drank it," Phoebe murmured once it was safe to talk again. Her voice dropped even lower. "Was it terribly bitter?"

"Horrid at first," Ellie said. "But after a while, it wasn't so bad. And oh, Phoebe, you should have seen Jack in the fountain. Splashing about like a happy child while Lucy and I sat watching and laughing."

The memory brought a smile to her face as her fingers moved mechanically through the familiar motions of hemming. Around them, the sewing room hummed with the usual quiet industry of nearly two dozen young ladies at their needlework. Late morning sunlight streamed through the tall windows, catching dust motes that danced in the air like tiny stars.

"I still can't quite believe you did it," Phoebe said, shaking her head. "Sneaking out at night, drinking in public houses, running through the streets like... like..."

"Like someone who's actually living a real life?" Ellie finished for her. "Instead of just existing behind these stuffy walls, learning how to be *proper*?" She infused the last word with all the disdain she could muster while still keeping her voice low.

Before Phoebe could respond, Lydia's annoying voice cut through the quiet murmur of conversation.

"Really, Miss Thompson," she declared, holding up her work with obvious distaste. "I simply cannot be expected to create anything worthwhile with such common materials. This fabric is hardly better than sackcloth."

A ripple of titters spread through the room as several girls nodded in agreement. Ellie's fingers tightened around her needle until she feared it might snap.

Miss Thompson looked up from where she had been examining another student's work.

Her grey eyes were cool as she regarded Lydia over the rim of her spectacles.

"My dear Miss Price," she said evenly. "True artistry lies not in the cost of one's materials, but in the skill of the hands that work them."

She paused, examining Lydia's uneven stitches. "Though in your case, I fear neither fine silk nor common cotton would make much difference to the end result."

Lydia's face flushed scarlet, but Miss Thompson had already moved on to inspect another student's work. In the awkward silence that followed, Ellie leaned close to Phoebe.

"If only Lucy had access to even half these materials," she whispered, running her fingers over the fine cotton before her. "You should see what she can create with just scraps and threads."

"So tragic," Phoebe sighed. "It seems terribly unfair, doesn't it? All these lovely fabrics here, and so many of the girls hardly appreciate them."

She glanced meaningfully at Lydia, who was now sullenly jabbing her needle through the cloth. "It's a pity we can't smuggle Lucy into our sewing class."

Ellie's hands froze. The sunlight streaming through the windows suddenly seemed brighter and more intense. As if they were shining on a path forward that had been hidden before.

"Phoebe," she breathed, her voice barely audible. "That's it."

"What's it?" Phoebe asked, then caught the gleam in her friend's eye. "Oh no. I know that look. Whatever you're thinking, Ellie, please don't–"

"We can't bring Lucy to the sewing room," Ellie said in an excited whisper. "But we could take some of these materials to her."

"Ellie, no." Phoebe's face went pale. "That would be stealing. Actually stealing. Not just taking leftover food or bits of thread, but real theft."

"Would it be though?" Ellie countered, her eyes fixed on the doorway that led to the supply room. "Think about it: most of these girls waste more fabric in one lesson than Lucy would use in a week. And she'd put it to such good use, Phoebe. She could make things to sell, earn some real money."

"Stop." Phoebe's needle trembled in her fingers. "Please stop. You know it's wrong, no matter how you try to justify it."

But Ellie barely heard her friend's protests. Her mind was already racing ahead, calculating possibilities. The supply room was rarely locked during lessons.

And Miss Thompson trusted her students. After all, who would dare to steal from the Bloomsbury Academy?

"All we need is a good distraction," she murmured, more to herself than to Phoebe. "Something to draw attention away from–"

"Miss Dubois?"

Both girls started guiltily as Miss Thompson's voice cut through their whispered conversation. The teacher stood at the front of the room, regarding them with raised eyebrows.

"I trust your hem is progressing well?" she asked pointedly.

"Yes, Miss Thompson," Ellie replied, forcing her hands to resume their work. "Very well indeed."

But even as she bent her head over her sewing, her thoughts remained fixed on the supply room door and the treasures that lay beyond it.

She could almost see Lucy's face lighting up at the sight of proper fabric. Real, beautiful material worthy of the girl's talents.

Beside her, Phoebe's nervous energy was almost palpable. But Ellie knew that her friend would help in the end. She always did.

When Miss Thompson turned away to examine Agnes's embroidery, Ellie took a deep breath. She gripped her fabric and pulled sharply. The sound of tearing cloth seemed deafening in the quiet room.

"Oh, fiddlesticks," she exclaimed, letting just the right amount of dismay colour her voice.

Miss Thompson turned back around. "Is something the matter, Miss Dubois?"

"I'm so terribly sorry, Miss Thompson." Ellie held up her work, displaying the ragged tear. "I'm afraid I've quite ruined it. Might I fetch another piece from the supply room?"

"Of course." Miss Thompson nodded distractedly, already moving to help Susan with a tangled thread. "But do be more careful this time."

"Phoebe, would you help me choose?" Ellie asked brightly. "Two minds are better than one, and I can never trust my own taste."

Before her friend could argue, Ellie was already rising from her chair. After a moment's hesitation, Phoebe followed.

The supply room was barely larger than a closet, its shelves lined with rolls of fabric in every imaginable texture and shade. A small window near the ceiling let in a shaft of dusty sunlight, illuminating the dancing motes in the air.

"Stand by the door," Ellie whispered urgently. "Watch for Miss Thompson. Or anyone else for that matter."

"Ellie, please," Phoebe pleaded one last time. "We could get expelled for this."

"Just keep watch," Ellie insisted, running her hands over a bolt of fine cotton lawn. The material was softer than anything she had ever seen Lucy work with, its pale blue colour perfect for a spring dress or perhaps a child's pinafore.

Her fingers trembled as she found the scissors. The metal felt cool and heavy in her hand, its weight a reminder of what she was about to do. For a moment, she hesitated.

What would Stuart think if he could see her now?

But then she remembered Lucy's face when she had touched Ellie's evening dress, the longing in her eyes as her fingers traced the fine stitching.

This wasn't really stealing, was it? Not when the fabric would be put to such good use.

The scissors made a soft snicking sound as she began to cut. Ellie worked as quickly as she dared, measuring out a generous length with shaking hands.

"Hurry," Phoebe hissed from her post by the door. "I think someone's coming down the hall."

Ellie's heart hammered against her ribs as she hastily folded the stolen cloth into a neat square. She tucked it into her sewing bag, forcing herself to move carefully despite her panic. A rushed job now would only draw attention later.

She had just closed her bag when Phoebe turned from the door, wringing her hands.

"Are you nearly finished?" she whispered. "I can't bear this another minute. What if–"

"Miss Dubois?"

Both girls jumped at Miss Thompson's voice. The teacher stood in the doorway, her head tilted in mild curiosity.

"Is everything all right? You've been in there for quite a while."

Ellie's heart seemed to stop, then started racing so fast she felt dizzy. She could feel the weight of her sewing bag, heavy with stolen fabric, pressing against her side like a guilty secret.

"I'm so sorry, Miss Thompson," Ellie managed, forcing her voice to remain steady despite the heavy thumping of her heart. "I was having trouble deciding."

She gestured toward the bolt of blue cotton lawn she had just cut from. "This one caught my eye, but... Well, it seems rather too fine for simple practice work."

Miss Thompson stepped into the small room, her skirts rustling in the confined space. Ellie shifted slightly, positioning herself between the teacher and the bolt of fabric where she had made her cut.

"Nonsense, my dear," Miss Thompson said, running her fingers over the material. "How else will you learn to work with fine fabrics if you never practice with them? And your stitching has shown marked improvement these past weeks."

"Has it?" Ellie's voice came out higher than usual. She cleared her throat. "That's very kind of you to say."

"Not kind at all, merely truthful." Miss Thompson reached for the bolt. "Here, let me help you cut a piece."

"Oh no," Ellie exclaimed, then quickly modulated her tone. "I mean... Perhaps you're right about the blue being suitable after all, but I think I prefer this cream cotton instead."

She moved toward a different shelf, desperate to draw attention away from the evidence of her theft. "It would show the stitching more clearly, don't you think?"

"An excellent choice," Miss Thompson nodded approvingly. "Very practical. And I must say, I'm pleased to see you taking such care with your selection. When you first arrived at Bloomsbury, I rather feared you might be another young lady who viewed scwing as merely a tedious obligation."

Guilt twisted in Ellie's stomach. "No, Miss Thompson. I've come to appreciate it very much indeed."

"Well then, shall we cut you a length of the cream?"

As Miss Thompson moved to help her with the new fabric, Ellie caught Phoebe's eye. Her friend's face was pale, but she managed a weak smile of relief.

Minutes later, they were back at their seats, the stolen fabric safely hidden in Ellie's bag. Her hands shook slightly as she threaded her needle, but no one seemed to notice.

"I can't believe we just did that," Phoebe whispered, her voice trembling.

"Think of how happy Lucy will be," Ellie whispered back.

But as she touched Stuart's locket through her dress, she couldn't quite suppress a twinge of shame. Her bag lay by her feet, and every time she shifted in her chair, the stolen fabric seemed to whisper of her guilt.

But it was too late for regrets now. She had made her choice, crossed another line. And somewhere in the back of her mind, a small voice wondered just how many more lines she would cross before this was all over.

Chapter Fifteen

Ellie hurried through the narrow streets of Spitalfields, her sewing bag clutched tightly against her side. Every few steps, her fingers strayed to touch the precious fabric hidden inside, smooth and fine as a feathery cloud compared to the coarse materials Lucy usually worked with.

The afternoon sun cast long shadows between the buildings, turning the familiar maze of alleyways into a stark pattern of light and darkness. She had walked this path so many times now that her feet carried her without conscious thought, leaving her mind free to imagine Lucy's reaction.

Would the gifted seamstress girl cry again, as she had over the simple needles and thread? Or would she be too overwhelmed for tears, running her skilled fingers over the cotton lawn in silent wonder?

"She'll make something beautiful with it," Ellie said to herself, while dodging a pile of rotting cabbage leaves. "Something far finer than anything Lydia or Susan could manage, even with all their expensive lessons."

The thought made her smile, easing the last traces of guilt about the theft. After all, wasn't this exactly what Miss Thompson had said about true artistry lying in the skill of the hands rather than the cost of materials?

As she rounded the corner into the street that led to St Mary's Mission, her steps quickened with anticipation. But the sight that greeted her stopped her dead in her tracks.

Jack and Percy stood waiting outside the mission doors. And there was something wrong about their postures. Something that made her breath catch in her throat.

Jack's easy smile was nowhere to be seen, replaced by a tightness around his mouth that transformed his whole face.

And Percy... Percy's expression was darker than she had ever seen it, his grip on his walking stick white-knuckled and rigid.

"Jack?" Her voice sounded hoarse as she hurried toward them. "What is it? What's wrong?"

The young man turned to face her, and the worry in his eyes made her heart skip a beat. "It's Lucy," he said simply.

"Lucy?" The fabric suddenly felt like lead in her bag. "What about Lucy? Where is she?"

"She's taken ill," Percy answered, his voice rougher than usual. "Started with a cough yesterday, but by this morning..." He shook his head grimly.

"The fever's got her something fierce," Jack added, his usual charm entirely absent. "She can barely lift her head from the pillow, and her breathing–"

He swallowed hard, unable to finish the sentence.

Ellie's hand flew to Stuart's locket, clutching it through her dress as if it might somehow help make sense of this jarring shift from joy to fear. All her excited plans about the fabric seemed suddenly childish and inadequate in the face of real suffering.

"But surely there's something we can do?" she asked, looking frantically between the two men. "Have you called for a doctor? Or at least gotten some medicine?"

The look they exchanged made her stomach twist uncomfortably. There was something in that silent communication she couldn't quite read, something that made the hair on the back of her neck stand up despite the fair weather.

"I have money," Ellie blurted out, already reaching for her reticule. "Enough for a doctor, and medicine too. We could send for one straight away–"

"Put that away," Percy grumbled. But then softened his tone at her startled expression. "It's not that simple, Miss Dubois."

"But why not?" Her fingers tightened around her purse. "If Lucy needs help–"

"You don't understand," Jack said quietly. "Our Lucy, she's got her pride, see? Won't take charity, not even from a friend."

"But this isn't charity," Ellie protested. "This is–"

"What?" Percy's bitter laugh cut through her words. "The kindness of a fine lady to her less fortunate acquaintances? A generous display of the privileged few performing their sacred duty of tending to the poor?"

Ellie flushed. "That's not fair. Lucy is my friend."

"Aye, she is," Jack agreed. "Which is why she would never forgive herself for taking your money. You've shown us kindness, Ellie, but Lucy... Well, she needs to feel she's earned her way. Even when she's burning up with fever, she's still the same stubborn girl who'd rather suffer than accept a handout."

Ellie's hand strayed to Stuart's locket as she absorbed Jacks' words. The weight of the stolen fabric in her bag seemed to mock her certainties about helping her friends. Was there really such a difference between giving money and giving stolen goods?

"There must be something we can do," she said at last.

Jack straightened suddenly, a familiar glint returning to his eye. "Well, as it happens, I might have a plan. Nothing too difficult, mind you. I just need a bit of help with a small... venture."

"What sort of venture?" Ellie asked cautiously.

"Simple, really. All you need to do is ask a few people for directions. That's all."

Seeing the doubt in Ellie's eyes, he gave her an encouraging smile. "Think of it like when we sold those flowers from the park, remember? Only this time, it's for Lucy."

Something in Jack's carefully chosen words made Ellie uneasy. But then she thought of Lucy, burning with fever in that cramped room, too proud to accept direct help.

"Will you do it, Ellie?" Jack asked softly. "For Lucy?"

Ellie took a deep breath and nodded. "Tell me what you need me to do."

"We'd better move somewhere more promising first," Percy said. "No one worth troubling around here."

Jack nodded. "Follow me."

They made their way through the warren of Spitalfields' streets, emerging gradually into wider, cleaner thoroughfares where the buildings seemed to stand taller and more respectable.

"This is more like it," Jack grinned. "Plenty of fine gentlemen about. Just need to find the right one."

"The right one?" Ellie asked hesitatingly.

Jack's eyes fixed on something over Ellie's shoulder. "See that gentleman by the bookshop? The one with the fine waistcoat and the gold watch chain?"

She turned slightly, catching sight of an elderly man examining the books displayed in the window. There was something kindly about his face, and he seemed like the sort of gentleman who surely wouldn't mind helping a lost young lady.

"All you need to do," Jack said sweetly, "is ask him the way to Church Street. Tell him you're looking for your aunt's house and you've got turned around somehow. Make it convincing like."

"That's all?" Ellie asked, unsure how this would benefit Lucy.

"That's all." Jack's hand brushed her elbow, gentle but insistent, guiding her forward. "Just keep him talking for a moment. Nothing to worry about."

Ellie took a few hesitant steps toward the gentleman, very aware of Jack moving quietly beside her, then dropping back into the shadows of a doorway. The weight of Stuart's locket seemed to grow heavier against her chest with each step.

"Excuse me, sir?" She clasped her hands together to keep them from fidgeting. The gentleman turned, revealing pale blue eyes behind gold-rimmed spectacles.

"I'm terribly sorry to trouble you," Ellie said. "But might you direct me to Church Street? My aunt lives there, you see, and I'm afraid I've got myself quite lost."

"Church Street?" The old man peered at her over the rim of his spectacles, smiling warmly. "Why yes, my dear. Though you're rather far from it, I'm afraid. You'll need to head back toward Bishopsgate, then–"

He half-turned to point the way, and that's when Ellie saw it. Jack's quick hands moved with terrible precision, silent as a shadow. The gentleman's coat shifted slightly, and something disappeared into Jack's sleeve.

The terrible reality of what was happening came crushing down on Ellie with bruising force. She wanted to cry out, to warn the kindly old man, but her voice seemed trapped in her throat. By the time she managed to draw breath, Jack had already melted back into the crowd.

"–and then it's your second right," the gentleman was saying. "You can't miss the church spire. Will you be able to find your way, my dear? You look a bit pale."

"Yes," Ellie managed, her voice barely more than a whisper. "Thank you. You've been most helpful."

She turned away quickly, afraid he might see the truth in her face. Forcing her feet to move, she started walking in the direction the old man had indicated. But her mind was a complete blank, as if her thoughts were frozen like ice in winter.

Suddenly, a hand caught her elbow, making her jump.

"Well done," Jack whispered, steering her into a quiet side street. "Couldn't have done it better myself. Here, look what our friend was carrying."

He produced a worn leather wallet with a flourish, and Ellie felt bile rise in her throat. The old man's kind smile flashed in her memory as Jack's fingers worked the clasp.

"A proper gentleman, that one," Jack said cheerfully, counting out several banknotes. "There's enough here to keep us comfortable for weeks. But I'd wager he won't even notice it's gone."

Ellie's hand flew to her mouth. "All that money. Jack, we've stolen his—"

"We've borrowed what we need for Lucy's medicine," Jack corrected smoothly, tucking a few notes into his jacket. "Nothing more."

The stolen fabric in Ellie's bag might as well have been a millstone around her neck. How could she protest Jack's theft when she herself had–

"But surely there must have been another way," she whispered. "He seemed such a kind old man."

"Kind, is he?" Percy's harsh voice cut in. He had been watching the exchange from the shadows, leaning heavily on his walking stick. "Kind enough to spare a few pennies for a sick girl in the rookery, do you think? To help a feverish seamstress get the medicine she needs?"

"I don't know." Ellie's voice trembled.

"Course you don't," Percy said, his tone softening slightly. "Because fine gentlemen like that don't venture into places like Spitalfields. They don't see what we see, don't they, Jack?"

"Right you are," Jack agreed while pocketing the wallet. "Now, I know just the place to get what Lucy needs. Fellow who doesn't ask too many questions, if you take my meaning."

"I'll come with you," Ellie offered quickly. "To help carry things, or–"

"Best not," Jack cut in. "These aren't the sort of establishments a young lady should visit." His usual charming smile returned. "Besides, you should be getting back to your academy before anyone misses you."

"But Lucy–"

"Lucy needs her rest," Percy interrupted smoothly. "She's in no state for visitors just now. The fever's got her sleeping most of the time anyway."

Ellie hesitated, torn between her desire to help and a growing sense of unease. The weight of what they had just done settled in her stomach like cold stone, and she found it impossible to think clearly.

"Go on now," Jack urged gently. "We'll take good care of our Lucy, don't you worry. That's what family's for, isn't it?"

"Oh, wait," Ellie called out suddenly, remembering her original purpose. She reached into her sewing bag with trembling fingers. "I brought something for Lucy. I thought... Well, before I knew she was ill."

She withdrew the stolen fabric, its pale blue cotton lawn looking oddly delicate in the grimy surroundings. How long ago it seemed since she had cut it from the bolt in the academy's supply room, so certain of the rightness of her actions.

"It's for her sewing," she explained, smoothing the material with nervous fingers. "I thought she might be able to make something beautiful with it."

Jack took the fabric, but something was different about his manner. "That's right thoughtful of you, Ellie. Our Lucy will be pleased to bits, once she's feeling better."

Percy watched the exchange with an unreadable expression, his eyes moving from the fabric to Ellie's face and back again. Something about that gaze of his made her want to snatch the cotton lawn back, to run away and never return to these dark streets.

But that was ridiculous, wasn't it? These were Jack and Lucy, her friends. And everything they had done today had been for Lucy's benefit.

Hadn't it?

The walk back to the academy seemed longer and lonelier than usual. Her bag, now empty of its stolen treasure, felt strangely light against her side. Like something vital had been taken from it. Or perhaps from her.

She found herself remembering the old gentleman's kind smile as he had given her directions. The way his gold-rimmed spectacles had caught the light. How he had worried about her looking pale.

"It was necessary," she whispered to herself, hurrying past the gas lamps that were already being lit for the evening. "Lucy needed medicine. And the fabric... She'll use it better than any of the girls at school would have."

But try as she might, she couldn't quite silence the small voice in the back of her mind that whispered something wasn't right. That same voice that had tried to warn her when Jack first mentioned his so-called plan.

She pushed the doubts away firmly. After all, what was done was done. And it had all been for Lucy's benefit. The pickpocketing, the stolen fabric, all of it.

Hadn't it?

The question followed her all the way back to Bloomsbury, as persistent as her own shadow in the gathering dusk.

Chapter Sixteen

Moonlight fell through the window of their small bedroom, painting silver stripes across Ellie's blanket as she lay staring at the ceiling.

Her fingers traced the surface of Stuart's locket, although its delicate swirls offered little of their usual comfort tonight. Every time she closed her eyes, she saw the elderly gentleman's kind smile. And Jack's swift, silent movements as he relieved the poor man of his wallet.

"It was for Lucy," she whispered into the darkness. But the words rang hollow in the quiet room.

Lucy.

The thought of her friend burning with fever made Ellie's chest tighten. Had Jack found the medicine he said he would buy? Was Lucy even now sleeping peacefully, her fever breaking under the influence of whatever mysterious remedy Jack had obtained with their ill-gotten gains?

Or was she tossing and turning like Ellie? Was each of her breaths a struggle in that cramped, airless room?

Ellie rolled onto her side, the bedsprings creaking beneath her. The sound seemed impossibly loud in the nighttime silence. She held her breath, listening for any sign that she had disturbed Phoebe or any of the other girls in the adjacent rooms. Luckily, everything remained still.

A moment later though, a quiet voice spoke from the other bed. "Ellie?" Phoebe whispered. "Are you awake?"

"I'm sorry," Ellie whispered back. "Did I wake you?"

"You've been fidgeting for hours." There was a rustle of blankets as Phoebe sat up. "What's wrong? You were so quiet when you came back from Spitalfields today. Usually you can hardly wait to tell me everything."

Ellie swallowed hard. The weight of everything left unsaid pressed against her chest like a piece of lead.

"It's Lucy," she managed at last. "She's ill, Phoebe. Terribly ill."

"Oh no." Phoebe's bed creaked as she leaned closer. "What sort of illness?"

"Fever." Ellie's voice caught on the word. "Jack says she can barely lift her head from the pillow. And her breathing..." She trailed off, remembering Jack's stricken expression.

A floorboard creaked somewhere in the darkness, making both girls freeze. But it was only the old building settling, and after a moment Phoebe spoke again.

"You're really worried about her, aren't you?" she asked softly. "I don't think I've ever seen you like this."

Ellie clutched Stuart's locket tighter, its edges pressing into her palm. "You should see where they live, Phoebe. That tiny room, with hardly any air or light. And now with Lucy so sick..."

She broke off, unable to continue. How could she explain the crushing weight of helplessness she felt? How could she describe the desperate measures it had driven them to?

But no, she couldn't tell Phoebe about the theft.

Her friend's tender heart wouldn't understand the cruel necessities of life in the rookery. Better to keep that part to herself, locked away with all the other small compromises she had made since entering Lucy and Jack's world.

"Oh, Ellie." Phoebe's voice was full of sympathy. In the dim light, Ellie could just make out her friend's troubled expression. "There must be something we can do to help."

"I did offer to pay for medicines and a doctor. But Jack and Mr Yates said Lucy would see it as charity. And she'd never accept that."

"Oh, I have just the idea," Phoebe said excitedly. "We could send her flowers. Nothing cheers up a sickroom like a lovely bouquet."

Ellie almost laughed at the suggestion, though there was nothing funny about it. "Flowers? In Spitalfields?"

"Why not?" Phoebe sounded slightly hurt. "When my cousin Margaret was ill last summer, we sent her the most beautiful arrangement of–"

"This isn't like your cousin Margaret's sickroom, Phoebe." Ellie sat up in bed, Stuart's locket swinging free on its chain. "Lucy doesn't have crisp white sheets or a nurse to tend her. She doesn't have windows that open properly to let in fresh air, or–"

She broke off, fighting back sudden tears.

"Perhaps some nice treats then?" Phoebe suggested tentatively. "Cook always says there's nothing like sugared almonds or crystallised fruit to whet an invalid's appetite."

"Sugared almonds?" This time Ellie couldn't hold back a bitter laugh. "Oh, Phoebe. Lucy needs real food. Something to give her strength."

She fell silent as a thought struck her.

Food.

Of course! That was it. Not dainty treats or expensive flowers. But hearty, nourishing food to help Lucy fight the fever. The kind of food that filled the academy's pantry every day, while Lucy lay weak and burning in her and Jack's tiny room.

"The kitchen," she said suddenly. "The pantry's always stocked with everything we need. Beef broth, preserves..." Her voice grew more excited with each word. "We could take enough to help her."

"Ellie, no." Phoebe's whisper was sharp with alarm. "You can't possibly be serious? Stealing from the kitchen?"

"Why not? We already take breakfast scraps."

"That's different. Those would only go to waste anyway." Phoebe's blankets rustled as she drew them tighter around herself. "But breaking into the pantry at night... We could be expelled."

"Only if we're caught." Ellie leaned forward, her voice urgent in the darkness. "Think about it, Phoebe. All that food just sitting there while Lucy wastes away with fever. Doesn't that seem wrong to you?"

"What seems wrong to me is breaking into the pantry like common thieves."

"Then I'll do it alone," Ellie declared, though her heart sank at the thought. She had grown so used to having Phoebe's help with her schemes that the idea of proceeding without her felt somehow hollow.

A long silence followed. Ellie could almost hear Phoebe's conscience wrestling with itself in the darkness.

"When?" Phoebe asked finally, her voice barely audible.

"Two nights from now. The night before my next visit to St Mary's." Ellie tried to keep the triumph from her voice. "That way the food will be as fresh as possible when I take it to Lucy."

"I haven't said I'll help," Phoebe protested weakly.

But Ellie knew from her tone that she would. Phoebe always did in the end.

"Thank you," she whispered, reaching across the space between their beds to squeeze her friend's hand.

Phoebe squeezed back, but her fingers trembled. "I have a terrible feeling about this, Ellie."

"It will be fine," Ellie assured her, though her own heart had begun to beat faster at the thought of what they were planning. "You'll see."

But as she lay back down, her fingers found Stuart's locket once more. What would he think of all this? The thought sent a shiver through her that had nothing to do with the cool night air.

Chapter Seventeen

"Are you sure about this?" Phoebe whispered, her nightgown rustling as she followed Ellie down the dark corridor. "We could still go back to bed and pretend this was all a bad dream."

Ellie didn't answer. Her bare feet moved silently across the floorboards. She had spent the past two days memorising which ones creaked. Three steps forward, one to the left, then another two steps. The route to the kitchen had become a complicated dance in her mind.

Behind her, Phoebe wasn't quite so careful. A board groaned beneath her foot, the sound as sharp as a gunshot in the midnight silence.

Both girls froze.

Seconds stretched like hours as they waited, hardly daring to breathe. But the academy remained still, its occupants lost in dreams behind closed doors.

"Sorry," Phoebe mouthed when Ellie glanced back at her.

Moonlight filtered through the tall windows, casting strange shadows on the walls. During the day, these corridors echoed with the chatter and laughter of dozens of young ladies. But now, in the depths of night, every portrait seemed to watch them with accusing eyes, while every shadow held potential dangers.

Ellie lifted Stuart's locket to her lips and pressed a kiss on it, for good luck. "This way," she breathed, gesturing for Phoebe to follow.

They crept past Mrs Bennett's office, their steps even lighter here where the stern headmistress ruled by day.

Past the music room where the old grand piano stood silent and ghostly in the darkness.

Past the sewing room where, only a few days earlier, Lydia had complained about the quality of their materials.

At last, they reached the kitchen stairs. Here, the carpet ended, leaving them exposed on bare wooden steps that might betray them with any careless movement.

Ellie went first, placing each foot with exquisite care. One step. Two. Three...

A sudden creak made her heart stop.

"Was that us?" Phoebe's terrified whisper barely carried the length of her arm.

Ellie shook her head slowly. The sound had come from above. Perhaps from the teachers' wing? They waited, frozen in place, until the silence convinced them it had been nothing more than the random creaks and groans any building was wont to make.

The kitchen, when they finally reached it, felt different in the dark. Moonlight gleamed on copper pots and iron pans, transforming familiar objects into lurking shapes. The great black stove hulked against one wall like a sleeping giant.

But it was the pantry they needed. Ellie moved toward the heavy wooden door, remembering how she had watched Cook unlock it. The key always went into the drawer beside the stove. She had seen it happen a dozen times over the past two days.

The pantry keys jingled softly against the other keys on the ring as her hand found them, making Phoebe gasp at the harsh sound.

"Careful."

"I've got it," Ellie whispered triumphantly, drawing out the key. It felt cool and heavy in her palm.

The lock turned with a soft click that nonetheless seemed to echo through the kitchen. Ellie pushed the door open slowly, wincing at each tiny creak of its hinges.

"What exactly are we looking for?" Phoebe asked, hovering anxiously in the doorway.

"Beef broth," Ellie replied, her eyes adjusting to the deeper darkness of the pantry. "Cook always keeps some in sealed jars. And perhaps some of that candied ginger she likes to give to anyone who's feeling poorly. Lucy might be able to keep that down even with a fever."

She moved carefully between the shelves, mindful of every step on the stone-flagged floor in the dark. The pantry smelled of spices and dried herbs, of sugar and tea and all the other luxuries that Lucy and Jack could never afford.

"Here," she whispered, reaching for a jar of broth. "Phoebe, can you—"

A sudden crash made both girls jump. Phoebe had backed into a shelf, sending several tins clattering to the floor.

They stood paralysed, barely breathing, as the sound seemed to go on forever in the darkness. Surely someone must have heard. Surely at any moment they would hear footsteps on the stairs, voices calling out in alarm.

The echo of the falling tins finally faded into silence. Ellie's heart thundered so loudly she was certain it must be audible throughout the entire academy.

"I'm sorry," Phoebe whimpered, pressing her hands to her mouth. "Oh, Ellie, I'm so sorry."

"Shh." Ellie strained her ears, listening for any sign that the noise had woken someone.

But the academy remained eerily quiet.

After what felt like an eternity, she dared to move again. "Help me gather these things quickly," she whispered. "Before our luck runs out."

Working as silently as they could in the darkness, they collected their precious cargo:

the jar of beef broth, still faintly warm from that day's cooking. A package of Cook's candied ginger, wrapped in waxed paper. And, most importantly, a bottle of cod liver oil that Ellie knew the kitchen staff kept on hand for when any of the students fell ill.

"Surely that's enough?" Phoebe pleaded as Ellie reached for a second jar of broth.

Before Ellie could answer, a creak sounded from the corridor above. Then another.

Footsteps!

"Someone's coming," Phoebe breathed, her voice tight with panic.

Ellie's mind raced. The pantry door stood open, evidence of their crime plain for anyone to see. But there wasn't time to close it without making noise. And even if they did, the fallen tins still littered the floor.

"Quick," she hissed, grabbing Phoebe's arm. "Behind those sacks of flour."

They squeezed into the narrow space between the flour sacks and the wall, where the girls were pressed so close together that Ellie could feel Phoebe's pulse racing. The rough burlap scratched against her cheek as she tried to make herself as small as possible.

The footsteps grew closer. Then, a warm glow appeared in the kitchen: lamplight.

Ellie held her breath.

"Really, Beatrice," Mrs Bennett muttered to herself. "These late-night cravings of yours are most unseemly."

Ellie felt Phoebe's fingers digging into her arm. Through the gap between the flour sacks, they watched their headmistress shuffle into view, wrapped in a dark dressing gown, her silver hair loose around her shoulders. She looked strangely vulnerable without her usual stern demeanour.

The lamplight threw wild shadows as Mrs Bennett moved toward the pantry. Ellie's heart seemed to stop altogether. Any moment now, their headmistress would spot the open door, the scattered tins...

But Mrs Bennett paused, frowning at something on the counter. "Now, what's this?"

She moved away from the pantry door, toward whatever had caught her attention.

"Ah, Cook's seed cake. Left out to cool, no doubt. Well, a small slice won't be missed."

The girls listened and watched, hardly daring to breathe, as Mrs Bennett cut herself a generous portion of cake. She stood there eating it with small, delicate bites, completely unaware of her students crouching mere feet away.

"Much better," she sighed at last, brushing crumbs from her fingers. "Although Cook really ought to use more caraway seeds."

She turned to leave, and the girls allowed themselves the tiniest sigh of relief.

But that small breath stirred up flour dust from the sacks surrounding them, tickling Phoebe's nose. Ellie felt her friend's body tense beside her.

No, no, no...

Despite Phoebe's desperate attempt to stifle it, a small sneeze escaped, barely louder than the squeak of a mouse.

Mrs Bennett whirled around, holding her lamp higher. "Who's there?"

The headmistress's face looked ghostly in the wavering light as she took a step toward the pantry. Ellie's heart hammered so hard she was certain Mrs Bennett must hear it.

Another step brought the headmistress closer to their hiding place, the lamplight now reaching the edge of the flour sacks.

A sudden thud made Mrs Bennett jump. Her lamp swung wildly as a large ginger tomcat leaped down from one of the counters, knocking over another tin in the process.

"Jasper," Mrs Bennett scolded, though her voice held more affection than anger. "You gave me quite a start."

Winding itself around her ankles, the cat meowed again, more insistently.

"Oh, very well," Mrs Bennett sighed. "I suppose if I'm to indulge in midnight feasts, you deserve a treat as well."

She turned away from the pantry, moving to the cupboard where Cook kept the cream. Ellie's legs trembled from being crouched so long in their hiding place, but she didn't dare move yet.

"Although I must say, Jasper," Mrs Bennett went on. "You're supposed to be keeping this kitchen free of mice, not prowling about causing mischief. What would Cook say if she knew I was rewarding you for such dereliction of duty?"

The cat didn't reply, enjoying its saucer of cream instead.

"But we'll strike a deal, you and I," Mrs Bennett chuckled softly. "I won't tell anyone if you keep mum about my nocturnal snacking habits."

At last, she gathered up her lamp and shuffled toward the kitchen door, Jasper trotting at her heels.

"Come along then," she said to the cat with a tired yawn. "Let's get back to bed before anyone discovers our little indulgence."

The lamplight faded. Footsteps creaked up the stairs. Still, the girls waited until the silence stretched long enough to convince them they were truly alone.

"I think I'm going to faint," Phoebe whispered as they extracted themselves from behind the flour sacks.

"Not yet," Ellie urged, though her own knees felt weak with relief. "We need to get everything back to our room first."

Working quickly now, they gathered their stolen supplies: the beef broth, the candied ginger, and the cod liver oil. Ellie set the fallen tins back in their place while Phoebe held their precious cargo. Then she locked the pantry door and returned the key to its drawer.

The journey back to their room seemed to take forever, each step measured and careful despite their desperate desire to hurry.

But at last they were safe behind their own door, their contraband hidden away at the back of their shared wardrobe.

Phoebe collapsed onto her bed, still shaking. "I never want to do anything like that again," she declared in a fierce whisper. "Never."

But Ellie barely heard her. She was already imagining Lucy's face when she brought her these healing tonics. The beef broth would help restore her strength, the ginger would ease her fever, and the cod liver oil...

Well, everyone knew how beneficial that was, no matter how foul the stuff actually tasted.

"It was worth it," she whispered, more to herself than to Phoebe. Her fingers found

Stuart's locket once more, but this time she didn't let its weight trouble her conscience.

"Everything will be fine now. You'll see."

Phoebe's only response was to burrow deeper under her blankets, as if trying to hide from what they had done.

But as Ellie lay in her own bed, listening to Phoebe's breathing grow slow and steady with sleep, she felt nothing but satisfaction.

Yes, they had taken risks. Yes, they had broken rules. But surely such small sins were forgivable when weighed against Lucy's needs?

She lay awake for a long time, watching the moonlight draw shifting patterns on the wall, until her eyes grew heavy and sleep finally claimed her.

Her last conscious thought was of Lucy, and of how tomorrow she would be able to help her friend in a way that really mattered.

Chapter Eighteen

Giddy with excitement, Ellie practically flew through the narrow streets of Spitalfields, clutching her basket of stolen goods close to her chest. The early morning air still held a bite of chill, but she barely noticed it, too focused on reaching Lucy with her precious bounty.

She's going to be so surprised, Ellie thought, dodging around a creaky cart laden with vegetables. The beef broth would provide Lucy with much needed nourishment. And if dear old Charlotte was to be believed, candied ginger could work wonders.

Her fingers brushed Stuart's locket through her dress as she quickened her pace. The streets that had once seemed so threatening now felt almost like home. She knew exactly which corners to round, which alleys to avoid, which cobblestones might trip unwary feet.

As she passed St Mary's Mission, the sound of voices drifted through its open doors. Mrs Collins would be expecting her help in manning the food queue again this morning.

Ellie's step faltered for a moment.

"Lucy needs me more," she whispered to herself, hurrying past. Though her conscience pricked at abandoning her usual duties, she pushed the feeling aside.

What good was ladling out thin stew to strangers when her friend lay burning with fever?

Soon, the familiar tenement loomed ahead, its crumbling brick walls dark with soot and age. Ellie gathered her skirts and started up the narrow stairs, trying not to breathe too deeply of the musty air. Her legs had grown used to this climb over the past weeks, though she still marvelled at how Lucy managed it several times each day.

As she neared Jack and Lucy's floor, an unexpected sound made her pause mid-step.

Laughter?

Clear and bright, it floated down the stairwell: Lucy's laugh, unmistakable despite her usual quiet nature.

Ellie's brow furrowed in confusion. Surely she must be mistaken. A few days ago, Jack had said his sister could barely lift her head from the pillow.

Taking the last few stairs more slowly now, she approached the door. More laughter spilled through the thin wood, along with the rumble of voices in cheerful conversation.

Ellie's fingers tightened around her basket handle as she knocked.

"Come in," Jack's voice called out.

She pushed open the door and stopped dead in her tracks.

Lucy sat in a chair by the window, looking remarkably well. Her cheeks held a healthy flush, and her long fingers were busy with needle and thread, working on what appeared to be a man's waistcoat.

Percy lounged against the wall nearby, while Jack sprawled on the floor, grinning up at his sister.

"Ellie," Lucy's face brightened at the sight of her friend, though something flickered in her expression. Was it embarrassment? "How lovely to see you."

Ellie stood frozen in the doorway, her mind struggling to make sense of the scene before her. Where was the sickbed? The burning fever? The laboured breathing that had worried Jack and Percy so much?

"Well, don't just stand there letting in the draft," Jack said cheerfully, springing to his feet. "Come in. Our Lucy's feeling much better today, aren't you, sister dear?"

"I... yes." Lucy's eyes dropped to her sewing as she spoke. "The fever broke yesterday morning. I'm feeling much stronger now."

"But when I–" Ellie moved into the room, still clutching her basket. "Jack told me you could barely lift your head. That your breathing was..."

She trailed off, watching Lucy's fingers tighten around her needle.

"Amazing what the right medicine can do," Percy said smoothly without leaving his position against the wall. "Remarkable recovery, wouldn't you say, Jack?"

"That's right," Jack nodded, his usual charm in full force. "That fellow I mentioned: the one who doesn't ask questions? His remedies might not be what your fancy doctors prescribe, but they do the trick."

Ellie studied Lucy's face. The girl certainly looked healthy enough, but there was something in her manner. A tension in her shoulders perhaps, or the way she wouldn't quite meet Ellie's eyes.

"I brought you some things," Ellie said at last, setting her basket on the rickety table. "Beef broth, and candied ginger. Oh, and cod liver oil. Though I have to warn you, it tastes absolutely dreadful."

Lucy's head snapped up, genuine surprise crossing her features. "You brought all that for me?"

"Quite the thoughtful friend you've made there, Lucy," Percy remarked, his tone difficult to read. "Going to such trouble on your behalf."

"Oh, but I couldn't possibly–" Lucy started, but Jack was already peering into the basket.

"Now, now, sister dearest," he said cheerfully. "No need to be proud about it. Not with a good friend like our Ellie here."

He pulled out the jar of broth, examining it with apparent delight. "My word, this looks better than anything we've had in weeks."

"I just wanted to help," Ellie said softly, watching as Lucy finally set aside her sewing and came to look at the provisions. The girl's face held an odd mixture of emotions, gratitude and shame seeming to war with each other.

"And help you have," Percy pushed himself away from the wall, moving to stand beside Jack. "Probably cost you a fair part of your allowance as well. Fine beef broth and candied ginger don't come cheap these days."

Ellie felt heat rise to her cheeks. "Oh, I didn't actually–" But she stopped herself, suddenly aware of how close she had come to admitting the theft.

"Shame on you, Percy," Jack admonished playfully. "No need to embarrass our friend by talking about money. What matters most is that our Lucy is on the mend."

He clapped his hands together, smiling. "I'd say this calls for a celebration, wouldn't you all agree? What with Lucy's recovery and Ellie's generosity. Seems like enough cause for a drink at the pub, don't you think?"

Ellie hesitated, her fingers twisting Stuart's locket. The morning was still young, and she hadn't exactly planned on spending it in a public house. But Jack's enthusiasm was infectious, as always.

"I suppose a quick visit wouldn't hurt," she said at last. "Though I'll need to be back at the academy by noon."

"Splendid," Jack replied, already reaching for his coat. "Come along, Lucy. You've been cooped up in this room long enough."

Lucy rose slowly from her chair, her movements careful. Though whether that was from lingering illness or something else, Ellie couldn't quite tell.

As she helped her friend to put her shawl over her shoulders, Lucy's fingers trembled slightly against hers.

"Thank you," Lucy whispered. "For the food and everything. You shouldn't have gone to so much trouble."

There was something in her voice – a catch, a hesitation – that made Ellie want to ask more questions. But Percy was already ushering them toward the door, while Jack led the way with his usual confident stride.

"Come along then," he called over his shoulder, grinning broadly. "Time to show our finishing school friend how we common folk celebrate a miraculous healing."

Chapter Nineteen

The pub's heavy door creaked open, releasing a wave of noise and tobacco smoke into the morning air. Ellie hesitated for a moment, but Jack's hand at her elbow guided her inside.

"Nothing like a bit of music to start the day," he grinned, raising his voice to be heard over what could charitably be called singing.

A group of dockworkers occupied the centre of the room, their faces ruddy and their voices raised in an enthusiastic if unmelodious rendition of 'The Wild Rover'. They swayed together, mugs held high, while their audience offered encouragement in the form of rhythmic table-thumping and occasional shouts.

"No, nay, never," the men bellowed, some rather behind the others. "No, nay, never no more!"

Jack shouldered his way through the press of bodies, guiding them toward an empty table in the corner. The wooden chairs scraped against the floorboards as they settled themselves, Lucy smoothing her skirts while Percy leaned his walking stick against the edge of the table.

"What'll it be then?" Jack asked, already half-risen from his seat. "The usual?" He glanced at

Percy and Lucy, then turned to Ellie with a grin. "And perhaps something a bit milder for our finishing school friend?"

Before Ellie could protest, he had disappeared into the crowd around the bar, returning moments later with four mugs of foaming beer. The liquid sloshed slightly as he set them down, leaving dark rings on the scarred tabletop.

"To Lucy's health," Jack declared, raising his mug with a flourish. Percy and Lucy lifted theirs in response, while Ellie hesitated before wrapping her fingers around the handle of her own mug. The beer looked darker than she remembered from their last visit.

Slowly, she brought the mug closer to her lips for a cautious sip. But then she winced as one of the singers managed to hit three different wrong notes in the space of two words.

Jack noticed and leaned close, his eyes dancing with amusement. "My deepest apologies. I fear this isn't quite up to your finishing school standards. Though they make up in spirit what they lack in skill, don't they?"

A particularly off-key note rang out, making Lucy press her hand to her mouth to stifle a giggle. Percy raised an eyebrow at the performance.

"Behold," he mocked. "The cultural refinements of our fair district. Though I must say, they're in rather good form this morning. Usually, they don't attempt harmony until after noon."

Lucy's quiet laugh turned into a proper chuckle at that, and Ellie found herself smiling despite her initial shock at the jarring noise.

There was something almost charming about the dockworkers' complete disregard for musical precision. And it was clear to see that they found tremendous joy in the simple act of singing together.

The men finished their song with more enthusiasm than accuracy, drawing scattered applause from the pub's other patrons. As the noise died down, a burly man with arms like tree trunks caught sight of their group.

"Well, if it isn't young Jack Mortimer," he called out, his voice still hoarse from singing. "Come to show us how it's done, have you, lad?"

Jack raised his hands in mock surrender. "Not today, Harrison. Wouldn't want to put you fine gentlemen to shame so early in the morning."

"Listen to him," Harrison chuckled to his companions. "Getting above himself since he started keeping such fine company." He nodded toward Ellie with a knowing wink.

"Merely trying to elevate the general tone of the neighbourhood," Jack replied with a grin. "Though I fear I'm fighting a losing battle, especially after that performance of yours."

More laughter greeted this sally, and Ellie found herself relaxing slightly. The rough camaraderie felt oddly comfortable compared to the stiff formality of the academy.

"Oh, you should hear him sing," Lucy said, touching Ellie's arm. "He's got a voice like..." She paused, searching for the right comparison. "Well, I've never heard anything quite like it, really."

Jack ducked his head, an unexpected moment of modesty that caught Ellie's attention. Before she could remark on it, though, her eye fell on the old upright piano in the corner of the room. Its wood was scarred and stained but it still appeared serviceable, maintaining a certain dignity.

Her face brightened. "Why don't you show me?"

"Only if you'll accompany me, Miss Dubois," Jack replied, executing a theatrical bow. His usual confidence returned as he gestured toward the instrument.

"Though I warn you," he said. "I'm not used to such fine accompaniment. Usually, I have to make do with old Joe banging away on that poor instrument like he's trying to punish it for some past offence."

Ellie made her way to the piano, lifting the lid to reveal yellowed keys, some of them chipped at the edges. She pressed one experimentally, relieved to find it at least somewhat in tune.

"Greensleeves?" she suggested, settling onto the worn bench. The familiar melody would be simple enough to play, even on this ancient instrument.

Jack nodded, positioning himself beside the piano with an exaggerated adjustment of his collar that made Lucy giggle. But when Ellie began to play, the transformation in his bearing was immediate and startling.

The first notes of his voice silenced the general chatter in the pub. Gone was the cheeky street rascal, replaced by something altogether different.

His tone was pure and clear as mountain air, each note perfectly placed, rising and falling with a control that seemed impossible for someone who had never had proper training.

"Alas, my love, you do me wrong..."

Ellie nearly missed a chord, so surprised was she by the depth of feeling in his voice. As she recovered, her fingers found their rhythm on the keys, and she began to truly listen.

There was something in his singing that reminded her of the Italian tenor who had performed at the Sheffield Assembly Rooms last winter. That same ability to make each word sound as if it carried the weight of real emotion.

"...for who but my lady Greensleeves..."

The pub had fallen completely silent now. At a nearby table, one of the dockworkers who had been bellowing so enthusiastically earlier sat with his mouth slightly open, his mug forgotten in his hand.

When Jack and Ellie finished, the stunned silence held for a moment longer. Then Harrison let out a long, low whistle.

"Cor, Jack," he said. "Where've you been hiding that voice, lad?"

A round of applause began, growing stronger as more patrons joined in. Jack gave a small bow, a genuine smile replacing his usual theatrics.

Just for a moment, Ellie caught a glimpse of something in his face: a flash of real pleasure that went beyond his customary charm.

Lucy beamed with obvious pride, while beside her, Percy's eyes moved between Jack and their appreciative audience.

The applause had barely died down when Harrison called out, "Another one, Jack. Give us a song about the ladies."

Jack glanced at Ellie, a question in his eyes. "Do you know 'Barbara Allen'?"

She nodded, her fingers finding the opening chords. This time, Jack turned slightly to face the room, standing straighter, as if the first song had awakened something in him.

"In Scarlet town, where I was born..."

His voice filled the pub like sunlight streaming through stained glass, turning the humble drinking house into something almost sacred. Even the hardened dockworkers seemed transfixed.

Jack shaped each phrase with natural grace, building the tragic tale of Barbara Allen with such conviction that Ellie found herself completely caught up in the story.

When he reached the final verses, describing the rose and briar growing from the lovers' graves, his voice took on a gentler quality that made something catch in Ellie's throat. She was suddenly grateful to have the piano to focus on, aware that her eyes had grown damp.

As the last note faded, someone sniffed loudly. Ellie looked up to see Harrison wiping his eyes with a large red handkerchief.

"Blasted tobacco smoke," he muttered unconvincingly, while his companions tactfully looked away.

The pub erupted in applause, even more enthusiastic than before. Several people called out requests for more, but Jack shook his head with his usual easy smile, though Ellie noticed his hands trembled slightly as he gripped the back of the piano bench.

"Best leave them wanting more," he said quietly. But there was a wistfulness in his voice that made her wonder. What sort of dreams lay hidden behind that charming smile of his?

Ellie rose from the piano bench, her eyes bright with excitement. "Jack, that was incredible. You could perform in concert halls with a voice like that."

"Now there's a thought," he chuckled, offering her his arm. "Jack Mortimer of Spitalfields, gracing the grandest halls in London."

They made their way back to their table, where Lucy was practically glowing with pride because of her brother's performance.

And even Percy had abandoned his trademark cynical expression, watching them with shrewd interest as they settled into their seats.

"I'm serious," Ellie insisted, still caught up in the lingering magic of Jack's song. "I've heard professional singers who couldn't hold a candle to what you just did."

He laughed, though something flickered in his expression before his usual mask of cheerful indifference slipped back into place. "Kind of you to say, but I'm hardly up to the standard of your fancy halls. Those performers, now they've got real talent."

"But you do have talent," Ellie said. "I've been to enough performances to know the difference between mere technical skill and true artistry."

"Do you hear that, Jack?" Percy grinned. "Sounds like we have what's called a connoisseur in our midst."

"Oh, I don't know about that," Ellie blushed. "What I'm trying to say is that some of these professionals aren't half as good as you might imagine. Why, I absolutely dread to think what we'll have to endure at the school soirée in two weeks' time."

"A soirée, you say?" Percy's eyebrows rose with careful precision.

"Nothing too grand, mind you," Ellie explained. "Just something the academy is organising. Various guests and performers, you know. An opportunity for us girls to practise our social graces."

She tried to make it sound dull and unimportant, but she could already see the keen interest sparking in Jack's eyes.

"Sounds wonderful," Jack sighed. "All those fine ladies and gentlemen, real classical music..." He gazed into the distance with an almost wistful expression. "What I wouldn't give to see something like that for myself."

"Perhaps," Percy suggested smoothly, "Miss Dubois might be able to arrange something."

"Oh, I couldn't possibly..." Ellie began, fidgeting with Stuart's locket through her dress. The soirée was meant to be an elegant affair, with a carefully selected guest list. Mrs Bennett would be watching everything like a hawk.

"Of course not," Jack said quickly. "I wouldn't dream of putting you in such a position."

But there was something in his tone that suggested otherwise, and his eyes still held that yearning look she had glimpsed after his performance.

"Surely there must be some way?" Percy asked. "After all, Miss Dubois, you've seen how talented Jack is. Seems a shame he'll never experience the kind of music he clearly appreciates."

Ellie hesitated, her caution at war with the sympathy she felt for Jack. The memory of his pure, clear voice was still fresh in her mind. "I suppose I could ask Mrs Bennett to include you as a performer."

Jack's laugh held a touch of bitterness. "Somehow I doubt your headmistress would welcome a performer from Spitalfields. Not quite the sort of entertainment she has in mind, I'd wager."

"I was wondering..." Percy mused, tapping his walking stick thoughtfully against the floor. "A large house like that must have a servants' entrance? A door for deliveries and such?"

Ellie found herself thinking aloud before she could stop herself. "The kitchen entrance. And with all the extra staff brought in for the evening..."

Her fingers kept twisting Stuart's locket unconsciously as her mind raced through the possibilities. The back of the house would be bustling with activity: hired waiters, musicians carrying instruments, delivery boys bringing last-minute supplies.

Jack leaned forward eagerly. "I can be quite the gentleman when I need to be," he said, his voice low and persuasive. "And I'm sure Lucy could work wonders with some toff's cast-offs from the ragman. Make me look all respectable and such."

Lucy nodded quickly. "Oh yes, I could alter something. No one would ever know."

"You've seen how these things work now," Percy said softly, his eyes fixed on Ellie's face. "Sometimes rules need to be adjusted. To let talent find its rightful place."

To Ellie's ears, his words carried a subtle reminder of their recent activities: the stolen food, the fabric, the old gentleman's wallet.

Her fingers traced the outline of Stuart's locket as she wavered on the edge of decision. The memory of Jack's voice still lingered in her mind, pure and true as a church bell.

What harm could it really do, letting him experience one evening of music and elegant company?

"The soirée starts at seven," she heard herself saying. "But if you come round to the servants' entrance half an hour or so earlier, it should be easy enough for you to slip in unnoticed. Everyone will be too busy with last-minute preparations to pay much attention to one more person coming and going."

Jack's face lit up with such genuine excitement that it pushed away the last of her doubts. "You won't regret this, Ellie," he said, reaching across to squeeze her hand. "I'll be on my very best behaviour. You won't even know I'm there. Just another face in the crowd, taking in all that fine music and culture."

"Like a proper gentleman," Percy added with a slight smile. "Sampling the delights of refined society."

Lucy was practically bouncing in her seat. "Oh, remember that grey suit we saw at the pawnbroker's recently? I know exactly what I can do with it," she said eagerly. "Just a few alterations here and there."

Watching Jack's animated face as he discussed his plans with Lucy, Ellie felt that familiar mixture of excitement and unease settling in her stomach. She had crossed so many lines already – what was one more?

Yet somehow, this felt different. Bigger, somehow. Like a door being opened that might prove difficult to close.

Chapter Twenty

Crystal glasses chimed like tiny bells as waiting staff wove between clusters of elegant guests. Gas lamps cast a warm glow over the academy's transformed dining hall, their light reflecting off on glittering ladies' jewels and gentlemen's watch chains.

"I still can't quite believe you actually invited him," Phoebe whispered, half-hidden behind a potted palm in their quiet corner. Her fingers twisted nervously in her white gloves. "A young man from Spitalfields, here at the Bloomsbury Academy. It's positively scandalous."

Ellie touched Stuart's locket through the ivory-coloured fabric of her gown. "You make him sound like some sort of criminal," she said, trying to laugh off Phoebe's words even as memories of the pickpocketing incident flashed through her mind.

"Isn't he, though?" Phoebe's eyes sparkled with barely suppressed excitement. "And isn't it at least a little bit dangerous? After all the stories you've told me about his adventures in the rookery."

A string quartet had begun to play, the music drifting over the pleasant hum of conversation.

Ellie watched Mrs Bennett moving among the guests, every inch the gracious hostess in her purple brocade.

"We have to be careful," Ellie warned, touching Phoebe's arm. "If Mrs Bennett sees us being too familiar with him, she might grow suspicious. We can't draw attention to—"

"Listen to you," Phoebe giggled, pressing her handkerchief to her lips. "Being all sensible and cautious. Usually that's my role."

Despite her nervousness, Ellie couldn't help smiling. "I suppose you're right. Though I never thought I'd see the day when you'd be the one eager to break the rules."

"Well, you can hardly blame me. After weeks of hearing about this mysterious Jack Mortimer." Phoebe's voice trailed off as her gaze fixed on something across the room. "Oh! Is that him? The handsome one talking to Lydia?"

Ellie turned, her heart skipping a beat as she caught sight of a familiar figure in a well-cut grey suit.

Jack stood with a small group of guests, gesturing animatedly as he spoke. Even from this distance, she could see his usual charm was working its magic on his audience.

"He looks like a perfect gentleman," Phoebe breathed, a blush creeping into her cheeks. "You would never guess he was from... Well, you know. His sister must be quite clever with a needle to manage such a transformation."

Ellie watched Jack laugh at something Lydia had said, all easy grace and perfect manners. No one would ever suspect that this charming young man regularly picked pockets in the shadows of Spitalfields.

"I should probably have a word with him," she said quietly. "Just to make sure everything's going smoothly."

"Oh yes, and do introduce us properly later," Phoebe urged, still watching Jack with undisguised fascination. "I'm simply dying to meet him."

Ellie hesitated, suddenly uncertain whether bringing these two parts of her life together had been wise. But it was too late for such doubts now.

She had barely made her way halfway across the room when a familiar voice stopped her in her tracks.

"Ah, Miss Dubois," Mrs Novak's thick accent sounded through the genteel murmur of conversation. The piano teacher swayed slightly, her glass of sherry threatening to slosh over its rim. "How sad it is that I never see you any more."

Ellie's throat went dry as she noticed Mrs Bennett standing beside the piano teacher, one eyebrow raised in a silent question.

"Mrs Novak," she managed, forcing her lips into a smile. "How lovely to see you this evening."

"Lovely?" Mrs Novak's laugh held a bitter edge. "When you have abandoned your poor teacher for so many weeks? After you showed such promise, such passion in your playing."

The string quartet had moved into a livelier piece, but Ellie could barely hear the music over the pounding of her own heart. She was acutely aware of Mrs Bennett's probing gaze moving between them.

"I don't quite understand," the headmistress said carefully. "Miss Dubois has been attending your lessons twice weekly, as arranged."

Mrs Novak blinked owlishly. "Attending? Why, I haven't–"

But as she began to reply, her arm swept out in an expansive gesture, sending sherry spilling over the rim of her glass onto the polished floor.

"Bother," she grumbled, staring forlornly at her now empty glass.

"I believe I saw a waiter heading toward the library with fresh drinks just a moment ago," Ellie offered quickly, seizing the opportunity. "Shall I show you the way?"

"No, no, I can manage. But it's very kind of you." Mrs Novak waved her off, dabbing ineffectually at the spilled sherry with her handkerchief. "You see, Mrs Bennett? Such a thoughtful girl."

She squeezed Ellie's arm as she moved past, muttering under her breath, "All the more the shame, really."

They watched Mrs Novak weave her way through the crowd, leaving an awkward silence in her wake.

"Miss Dubois?" Mrs Bennett's voice was sharp as a needle. "Would you care to explain that rather peculiar exchange?"

Ellie's fingers found Stuart's locket, clutching it through her gown. "I fear Mrs Novak has been... Well, you've seen how she can be in the evenings."

She forced herself to meet the headmistress's eyes. "It must be the sherry, you understand. Sometimes I think she hardly knows what day of the week it is."

"Indeed." Mrs Bennett's tone suggested she wasn't entirely convinced. "Though she seemed quite sure of herself."

"Poor Mrs Novak." Ellie shook her head sadly, hating how easily the lies came to her lips. "She often dozes during our lessons. And I rather suspect she doesn't always remember who was there and who wasn't. Why, just last week she insisted that Queen Victoria herself had attended her morning class."

After what felt like an eternity, Mrs Bennett's severe expression softened slightly. "Yes, I suppose you may be right. The woman's habits have become rather concerning of late."

"If you'll excuse me," Ellie said quickly, seizing her chance to escape. "I believe I see Phoebe trying to catch my attention."

She turned away, her heart still racing. But she could feel Mrs Bennett's eyes following her as she moved through the crowd, and Ellie forced herself to move with grace, as if she had nothing to hide.

She made her way across the room with orchestrated indirection, pausing every now and then as if admiring the decorations or greeting fellow students. Each casual stop took her a little closer to where Jack stood charming his cluster of admirers.

She thought she could still feel Mrs Bennett's gaze burning into her back. Or perhaps that was merely her imagination. More and more often these days, she seemed to see suspicion lurking in every corner.

The string quartet had begun a gentle waltz. Ellie used its rhythm to guide her meandering path, stopping to examine a flower arrangement here, to straighten a table setting there. Her reflection flickered in the tall mirrors lining the walls, making her movements seem multiplied and strange.

When she finally reached Jack's group, she hung back for a moment, watching him dazzle his audience.

"And then," he was saying, his refined accent perfect as any gentleman's, "the Archbishop himself commented on the exceptional quality of the performance. Though naturally, one hesitates to repeat such praise."

Lydia and Susan hung on his every word, while their sewing teacher Miss Thompson appeared thoroughly charmed.

Looking over their heads, Jack caught Ellie's eye. And for a moment his carefully constructed mask slipped, revealing a flash of pure excitement.

Miss Thompson noticed Ellie hovering at the edge of their little group. "Ah, Miss Dubois," she said warmly. "You have quite an interest in music, don't you? We were just discussing the most fascinating performance at St James's Hall."

She gestured toward Jack. "Mr Mortimer here was sharing his insights. He appears to be quite the musical authority."

"You're too kind, Miss Thompson," Jack demurred with perfect modesty. "Though I confess I do take great pleasure in fine music when the opportunity presents itself."

His eyes met Ellie's as they exchanged a polite greeting, each playing their part to perfection.

"Do you play any instruments yourself, Miss Dubois?" he enquired, his refined accent never wavering.

"I dabble at the piano a bit," Ellie replied. "Though I fear my talents are rather modest."

"Nonsense," Miss Thompson said. "Miss Dubois is being far too humble. I'm told she's a gifted pianist."

Jack's expression brightened with seemingly genuine interest. "In that case, might I beg your opinion on this evening's musical selections, Miss Dubois? I found the quartet's choice of tempo in that Mozart sonata particularly intriguing."

"Of course," Ellie replied politely, allowing the conversation to draw them naturally toward the edge of the group.

Lydia and Susan had already lost interest, turning their attention to a young gentleman who had just approached with glasses of punch.

As their discussion of Mozart carried them further from Miss Thompson's group, Ellie and Jack moved towards a quieter corner near the French windows.

The night air drifted in, carrying the scent of the academy's rose garden. Jack was practically bouncing on his heels, his usual easy grace temporarily forgotten in his excitement.

"Enjoying the soirée?" Ellie asked quietly, though she already knew the answer from his beaming face.

"Oh, Ellie," he replied cheerfully, dropping the refined accent now they were alone. "It's better than I could have imagined. The music, the conversations. The way everyone just accepts me as one of their own."

His joy seemed so genuine that Ellie felt her earlier tensions beginning to fade. This was why she had helped him to be here tonight: to give him a glimpse of a world he could only dream about.

But then his grin shifted into something sharper, revealing the streetwise rascal behind the gentleman's disguise.

"And," he whispered, leaning closer, "you'll never guess what else I've already managed to accomplish during this splendid evening."

Jack reached into his coat pocket, his eyes dancing with triumph. "Look at this lovely little haul."

For a moment, Ellie didn't understand what she was seeing. Then her blood ran cold as Jack's fingers revealed the glint of a gold watch chain, a delicate pearl brooch, and what looked suspiciously like Lydia's favourite cameo.

"You've been stealing?" The words came out as barely more than a whisper. Nevertheless, her gloved fingers flew to her mouth as she glanced around frantically. But the music and chatter had swallowed up her shocked response before anyone could hear it.

"Now, don't look at me like that." Jack's voice remained light, though his eyes had taken on a harder edge. "I'm just making the most of an opportunity. After all, it's not as if these fine folks will miss a trinket or two."

Ellie's eyes darted nervously around the room, but no one seemed to be paying them any attention. The quartet had started another waltz, and couples were moving on the dance floor.

"But that's not why I helped you come here," she protested. "I thought you wanted to experience the music, the culture–"

"Oh, I am experiencing it." Jack's grin widened as he watched Lydia twirl past them, laughing at something her dance partner had said. "See how happy that one looks? She doesn't even realise her pretty little brooch is gone. Probably won't notice till morning."

"Jack, please." Ellie's voice shook. "You have to put these things back."

He laughed softly, tucking the stolen items away. "Back? To people who have so much they don't even notice what they've lost?"

His expression hardened. "Look around you, Ellie. All this fancy food, these sparkling jewels, those silk dresses: they cost more than Lucy and I can ever hope to make in a whole lifetime."

The string quartet's music seemed to fade into a distant hum as Jack continued, his voice dropping lower.

"You know what I'm going back to tonight? A cold room in Spitalfields where the wind and the rain come in through cracks in the wall. Where Lucy sits by candlelight, sewing her fingers bloody just to earn a few pennies."

He gestured at the elegant crowd. "These people spend more on one evening's entertainment than we see in a year."

"But stealing from them won't make things right," Ellie said, though her conviction wavered as she watched a waiter pass by with a tray of untouched delicacies.

"Won't it?" Jack's eyes glittered. "That watch chain alone could keep us fed for a month. And Lydia's trinket might pay for proper medicine next time Lucy falls ill."

He paused, letting his words sink in. "Or perhaps you'd prefer I find another kindly gentleman whose wallet we might relieve him of?"

Ellie flinched at the reminder of their last theft together. "That's not fair."

"Fair?" Jack's laugh held no humour now. "Nothing about any of this is fair, Ellie. In a few hours, all these fancy ladies and fine gentlemen will return to their comfortable homes. But I'll go back to the rookery, where children die of hunger and cold."

She watched him straighten his suit jacket, the one Lucy had so expertly altered to make him look like he belonged here.

"So yes," he continued, his voice softening. "I'm taking advantage of this opportunity you've arranged for me. Just not in the way you had imagined."

Across the room, Mrs Bennett was raising her glass in a toast to the academy's refined young ladies. The crystal sparkled in the gaslight as guests murmured their approval.

"I suppose," Ellie said slowly, "there's nothing I can say to change your mind?"

"Nothing at all." Jack's charming smile returned, though it didn't quite reach his eyes. "Now, if you'll excuse me, I believe I spotted a rather promising watch chain on that toff over there by the punch bowl."

Before she could stop him, he melted back into the crowd, every inch the perfect gentleman once more. Ellie watched him go, her heart heavy with the knowledge that she had helped make this evening's thefts possible.

The music played on, the dancers twirled, and somewhere in the crowd, Jack continued his own particular dance of deception.

Ellie moved to one of the French windows, needing the cool night air on her face. The garden beyond lay in shadow, broken only by the warm rectangles of light spilling from the dining hall.

From here, she could see both worlds at once: the elegant party behind her, and the darkness ahead where London's streets eventually led to Spitalfields. The contrast made her head spin. Or perhaps that was just the evening's revelations catching up with her.

Her fingers found Stuart's locket again. What would her levelheaded, sensible engineer from Sheffield think about all this? Would he have stood silently by while Jack relieved the guests of their valuables, like she had just done?

But then she caught sight of Lydia twirling past in her expensive gown, with jewels glittering at her throat. And Jack's words echoed in her mind.

These people spend more on one evening's entertainment than we see in a year.

Was he really so wrong? The food alone being served tonight could feed Jack and Lucy for a month. While the jewels worn by just one guest could probably pay their rent for a decade.

The chimes of a distant church bell drifted through the window, making her shiver. In a few hours, all this would be over. The guests and the girls would go to their warm beds.

And Jack would fade back into the shadows of Spitalfields, where Lucy waited in their draughty room with her needle and thread.

Perhaps that was why Ellie couldn't bring herself to raise the alarm. After all, hadn't she herself stolen food from the kitchen, as well as fabric from the sewing room?

At least Jack was honest about his intentions, in his own way.

Through the window's reflection, she watched him charm another group of guests, his borrowed gentility sitting as naturally on his shoulders as his fine grey coat. No one would ever suspect the truth behind that easy smile.

Her fingers tightened around Stuart's locket as she realised she could no longer tell which version of Jack was the real one: the charming young man who sang like an angel in a dirty pub, or the ruthless thief who spoke such bitter truths about the world's unfairness?

Perhaps they were both equally real, like the double reflection she saw in the window: the elegant young lady in a fine evening gown, and the girl who helped steal an old man's wallet in the streets near Spitalfields.

The quartet began a slower piece, and Ellie turned back to the bright room, knowing she would keep Jack's secrets. Not because she believed he was right, but because she no longer knew if he was entirely wrong.

She touched Stuart's locket one last time, then let her hand fall to her side. The night was far from over, and she had her own part to play in this elegant deception.

After all, wasn't that what they were all doing? Playing parts in a world where some people had everything, and others had nothing at all?

The thought followed her back into the warmth of the party, as persistent as a shadow on a moonlit night.

Chapter Twenty-One

The morning after the soirée dawned grey and restless, matching the atmosphere that pervaded the academy's halls. Whispers darted between clusters of girls like nervous starlings, carrying fragments of scandal on swift wings.

As Ellie and Phoebe descended the main staircase, snatches of excited conversation drifted up to meet them.

"Did you hear? Valuables stolen during the party itself."

"I heard that Mrs Bennett is beside herself."

"At least three separate guests. And right under everyone's noses, too."

Ellie's stomach twisted at each new revelation. She had hoped, somehow, that the events of last night might fade like a bad dream in the morning light.

But now the consequences of Jack's actions were spreading through the academy like wildfire.

In the day room, girls huddled together in small groups, their heads bent close in feverish discussion. The usual quiet refinement of their morning tea had shattered under the weight of the brewing scandal.

Mrs Bennett stood near the fireplace, her purple day dress practically bristling with suppressed agitation as she attempted to restore order.

"Young ladies, please." Her voice carried a note of forced calm that failed to fool anyone. "I must insist upon proper decorum. These wild speculations are most unbecoming."

But even as she spoke, fresh whispers rippled through the room.

Ellie sank into a chair near the window, trying to make herself as small and unremarkable as possible. From this vantage point, she had a clear view of Lydia holding court in the centre of the room, surrounded by her usual admirers.

"It was my grandmother's cameo." Lydia's voice trembled – a little too perfectly – as she pressed a handkerchief to her eyes. "Passed down through the generations."

Susan Harris clutched dramatically at her own throat, as if to protect her jewellery from invisible thieves. "How absolutely dreadful. And to think it happened right here, in our very own academy."

"Indeed." Mrs Bennett's lips pressed into a thin line. "Though I feel compelled to remind you all that nothing has been definitively proven. A few misplaced items at a large gathering hardly constitute–"

"Misplaced?" Lydia's eyes widened with tactical precision. "My cameo was not misplaced, Mrs Bennett. It was stolen. Along with Mr Ashworth's pocket watch and Lady Pembrooke's sapphire brooch."

Fresh murmurs swept the room at this revelation. Mrs Bennett's face tightened further, but before she could respond, Emily Baker spoke up eagerly.

"Who could have done such a thing?" she asked, her voice pitched to carry. "Surely none of the regular staff would dare to steal from us?"

Mrs Bennett cleared her throat sharply. "That is quite enough speculation for one morning. Need I remind you that refined young ladies do not indulge in idle gossip? I suggest you turn your attention to more appropriate topics. The weather, perhaps, or your progress in French composition."

As soon as she had left the room however, the tide of whispers rose again. Lydia dabbed at fresh tears from her eyes, though Ellie noticed they never quite fell.

"If you could have seen my dear grandmother wearing it," Lydia sighed. "She looked so elegant, so refined. Everything a lady should be."

Her gaze drifted meaningfully toward the maid clearing tea cups from a nearby table. "Though I suppose some people simply can't resist taking what isn't rightfully theirs. They spend all day handling things they could never hope to own themselves. The temptation must be quite overwhelming."

Lydia paused to adjust her sleeve with delicate precision. "Such base instincts. But then again, what else can one expect from their sort?"

The maid's hands trembled slightly as she gathered the cups, making the fine china rattle against the saucers.

Ellie watched the girl's shoulders hunch under the weight of Lydia's implications, and something hot and angry began to twist in her own stomach.

She thought of Jack's swift fingers the night before, his bitter words about inequality still echoing in her mind. Looking at Lydia now, surrounded by sympathetic admirers and radiating wounded privilege, Ellie wasn't entirely sure he had been wrong.

"Are you quite all right?" Phoebe's quiet voice interrupted Ellie's brooding. "You've hardly touched your tea."

Ellie forced her fingers to release their grip on Stuart's locket, trying to summon a smile for her friend.

"Just tired. The soirée went rather late, didn't it?"

"Oh yes, about that." Phoebe leaned closer, her voice dropping to a conspiratorial whisper.

"You failed to introduce me to Jack. After all those stories you've told me about him, I was quite looking forward to making his acquaintance."

"He was... occupied." Ellie stared into her cooling tea, watching the light ripple across its surface.

"I'm sure he was." A faint blush crept into Phoebe's cheeks. "Though I did catch a glimpse of him speaking with Miss Thompson. He cut quite the striking figure in that suit of his. No one would ever have guessed his true origins."

Ellie thought of Lucy's clever fingers, and how the poor girl must have worked late into the night for days to pull off such an impressive transformation. How easily fine clothes could make the world see what it wanted to see.

Phoebe glanced around at the gossiping girls, then shifted even closer. "Ellie," she whispered, her voice barely audible above the general murmur of conversation. "You don't suppose... That is, your friend Jack... He wouldn't have had anything to do with these thefts, would he?"

The tea cup rattled slightly against its saucer as Ellie set it down. "What a strange question," she said, keeping her voice carefully level. "Whatever made you think that?"

But she couldn't quite meet Phoebe's concerned gaze. Instead, she turned her attention back to where Lydia held court, letting her friend's worried silence fade into the general buzz of speculation that filled the room.

"But who do you suppose could have done it?" Susan was asking, her eyes wide with delicious horror. "Could the thief have somehow slipped in among the guests?"

"More likely it was one of the extra staff brought in for the evening," Emily suggested. "That tall one with the dark hair looked rather shifty."

"Unless..." Susan's voice dropped ominously. "What if it was someone from the academy's household staff?"

A collective shudder passed through the group. Lydia straightened in her chair, arranging her skirts with precise movements.

"That would be far worse," she declared. "To think we might have a thieving crook living under this very roof."

She paused for effect, then added, "And what with my birthday in just a few days and all. Papa always sends me the most exquisite gifts, you know."

"Oh, how dreadful." Emily clasped her hands together. "You don't think... Surely, the thief would never dare–"

"I certainly hope not." Lydia's tone suggested she hoped exactly that, if only for the drama it would provide. "Though with a thief lurking about, who can say what might happen?"

Murmurs of sympathy rippled through her audience. The maid who had been hovering nearby with her tray of cups began to move toward the door, her face burning.

"So you do think it was one of the servants?" someone asked from the edge of the group.

Lydia's eyes followed the retreating maid with deliberate slowness. "More than likely," she replied, her voice carrying clearly across the room.

"But what do you expect when you let these creatures anywhere near decent society?" Her lip curled slightly. "It's like Father always says: you can't trust people who were born in the gutters. They're like rats, really. Even when they manage to crawl out of their slums and rookeries, they still carry the stink of poverty with them."

The words struck Ellie like a slap in the face. Before she could stop herself, she spoke up loudly, her voice sharp with anger.

"And I suppose being born with a silver spoon in your mouth makes you naturally superior?"

The room fell silent. Lydia turned slowly, a smile playing at the corners of her mouth as if she had been waiting for just such an outburst.

"Why, Miss Dubois," she said sweetly. "I didn't realise this topic would upset you so." Her eyes glittered with malice. "Though I guess, coming from... Where was it again? Ah yes, Sheffield. All those factories and common labourers. One does tend to forget that not everyone here comes from proper breeding."

Ellie's hands clenched at her sides. "At least in Sheffield people earn their wealth through honest work. Rather than inheriting both their money and their prejudices."

A cold smile spread across Lydia's face. "Honest work? Is that what they call it?" She let out a delicate laugh. "How fascinating. Though I must say, if your mother's factory is so successful, one would think she could afford to dress you properly."

Her gaze fixed on the silver chain at Ellie's throat. "That locket you're always fingering: brass, isn't it?"

"It's silver," Ellie said, her voice tight. Her fingers moved instinctively to touch it, then dropped away as she realised she was proving Lydia's point about her habit.

"Silver. Of course it is."

Lydia turned to her friends with exaggerated concern. "Polished tin, more likely." Her lips curved in a cruel smile. "Although I suppose when one doesn't know any better, even cheap trinkets can seem precious."

The casual dismissal of Stuart's gift sent a wave of heat rushing through Ellie's body. Her hands trembled and she pushed them down to her lap with clenched fists.

"Better a simple locket given with love than a family heirloom worn by someone with a heart of stone."

"Given with love?" Lydia's voice was silky smooth. "By whom? That engineer boy you're always swooning over?" She sighed theatrically. "How romantic. I'm sure he means well, even if he can't afford any better. After all, one must make allowances for... limited circumstances."

The words seemed to echo in the suddenly still room. Ellie shot to her feet, her chair scraping backwards across the floor with a harsh screech.

"You wouldn't recognise real worth if it was standing right in front of you, Lydia." Her voice shook with fury. "You're too busy hoarding your possessions to appreciate your blessings."

Without waiting for a response, Ellie turned and stormed toward the door. She could feel every eye in the room following her, and she could hear the whispers already beginning to stir in her wake.

But she didn't care. She had to get out. Away from Lydia's smug superiority, away from the suffocating weight of all that privilege and prejudice.

The door slammed behind her with a satisfying bang that would have scandalised Mrs Bennett. But Ellie couldn't bring herself to care about proper behaviour or refined manners.

Not when Jack's words from the night before seemed to ring more true with every passing moment.

Ellie hurried through the hallway and up the stairs, her pulse still thundering in her ears. Jack's voice echoed in her mind: *These people spend more on one evening's entertainment than we see in a year.*

"Perhaps you were right all along," she muttered under her breath as she took the steps two at a time. "When the divide between rich and poor is so vast, so unfair–"

The collision caught her completely off guard. She had been so lost in her thoughts that she hadn't noticed the maid struggling up the stairs with an armful of letters and parcels. Their shoulders connected, and suddenly paper and packages were tumbling everywhere.

"Oh, I'm so sorry, Miss." The maid dropped immediately to her knees, scrambling to gather the scattered items. "It's entirely my fault, I should have been more careful."

"No, please," Ellie interrupted, kneeling beside her. "I'm the one who wasn't watching where I was going." She reached for a letter that had slid against the bannister. "Let me help you."

As she gathered the fallen items, her hands closed around a sizeable parcel wrapped in thick brown paper. The address caught her eye – the elegant handwriting, the obvious quality of the paper.

But it was the name that made her pause: *Miss Lydia Price*.

Lydia's smug voice drifted back to her: *Papa always sends me the most exquisite gifts.*

Ellie's fingers tightened on the package as an idea began to form.

"Here," she told the maid, keeping her voice carefully casual. "You've got your hands full with all the rest. I can take this one to Miss Price myself."

The maid hesitated, shifting her newly gathered burden. "Oh, but Miss... I couldn't ask you to–"

"It's no trouble at all." Ellie managed a smile, though her heart had begun to beat faster. "Consider it my way of making amends for nearly knocking you over."

"That's very kind of you, Miss," the maid said with visible relief, balancing her remaining armful of post. She bobbed a quick curtsy before continuing up the stairs.

Ellie stood still for a moment, feeling the solid weight of Lydia's parcel in her hands. A rather large package, she thought. No doubt containing something exquisite, as Lydia had said.

Something that Lydia, with all her wealth and privilege, probably didn't deserve at all.

Ellie's feet carried her to the small bedroom she shared with Phoebe. *Just a peek,* she told herself.

Just to see what sort of gifts were considered suitable for someone like Lydia Price.

She closed the door behind her and moved to sit on her bed, the parcel balanced across her knees. The brown paper was thick and expensive, carefully wrapped and secured with string that had been tied with precise corners.

Her fingers worked at the knots slowly, carefully. She could rewrap it afterward, she thought. No one would ever know.

The string came away easily, coiling like a snake on her bedspread. The paper made a soft crinkling sound as she unfolded it with delicate movements, taking care not to tear a single edge.

Inside, tissue paper rustled beneath her touch, revealing first one item, then another. A beautifully carved wooden box caught the morning light, its brass fittings gleaming.

Ellie opened it to find row upon row of expensive sewing supplies: delicate scissors with mother-of-pearl handles, silver thimbles, needles of the finest quality, and dozens of spools of thread. Precious treasures that Lucy could only dream of touching.

She remembered Lydia's criticism about the school's supposedly 'common' supplies, and a bitter laugh escaped her.

Probably wrote a letter to Papa and Mama to complain, she thought sarcastically.

But it was the next item that made her breath catch. A shawl, impossibly fine, in a shade of blue that reminded her of summer skies. The fabric was so delicate it seemed to float as she lifted it from its wrapping.

Lucy's face flashed through Ellie's mind. Lucy, who worked miracles with a needle despite having to make do with cast-off threads and third-rate fabrics. Lucy, whose own shawl was more darning than original fabric.

Ellie's fingers clutched the fine material as Jack's words from the night before came back to her: *That watch chain alone could keep us fed for a month.*

She began to rewrap the parcel, her movements mechanical. But halfway through, her hands stopped.

Why should Lydia have such beautiful things when Lucy had nothing? What right did Lydia have to these exquisite sewing supplies when Lucy's talented fingers were forced to work with whatever she could scrounge?

The unfairness of it all seemed to crystallise in that moment. Lydia's cruel words about people born in the gutters, her dismissal of

Stuart's loving gift, her casual cruelty to the maid.

And now these pretty things that she would likely never fully appreciate.

Ellie's decision formed slowly, then all at once. Lucy would put these things to better use. Lucy would treasure them, and use them to create true beauty. Instead of treating them as just another symbol of wealth and privilege.

It wasn't stealing, Ellie told herself as she gathered the items close. It was justice. Redistribution. Setting right, in some small way, the imbalance that Jack had spoken of with such bitter knowledge.

Moving quickly now, before she could second-guess herself, Ellie crossed to the wardrobe. She pushed aside the neat row of dresses, creating a space at the very back where the shadows would hide her secret.

The parcel seemed to whisper against the wood as she set it down, like a guilty conscience trying to make itself heard.

She closed the wardrobe doors firmly, already planning her next visit to Spitalfields. Lucy's face would light up when she saw the sewing supplies. And that shawl. How beautiful it would look on her. So much lovelier than her current threadbare one.

But as Ellie turned to leave, her own reflection in the mirror stopped her short. The same dark curls framed her face, the same blue eyes gazed back at her. Nothing had changed, and yet...

Everything had changed.

The girl in the mirror wore the same dress, the same carefully pinned hair, but something was different in the way she held herself. As if she had crossed some invisible line and could never quite find her way back.

Her fingers found Stuart's locket. She thought of his honest face, his steadfast nature, his belief in doing what was right.

The weight of it suddenly felt unbearable against her throat.

Ellie turned away from her reflection, flinching from the sight of Stuart's gift catching the morning light. That simple symbol of love, now tarnished by what she had become. By what she had chosen to do.

She hurried from the room, leaving her old self behind in the mirror, along with all the certainties she had once held dear about right and wrong.

Chapter Twenty-Two

As the hansom cab rattled through London's busy streets, the parcel lay on Ellie's lap like a silent judgment. It felt heavy and impossible to ignore. The fine sewing supplies and delicate shawl barely weighed anything at all, of course. Yet they seemed to press down on her very soul.

She tried to focus on her destination instead, imagining the look on Lucy's face when she would see these beautiful things. But her thoughts kept circling back to the moment she had slipped the parcel into her wardrobe. Another step, another decision that could no longer be undone.

The cab jolted over a rough patch of cobblestones, making the parcel shift slightly. Ellie's fingers tightened around it.

Too late for doubts, she told herself. Too late to turn back. What was done was done, and surely, using these things to help Lucy was better than letting them gather dust in Lydia's privileged hands?

But the burden remained, weighing on her conscience as the cab carried her deeper into the heart of London's poorer districts.

The hansom cab finally drew to a halt at the street corner nearest St Mary's Mission. Ellie gathered her skirts with one hand, clutching the parcel close with the other as she descended.

She kept her eyes fixed ahead, unable to bear even a cursory glance toward the mission where, once again, Mrs Collins would be organising today's food queue without her.

Ellie quickened her pace, weaving between puddles of questionable origin. When she reached the tenement building where Jack and Lucy lived, she slipped inside and started up the creaking stairs, the parcel clutched tightly to her chest.

By the time she reached Jack and Lucy's floor, her heart was racing. Though whether that was from the climb or from anticipation, she couldn't quite tell.

The door to their room stood slightly ajar, spilling a thin wedge of light into the dim hallway. Ellie tapped lightly on the wooden frame before stepping inside.

She found Lucy exactly where she had expected: perched on a chair beside the window, making the most of the weak sunlight that managed to filter through the soot-stained glass. The girl's fingers moved swiftly and steadily as she worked on what appeared to be a gentleman's shirt.

The sight of Lucy in her faded dress, surrounded by the room's meagre furnishings, eased some of the weight from Ellie's conscience. Especially when she noticed how Lucy had to squint in the poor light, her face drawn with concentration as she worked.

"Ellie!" Lucy brightened as she looked up, though something flickered in her expression. Surprise at this unexpected visit perhaps? "I didn't think we'd see you today."

"I wanted to bring you something," Ellie said, still holding the parcel close. "Is Jack not here?"

"He and Percy are off trying to sell those things from your school's party." Lucy shook her head slightly, her voice taking on a rueful tone. "No doubt they'll end up celebrating their success at The Dog and Duck afterwards, drinking away part of the profits."

"Well, perhaps it's better they're not here," Ellie said, moving closer to the window. "Because this is just for you."

She held out the parcel with unsteady hands, betraying her nervousness. The brown paper crinkled softly in the quiet room, its expensive quality somehow more obvious here than it had seemed in her bedroom at the academy.

Lucy set aside her sewing, careful to secure her needle first: a habit born of someone who couldn't afford to waste even the smallest scrap or shortest length of thread.

"For me?" Her voice held a note of wonder, as if unused to receiving gifts of any kind.

"Open it," Ellie urged, perching on the edge of the room's narrow bed. Her heart began to race again as Lucy's careful fingers worked at the string, untying each knot with delicate precision rather than simply cutting the bindings.

The paper fell away to reveal the wooden box first. Lucy's soft gasp as she opened it sent a wave of warmth through Ellie's chest, momentarily drowning out her lingering guilt.

"Oh, Ellie..."

Lucy took out the pearl-handled scissors with reverent fingers, turning it so the weak sunlight caught its polished surface.

"I've never seen anything so fine."

Her other hand drifted over the silver thimbles, the gleaming needles, the spools of thread in every imaginable shade.

But it was the shawl that drew the biggest reaction. As Lucy unfolded the delicate blue fabric, her eyes went wide.

"It's like holding a piece of sky," she breathed, letting the fine material glide between her fingers.

The joy in Lucy's face made everything seem worth it: the theft, the deception, the weight of guilt that had pressed down on Ellie during the cab ride. This was why she had done it. This moment, this happiness.

But then Lucy paused. Her fingers sampled the softness of the tissue paper, and her expression shifted. She turned the expensive wrapping over in her hands, her movements slowing as she noticed the careful creases, the precise folds, the quality of the paper itself.

"Ellie," she said softly, her voice changing. "Where did all this come from?"

The question hung in the air between them, heavy with unspoken implications. And suddenly the room felt colder, as if a cloud had passed over the weak sunlight streaming through the window.

Ellie's fingers found Stuart's locket, twisting it nervously through her dress. "Oh, I just... happened to come across them."

Lucy's quiet gaze didn't waver. She smoothed the tissue paper with the kind of gentle touch that spoke of someone who understood the value of fine things precisely because she so rarely encountered them.

"You happened to come across them?" Lucy repeated. There was no judgment in her voice, only a sad kind of knowing that made Ellie's carefully constructed justifications crumble.

"They were meant for Lydia," Ellie burst out, the words tumbling forth like water through a broken dam. "A birthday gift from her father.

But you should have heard her this morning, Lucy. The horrible things she said about people who weren't born into wealth. About how they're like rats crawling out of the gutter."

She gestured at the shawl still draped across Lucy's lap. "She has dozens of fine things already. Probably wouldn't even appreciate these properly. Whereas you... You could do such wonderful things with them. Your talent deserves proper tools, not broken needles and thread that keeps snapping."

Lucy's face however had grown paler with each word. She gathered the shawl with trembling hands, folding it back into its tissue paper with the same care one might use to wrap a sleeping child.

"A birthday gift," she whispered. "From her father."

"Yes, but–"

"Ellie." Lucy's voice cracked slightly. "This isn't like taking leftover food. Or even like the fabric from your sewing room."

She closed the wooden box of sewing supplies with a soft click that seemed to echo in the sudden stillness. "This is different."

"How is it different?" Ellie demanded, though her voice lacked conviction. "It's merely redistributing things from people who have too much to people who–"

"To people like me?" Lucy's quiet interruption cut deeper than any shout could have. "People who live in places like this?" She gestured at the cramped room with its peeling wallpaper and rickety chairs. "Is that how you justify it to yourself?"

The compassion in Lucy's eyes made it somehow worse. "They'll know exactly when and where it went missing, Ellie. They'll be asking questions. Looking for someone to blame."

Ellie felt the blood drain from her face as the full implications of Lucy's words sank in. She thought of Mrs Bennett's shrewd gaze, of the servants who would be questioned. And of the maid who had seen her take the parcel.

"I didn't think–" she began.

"No," Lucy said gently. "I don't suppose you did." She sighed, slowly gathering the gifts into a neat pile.

"You need to be careful," Lucy warned. "All this stealing. The food, the fabric, and now this." She pushed the parcel back toward Ellie. "We're not worth getting yourself into serious trouble over."

"Don't say that." Ellie's voice caught in her throat. "Don't ever say you're not worth it."

"But it's true, isn't it?" Lucy's fingers traced the edge of the wooden box, a gesture of longing quickly suppressed. "Look at me, Ellie.

Really look. I'm just a girl from the rookery who's good with a needle. That's all I'll ever be."

"That's not true." Ellie took Lucy's hands in hers, forcing her to stop pushing the gifts away. "You're so much more than that. You're talented and kind and–"

"And poor," Lucy finished quietly. "Poor enough that having these lovely things would only raise questions. Questions I couldn't answer without getting you into trouble."

"I don't care about trouble." Ellie's chin lifted stubbornly. "And I won't take them back. They're yours now."

Lucy's resistance wavered. She glanced at the shawl, then back at Ellie's determined face. "You really don't understand what you're risking, do you?"

"I understand perfectly well. And I still say you deserve these things more than Lydia ever will." Ellie squeezed Lucy's hands. "Think what you could make with proper tools. The kind of work you could do."

Something shifted in Lucy's expression, a flicker of long-buried hope breaking through her practical exterior. She bit her lip, then seemed to come to a decision.

"Can you keep a secret?" she asked softly.

When Ellie nodded, Lucy released her hands and moved to the old wardrobe with its creaky doors. From beneath a stack of neatly folded clothes, she withdrew a small, worn notebook.

"I've never shown this to anyone," she said, her voice barely above a whisper. "Not even Jack."

Her fingers rested on the cover of the closed notebook for a heartbeat before opening it slowly. "Sometimes, when I can't sleep, I draw things. The kind of dresses I'd make if..."

She trailed off, but Ellie understood. If circumstances were different. If life had dealt Lucy a different hand.

"If you had your own shop," Ellie finished.

"Yes," Lucy nodded sadly. "If I had my own shop. Which will never happen."

"But that's exactly what these designs deserve." Ellie moved closer, looking at the detailed sketches that filled the notebook's pages. "A proper shop, with a window to display your work. And customers who appreciate real talent."

A flush crept into Lucy's pale cheeks. "It's just a silly dream."

"It's not silly at all."

Ellie turned another page, marvelling at the intricate details Lucy had captured with just a stub of pencil. "And these supplies, they're only the beginning. The first step toward making that dream real."

A sudden crash from the neighbouring room made them both jump. A man's voice rose in anger, followed by the sound of breaking crockery and a woman's frightened cry.

"Leave off, you drunken fool," the woman shouted. "That was our last decent plate."

More crashes followed, punctuated by cursing and the thud of someone stumbling against a wall. Lucy's shoulders hunched as if she could make herself smaller, her fingers automatically closing the precious notebook.

"The Burtons," she explained quietly, sliding the notebook back into its hiding place. "He usually doesn't start drinking until the evening. But I suppose he got paid early today."

The sounds of the fight grew louder. A child began to cry somewhere in the building, its wails mixing with the shouts and crashes next door.

Lucy smoothed her skirts with practiced composure, but the nervous uncertainty in her movements was plain to see.

"This is my world, Ellie," she said softly. "Fine shawls and silver thimbles don't belong here. Neither do fancy dreams of dress-making shops."

She gestured at the thin walls that did nothing to muffle the violence next door. "This is what's real. People like the Burtons, drinking away their wages. Children going hungry. Women working their fingers to the bone just to keep a roof over their heads."

A particularly loud crash rattled the empty teacup on the table. Lucy smiled sadly. "What wealthy lady would order a dress from someone who lives in a place like this? Who would trust their fine fabrics to a seamstress from Spitalfields?"

The sad acceptance in her voice made Ellie's heart ache with sorrow. This was Lucy's reality. Not the beautiful drawings in her secret notebook, but the harsh sounds of poverty and desperation seeping through these thin walls.

"I should go," Ellie said softly, though her mind was already racing ahead, refusing to accept Lucy's resignation.

"But promise me you'll keep these things." She touched the wooden box of sewing supplies. "Hidden away if you must, but keep them. Please."

Lucy hesitated, then nodded. "Thank you," she whispered. "Even if I shouldn't accept them. Thank you for believing in me."

The stairs creaked under Ellie's feet as she descended, each step carrying her further from Lucy's world and closer to her own. But her thoughts remained in that draughty room with its rotting floorboards, and its secret notebook full of dreams.

No, she thought fiercely as she emerged into the grey London afternoon. Lucy was wrong about one thing: talent like hers didn't belong trapped in a tenement room, any more than those wonderful designs belonged hidden in a drawer.

A passing cart scattered a group of ragged children playing in the gutter. They darted away like sparrows, their laughter echoing off the sooty walls. Ellie watched them disappear down an alley, thinking of all the dreams that died in places like this.

But not Lucy's. Not if she could help it.

Her fingers found Stuart's locket as she walked, but for once its familiar shape didn't bring guilt or doubt. Instead, it felt like a lucky charm, strengthening her resolve.

She would find a way to help Lucy escape this place. And to transform those pencil sketches into real dresses hanging in the window of a real shop.

She didn't know how yet. But she had already crossed so many lines, broken so many rules. What was one more impossible thing, if it meant giving Lucy's dreams a chance to fly?

Chapter Twenty-Three

The candle flame wavered as Ellie dipped her pen into the inkwell, casting strange shadows across the blank paper before her. In the other bed, Phoebe's steady breathing provided a gentle counterpoint to the scratching of her nib.

My dearest Stuart,

With a sigh, she stopped. Opening his locket, she stared at Stuart's miniature portrait inside and kissed it.

How could she explain the thoughts that had been keeping her awake these past nights? The things she had seen, the truths she had learned about London's darker corners?

I hope this letter finds you well, and that the work at the factory continues to challenge and inspire you. Though we have been apart these many weeks, I find my thoughts constantly returning to the conversations you and I have had about justice and fairness.

Ellie paused, watching a drop of ink gather at the pen's tip. In the candlelight, it looked almost like a tear about to fall.

Do you remember that day last summer, when we watched a handful of children playing outside the factory gates? You spoke then about wanting to improve their lives through your engineering work.

About making the machines safer, the hours more reasonable.

Her fingers traced the locket's delicate engravings as she searched for the right words.

I understand that desire better now, Stuart. Here in London, I've seen things that would break your gentle heart. Children wearing shoes full of holes, young girls bent over needlework in rooms so dark they can barely see the stitches. Talented people trapped by circumstances beyond their control, their dreams dying slowly like flowers without sunlight.

The candle sputtered, making her start. She looked over at Phoebe, who was softly murmuring something in her sleep. Then she returned to her letter.

Sometimes I lie awake at night, wondering how we can call ourselves civilised when such inequalities exist. When some people have so much while others survive on so little. When a girl with real artistic talent must waste away in a tenement room, never having the chance to–

Ellie's pen hovered above the paper. She was saying too much, revealing too much of what she had seen in Spitalfields.

And of what she had done.

Carefully, she crossed out the last few lines until they were illegible. Stuart had an honest nature, and he believed in doing things the right way. But how could she possibly explain to him that sometimes the right way wasn't enough?

I suppose what I'm trying to say is that I understand now why you're so passionate about improving living conditions for the working classes. And why you believe so strongly in making things better and more fair.

A floorboard creaked as she shifted in her chair. Here she was writing to Stuart about fairness when some of her own actions had been so dishonest.

Sighing miserably, she shook her head.

There are times when the contrast between wealth and poverty in this city seems almost obscene. When I see my fellow students carelessly wasting food while children go hungry in the streets. When I watch them complain about the quality of their silk ribbons while others make do with–

Again she stopped, realising how bitter her words had become. This wasn't what Stuart would want to hear. Not from the sweet girl he had given his locket to on that sunny afternoon in Sheffield, when everything had seemed so much simpler.

Taking a fresh sheet of paper, Ellie began again:

My dearest Stuart,

I miss you more with each passing day.

But the other words remained unwritten, drifting in the candlelight like shadows she couldn't quite grasp.

How could she make him understand when she barely understood herself? When every justification for her actions seemed to slip through her fingers the moment she tried to capture it on paper?

The candle flame danced. And in its unsteady light, Ellie saw her own reflection in the window glass. A stranger stared back at her, barely recognisable as the innocent girl who had left Sheffield only such a short time ago.

Her fingers closed around Stuart's locket as she watched that reflection fade into darkness, taking with it all the things she couldn't bring herself to write.

The next morning, the breakfast room hummed with nervous whispers, like leaves rustling before a storm. Where there would normally be cheerful chatter about lessons and letters from home, now there were only darting glances and half-finished conversations.

"But what if it happens again?" Emily Baker demanded loudly, wanting to be heard by everyone in the room. "What if the thief is still here? Why, they could be walking among us as we speak?"

Ellie stirred her porridge without appetite, watching the servants move between the tables with unusual caution. They seemed almost frightened this morning, shrinking beneath the weight of everyone's suspicious glances. She knew they didn't deserve this.

"Did you see how the maid looked at my rings just now?" Susan Harris whispered, hiding her hands beneath the table. "I swear she was counting them."

"Shame on you, Susan," Phoebe protested. "You can't just go around throwing wild accusations at people."

"Well, someone took Lydia's cameo at the gala, didn't they?" Emily insisted. "Right here, in our own academy. Heaven knows when they will strike again. None of us are safe any more."

A maid approached their table with fresh tea. "Would you care for more, Miss?" she asked Susan politely, holding the silver teapot.

"No, thank you," Susan said, her voice as cold as ice. "I would rather go thirsty than be served by a thief."

The maid's face crumpled slightly before she moved on. The sight made Ellie's blood boil as she watched the poor girl's retreating back.

The servants were completely innocent. She knew that for a fact. Yet they were being treated like convicted criminals.

All because of Jack's actions.

Actions she had helped make possible.

"This is getting ridiculous," Phoebe grumbled. "I hear they're questioning the entire staff. Down to the scullery maid."

"Well, naturally." Lydia's voice dripped honey-coated venom. "Though I must say, after what happened at the soirée, I'm astonished that Mrs Bennett still allows them in our presence at all. She would have been better off dismissing the whole lot of them."

"Why would you want her to do that?" Phoebe demanded. "There's no proof any of them are guilty."

"Proof? Pah! You simply can't trust these lower classes. It's like inviting thieves into one's home and then acting surprised when things go missing. Though I suppose some people simply don't know any better than to steal when given the chance."

Ellie threw down her napkin and pushed back her chair. She'd had quite enough of all this nastiness. But before she could speak, Mrs Bennett appeared in the doorway.

"Young ladies, your attention, please."

The room fell silent while her sharp gaze swept across the breakfast tables.

"I have an announcement to make."

"Have you found the culprit, Mrs Bennett?" Emily asked breathlessly.

"Not yet, Miss Baker," the headmistress replied evenly as she stepped towards the centre of the room. "But in light of recent events, I have decided that anyone who wishes to ensure the safety of their valuables may bring them to my office following breakfast. I will personally see to their safekeeping until this unfortunate situation is resolved."

A rush of whispers went through the room. Lydia's voice rose above the others, sharp with calculated outrage.

"If only you had made this offer before the soirée, Mrs Bennett. Then my grandmother's cameo might still be—"

"Yes, thank you, Miss Price." Mrs Bennett's tone could have turned water into ice. "I trust this arrangement will help ease everyone's minds."

Ellie barely heard the rest of the headmistress's words. Her attention had fixed on something else entirely: the steady stream of girls already reaching for their jewellery, preparing to surrender their precious things into Mrs Bennett's care.

"Look at them all," Phoebe whispered to Ellie. "They can't seem to hand over their valuables fast enough."

Ellie watched Emily Baker slip a heavy gold bracelet from her wrist. Susan Harris had already left the room to gather her brooches. And others were discussing what else they might bring down from their bedrooms: rings, pearls, necklaces, family heirlooms.

All those valuable things, Ellie thought. All in one place. Most convenient.

Her fingers found Stuart's locket, while her mind filled with images of Lucy bent over her secret notebook, drawing dreams in the dim light of that cramped tenement room.

One single theft, a voice whispered in her head. One final act that could change everything.

"Ellie?" Phoebe touched her arm gently. "You're awfully quiet this morning. Are you feeling ill?"

"No," Ellie said softly, watching another girl remove a pearl ring. "No, I'm perfectly well."

But her heart had begun to beat faster, while her thoughts raced ahead to Mrs Bennett's office. And to all those precious things that could pay for turning Lucy's drawings into reality.

Just one more time, she told herself. One last crossing of that line she had already crossed so many times before.

She rose from the table, her decision made.

"Where are you going?" Phoebe asked.

"I need to think," Ellie replied, already moving toward the door. But she knew it wasn't really thinking that she needed to do.

It was planning.

Chapter Twenty-Four

Moonlight shone through the small bedroom window, casting a soft, silver light across Ellie's bed. She lay perfectly still, listening to Phoebe's steady breathing from the other side of the room while her own heart hammered against her ribs.

The church bells had struck midnight long ago. By now, surely everyone else must be asleep.

She reached up to touch the silver chain at her neck, but then she stopped herself. Tonight of all nights, she couldn't bear to feel Stuart's gift of love while plotting to steal from her fellow students.

It's for Lucy, she told herself.

It wasn't just scraps of food or cast-off fabric this time, but enough money to give talent a chance to bloom. To rescue someone from a life of poverty. To set right the terrible unfairness that she had witnessed in this loathsome city.

She thought of Lucy's secret notebook, filled with those beautiful designs. What a remarkable gift her poor friend had.

But Lucy remained trapped in that cold tenement room, condemned by fate, while ungrateful girls like Lydia lived in carefree luxury.

This isn't theft, Ellie repeated to herself. This was making things right. Lucy deserved a better future. All the girl needed to achieve her dream was a little help from Ellie.

But even as she formed the thought, Stuart's face seemed to float before Ellie's eyes in the darkness. Her darling Stuart, who believed so strongly in earning your way through hard work and patience.

The floorboards creaked somewhere in the vast building, making her start. How long had she been lying here, arguing with her conscience?

Drawing in a long breath, she pushed away her doubts.

Too late for second thoughts now.

Too late to listen to the part of her that still believed in rules and proper behaviour.

Rules were for people who had never seen children playing in gutters while wearing shoes full of holes. For people who had never watched someone like Lucy working her fingers raw by candlelight, squinting over endless mending just to earn a few pennies.

Somewhere in the darkness, a clock struck to mark the passing of another hour. Time to move, she decided. Ellie slipped from beneath her covers, already fully dressed.

She crept to the window, treading as lightly as she could. The moon hung low and bloated in the sky, like a distorted face watching her every move.

Now or never, she thought. Before her courage failed. Or before common sense and conscience could talk her out of it.

She moved to the bedroom door and paused, glancing back at Phoebe's sleeping form. Her friend would never forgive her for this.

But then again, there were so many things Phoebe might never forgive her for, if she knew the whole truth.

The door hinges protested softly as she eased it open, making her wince at even that small sound. But Phoebe didn't stir, and no other noises suggested anyone else was awake.

Ellie slipped into the darkened corridor, where the moonlight created strange shadows that seemed to reach for her with grasping fingers.

For Lucy, she reminded herself as she started on her slow and cautious path toward Mrs Bennett's office. *For dreams that deserve a chance to become real.*

Each step felt like an eternity as Ellie crept forward, one hand trailing along the wall for guidance.

A floorboard groaned beneath her foot, the sound echoing through the quiet house. She froze, heart thundering in her chest.

Slowly, she counted to ten, waiting for any sign that someone had heard. But only silence answered.

Another step. Another creak. The sound of her own breathing seemed frighteningly loud to her ears, while every shadow made her heart jump, her frightened mind turning ordinary shapes into lurking figures ready to raise the alarm.

At the top of the main staircase, Ellie hesitated. The steps were treacherous enough in daylight, with their polished wood and deceptive shadows. But now, in the darkness, she could barely make out where one ended and the next began. One wrong move on these stairs could wake up the entire house.

She gripped the bannister, easing her weight onto each step with excruciating slowness. Halfway down, the wood gave a sharp crack that made her blood run cold.

Again she waited, counting heartbeats, expecting at any moment to hear Mrs Bennett's door open or a maid's startled cry.

But the house remained silent.

When she finally reached Mrs Bennett's office door, her hands were trembling so badly she could barely grip the handle. The brass felt ice-cold against her palm as she turned it with infinite care.

The door swung open on well-oiled hinges, revealing deeper darkness beyond. Ellie slipped inside, letting her eyes adjust to the gloom.

Mrs Bennett's massive desk stood like a dark island in the centre of the room. Moving closer, Ellie's heart began to beat faster while she searched for any sign of where the headmistress might have hidden the valuables.

She tried a few drawers, easing them open slowly to avoid making any noise. But they revealed nothing useful: only papers, letters and a half-empty box of chocolates.

Then she spotted it: a heavy cabinet against the far wall. Perfect for keeping precious things secure.

A brass key glinted on Mrs Bennett's desk, placed there with such careful precision it almost seemed like an invitation.

Too easy, a voice whispered in Ellie's mind. But she ignored the thought, and took the key with unsteady fingers.

Holding her breath, she went over to the cabinet and slid the key into the lock. One turn, a faint click, and the cabinet door opened.

In the dim light, she could just make out the shapes of jewellery boxes and velvet pouches. Enough treasures to change Lucy's life forever.

Ellie reached out her hand–

"I must say, Miss Dubois," Mrs Bennett's voice cut through the darkness like a knife. "I had rather hoped I was wrong about you."

A lamp flared to life, flooding the room with sudden brightness that made Ellie stagger back. Mrs Bennett rose from the shadow of a high-backed chair, cold disappointment written all over her face.

"Though I suppose," the headmistress said, "one can never be too careful about these things."

With a sickening heaviness in her stomach, Ellie realised that she had walked straight into a trap.

"I did wonder who our mysterious thief might be," Mrs Bennett continued, setting the lamp on her desk. "But you, Miss Dubois, were not my first suspect."

The headmistress came closer, her shadow stretching tall against the wall. "After that theft at the soirée, I decided to lay a trap," she said coldly. "Announce that students could store their valuables here, then wait to see who would take the bait."

The reality of how completely she had been deceived crashed over Ellie like a wave of icy water. Mrs Bennett had used everyone's genuine fear and panic to set up this trap.

But as the shock faded, something else rose to take its place: a hot, defiant anger that burned away her fear.

"You arranged all this just to catch me?" Ellie's voice shook, but not with shame. "While children are starving in the streets outside these walls? While people with real skills and talents waste away in poverty, simply because they weren't fortunate enough to be born into the right family?"

"Miss Dubois—"

"No." Ellie gripped Stuart's locket, drawing more strength from it. "There are mothers out there who can't feed their children as well as you feed your cat, Mrs Bennett. I've seen talented people working their fingers raw for pennies, while we throw away more food at breakfast than they get to eat in a week."

Mrs Bennett's lips tightened. "Ah yes. Your interest in London's poor. Is that who you've been spending your time with, instead of attending your piano lessons with Mrs Novak?"

Reading the stunned surprise on Ellie's face, the headmistress fixed her with cold, glaring eyes. "You see, Miss Dubois, after that rather peculiar exchange with Mrs Novak during our soirée, I decided to pay her a visit."

Mrs Bennett's voice held the quiet satisfaction of someone who has finally confirmed a long-held suspicion. "Imagine my surprise to learn you haven't attended a single lesson in weeks. Though apparently Miss Greenwood has been most diligent in taking your place."

The mention of Phoebe made Ellie's stomach clench. She wouldn't let her friend be punished for her deceptions.

"Phoebe had nothing to do with it," she said quickly. "I convinced her to help me. She didn't know what I was really doing."

"And what exactly were you doing, Miss Dubois? Besides lying to your teachers and abandoning your studies?"

Ellie lifted her chin. "I was volunteering at St Mary's Mission, trying to help people who actually needed it."

"So much deception." Mrs Bennett shook her head. "And I suppose you imagine this makes you some sort of hero?"

"At least I was doing something useful." Ellie's voice rose with passion. "There's a girl I met there, Lucy. She has such a gift for dressmaking. If she just had the money to open her own shop, to escape that horrible tenement–"

"Enough." Mrs Bennett's voice cracked like a whip. "Do you imagine you're the first young lady to be moved by the plight of the poor? When we visited that rookery, it was to show you how the lower classes live. So you would appreciate your own good fortune. Not to encourage you to become one of them."

"One of them? Ha!" Ellie's laugh held no humour. "You mean honest, hardworking people who will never have the chances we take for granted?"

"I mean thieves, Miss Dubois." Mrs Bennett's eyes were cold. "Whatever noble intentions you claim, you have proven yourself to be nothing more than a common criminal. One who has betrayed not only my trust but that of your fellow students."

She moved behind her desk, straightening papers with precise movements. "I will, of course, be writing to your parents immediately. They will be asked to collect you as soon as possible. Until then, you will remain confined to your room, and you are not to have any contact with the other girls."

"Don't trouble yourself." Ellie met Mrs Bennett's gaze without flinching. "I'll leave. Now, in fact. I'd rather sleep in the streets than spend another moment in this temple to privilege and prejudice."

Mrs Bennett's face hardened. "As you wish. Though I rather doubt you will find the streets as romantic as your imagination has painted them."

The headmistress paused, something almost like pity crossing her features. "I fear you will learn that lesson soon enough."

"Better that than to hide behind these walls," Ellie shot back. "Pretending the world outside doesn't exist."

She turned toward the door, her voice steady despite the trembling of her hands. "At least I tried to help someone. What have you ever done except teach girls how to ignore other people's suffering?"

She didn't wait for Mrs Bennett's response. Head held high, she strode from the office, leaving the headmistress at her desk in the cold lamplight.

Ellie's determined footsteps echoed through the dark hallways as she climbed the stairs, abandoning her earlier caution.

Let them wake up now.

Let them all see her leave. She no longer cared.

When she reached the bedroom she shared with Phoebe, her friend was already awake, sitting up in bed with wide, frightened eyes.

"Ellie?" Phoebe's voice trembled. "I heard noises. Where have you–" She broke off, taking in Ellie's fully-dressed state. "What's happening?"

"I'm leaving." Ellie yanked her travel bag from beneath the bed, the scraping sound harsh against the floorboards. "Mrs Bennett made sure I was caught trying to steal from her office.

Though I suppose you'll hear all about it at breakfast tomorrow."

She wrenched open the wardrobe, pulling out dresses and throwing them haphazardly into her bag. A glove fell to the floor, and she left it there.

"Stealing?" Phoebe slipped from her bed, wrapping her shawl tightly around her shoulders. "But why would you–"

"For Lucy." Ellie's fingers caught on a hook, tearing her sleeve. "To help her escape that awful place. To give her a chance at the life she deserves."

Her hands shook as she gathered her books, her letters from Stuart, the little treasures that had made this room feel a bit more homely. Behind her, she could hear Phoebe's quiet sniffling.

"Please don't cry," Ellie said, even though her own voice cracked. "I can't bear it if you cry."

"How can I not?" Phoebe moved closer, touching Ellie's arm with gentle fingers. "You're my best friend. And now you're leaving like this, in the middle of the night, in disgrace."

Ellie stopped.

Disgrace.

Hearing Phoebe say it like that suddenly made everything terribly real. She sank onto her bed, a dress still clutched in her hands.

"I'm sorry," she whispered. "I know I've disappointed you. Just like I've disappointed everyone else."

"No." Phoebe sat beside her, taking the crumpled dress and smoothing it with trembling hands. "I'm not disappointed. I'm frightened for you." She let out a sad sigh and then asked, "You'll go home then?"

"Back to Sheffield? What would Mother and Pierre say? What would Stuart think?" Ellie shook her head. "No, I simply can't."

"But where will you go? What will you do?"

"I'll find somewhere. The streets can't be worse than staying here, pretending to be something I'm not."

Phoebe gave her a searching look. "You're serious about this, aren't you?"

"Yes, I am."

"Thought so," her friend sighed. "Then let me help you, at least this once more." She stood, brushing away tears with quick fingers.

Together they folded Ellie's clothes and tucked away her small possessions. Neither of them spoke as they worked, the silence broken only by Phoebe's occasional sniff.

When Ellie closed her travel bag, they stood facing each other in the moonlight. Phoebe's tears fell freely now, and Ellie felt her own eyes burning.

"I'll write to you," she promised. "Once I'm settled somewhere."

"You'd better." Phoebe pulled her into a fierce embrace. "And promise me you'll be careful. London can be so dangerous."

Ellie hugged her back, remembering all the times Phoebe had covered for her, had worried about her, and had tried to keep her safe. "I'm sorry," she whispered again. "For everything."

"Never mind that now." Phoebe's voice sounded muffled against her shoulder. "You're still my dearest friend."

They held each other for a moment longer, neither wanting to be the first to let go. But finally, Ellie stepped back, picking up her travel bag.

"Goodbye, Phoebe."

She turned quickly, not wanting to see fresh tears in her friend's eyes. But Phoebe's quiet sob followed her into the hallway, a sound she knew would haunt her for a long time to come.

Ellie paused at the academy's front door, her bag feeling heavier than before. Beyond the solid oak panels of the door, she could hear the first stirrings of dawn: a distant birdcall, the rattle of an early milk cart.

This is it, she thought.

No more safe walls, no more easy routine of lessons and meals. No more steadfast friendship from Phoebe.

Drawing a deep breath, Ellie straightened her back and opened the door. A rush of cold morning air met her as she stepped outside. Grey fog swirled around her skirts as she descended the few steps to the street, each one taking her further away from the warm comfort of the academy.

Where will you go? Phoebe's voice echoed in Ellie's mind.

She had no plan, no destination. Nothing but her own stubborn pride.

The vastness of London stretched before her, suddenly more threatening than exciting. But she gripped her bag tighter and forced herself forward into the swirling mist. Whatever waited ahead, she had chosen this path.

And now she would walk it.

Chapter Twenty-Five

Spitalfields was already awake when Ellie arrived. Market traders were calling out to people, trying to attract business, while factory workers hurried past with their collars turned up against the morning chill.

The fog that still clung to the ground muffled her footsteps as she made her way through the maze of streets, her legs feeling heavy with exhaustion.

The walk from Bloomsbury had taken far longer than she had expected, and her arms and shoulders were aching from the weight of her travel bag. She hadn't dared to spend precious money on a hansom cab. Not when she had no idea how long her remaining funds would need to last.

But despite her painful feet and the gnawing emptiness in her stomach, each step seemed to bring fresh ideas. During her long walk through London's gradually brightening streets, the skeleton of a plan had formed.

We could start small, she thought as she navigated around a cart stacked with baskets full of turnips and potatoes. *Take in mending at first, save every penny...*

The plan grew clearer as she continued her journey, filling her with a fierce energy that helped her to ignore her dishevelled appearance and the curious glances from passers-by. Her hat had slipped askew, and she knew that her hair must be escaping its pins.

But appearances hardly mattered any more. Those concerns belonged to another lifetime now.

When she finally reached the familiar tenement building, Ellie paused to catch her breath. Setting down her bag for a short moment, she rubbed the red marks on her palms.

The old stairs that she had climbed several times before suddenly looked like a mountain to be conquered. But the thought of Lucy's secret notebook, filled with those beautiful designs, gave her the strength to begin the ascent.

Her legs burned with each step, the tired muscles protesting after her nighttime adventure and the long walk.

At last, she reached Lucy and Jack's door. Softly, Ellie knocked before pushing it open.

Three heads turned toward her. Lucy was sewing at her place by the window, while Jack sat at the table, with his chair tipped back and his legs stretched out in front of him. Percy stood near the cold fireplace, his face set in its usual scowl.

Their expressions shifted from surprise to shock as they took in her appearance: the heavy travel bag, the wrinkled dress, the loose strands of hair falling around her face.

"Good grief," Jack said, straightening in his chair. "What happened to you?"

Lucy set aside her sewing and rose quickly. "Ellie? Are you all right?"

"I've left the academy," Ellie announced, letting her bag drop to the floor with a solid thud. "Or rather, they were about to expel me, so I saved them the trouble."

"Expel you?" Percy's eyes narrowed. "Whatever for?"

Ellie explained about Mrs Bennett's trap, and how she got caught red-handed.

"So I decided to leave," she concluded her story. "Rather than face the shame of being sent home in disgrace."

As she spoke, she watched the colour drain from Lucy's cheeks as understanding dawned.

"Those things you tried to steal," her friend asked. "That was for me, wasn't it? For the shop I told you I was dreaming about?"

Ellie nodded. "You deserve a chance, Lucy. A real chance to make those beautiful drawings come true."

Lucy sank back into her chair. "Oh, Ellie. What have I done? My silly dreams aren't worth ruining your life over."

"Your dreams aren't silly," Ellie insisted. "And my life isn't ruined. It's just... taking a different path than expected."

"That's the spirit," Jack said. "But where exactly were you planning to stay?"

"I thought I'd look for a room somewhere nearby," Ellie replied. "Something small and simple, of course."

"Small and simple, eh?" Jack snorted. "How much money have you got?"

Ellie reached into her reticule and pulled out her coins. She had counted them carefully during one of her rest stops on her gruelling walk.

"This is all I have," she said, showing the coins in her outstretched hands. "Surely, that ought to be enough for a few months' lodgings?"

Jack and Lucy exchanged a look that made Ellie's confidence waver.

"Months? That money might get you a few weeks in a decent boarding house," Jack said. "If you're lucky, that is. London ain't cheap, Ellie. Most working folk have to share rooms just to afford the rent. Even the maids at your fancy academy probably sleep three to a chamber."

"Oh." The word came out small and uncertain.

Percy pushed away from the fireplace and came limping over in her direction. "This is madness," he said. "You need to go home, girl.

Back to Sheffield. Back to your mother and that comfortable life you were born to."

Something hot and fierce rose in Ellie's chest. "I will not."

"Be sensible," Percy pressed. "What do you know about surviving in a place like this? About going hungry, or working until your fingers bleed?"

"I'll endure." Ellie lifted her chin. "I'm not afraid of hard work."

"This isn't about being afraid." Percy's voice held an edge of frustration. "This is about understanding what you're giving up. That academy might have been full of stupid rules and spoiled girls, but at least it was safe. Protected."

"Protected?" Ellie let out a short, hollow laugh. "Protected from what? From seeing how other people live? From understanding what it means to struggle?" She gestured at the room around them. "I'd rather face this reality than hide behind walls of privilege."

"He's right though, Ellie," Lucy said. "This isn't the sort of life you're used to."

"Then I'll get used to it."

Jack rubbed his chin thoughtfully, then slapped his palms against his knees and stood up. "In that case, it seems to me that the simplest solution is for you to stay here with us."

"Jack," Lucy protested. "We can't–"

"Why not? We've got the space for an extra person. And it's better than letting her spend all her money on some flea-ridden boarding house."

"But–" Lucy glanced around their cramped quarters and at her own small sleeping area sectioned off by a faded sheet hanging from a string. "This isn't... I mean, she shouldn't have to–"

"I don't mind," Ellie said quickly. "I would rather stay here with friends than anywhere else."

Lucy frowned and bit her lip. "That's because you don't understand what you're agreeing to. The cold, the rats, the noise at all hours."

"Then I'll learn to endure them," Ellie replied firmly. "Just as you have done."

Neither of the siblings spoke. Lucy turned back to her sewing, her fingers working faster than before. Then Jack nodded with something like approval in his expression.

"That's settled then," he declared. "Welcome to your new home, Miss Ellie Dubois."

But Lucy shook her head. "I never should have shown you that notebook," she muttered. "My foolish drawings. If I'd known they would lead to this..."

"Don't you dare call them foolish." Ellie moved to kneel beside Lucy's chair. "Those designs are wonderful. They deserve to be more than just sketches in a hidden notebook."

She caught Lucy's hands in hers, squeezing them earnestly. "That's why I'm going to help you raise the money for your shop."

The room fell silent. Jack and Percy exchanged a long look that Ellie took for skepticism.

Let them doubt me.

She would prove them wrong.

"Ellie," Jack began carefully. "You don't understand how things work here. Getting that kind of money together... It's not like in your world. People in the rookery can work their whole lives and barely scrape enough together for bread and coal."

"My father always said the hardest part of any successful business is getting started." She smiled and her eyes brightened. "But the end result is worth all the effort and hard work you put into it."

"Your father?" Percy interrupted. "Would that be the Frenchman? What was his name again? Pierre, wasn't it?"

"Pierre is my stepfather," Ellie replied. "My real father founded a steam engine factory in Sheffield."

"A proper businessman," Percy nodded approvingly. "But then he died?"

"Yes, only a few years ago, as a matter of fact." Her eyes began to glaze over. Sometimes it felt far longer than that. So much had happened in the meantime.

"Tragic," Percy said sympathetically. "Can't have been easy for your mother and you."

"It wasn't," Ellie admitted. "Father left his share of the factory to Mother, but she struggled at first. Lots of people didn't think a woman could understand the business."

"People can be quite small-minded," Percy said.

"Mother proved them wrong though. Well, she and Pierre together. He came along at just the right moment, and helped her to keep the business going."

"How fortunate," Percy replied with a smile. "And how very kind of him."

"Yes, Pierre was a blessing." Ellie turned back to Lucy. "That's what I mean about getting started. Sometimes you just need someone to believe in you, to help you take that first step."

"It's not that simple," Jack protested. "The kind of money it would take to rent a shop, to buy materials–"

"Money isn't everything," Ellie insisted, the fierce energy that had carried her through London's streets surging again. "Lucy's got more talent than half the dressmakers in Mayfair. We just need to show people what she can do."

"And how do you suggest we do that?" Jack asked.

"I don't know. But we'll find a way."

Ellie looked at the three of them with a hopeful, confident smile. When her gaze drifted to Percy, his hard features softened unexpectedly. He gave her an encouraging nod, the corner of his mouth lifting in what might have been approval.

"Well," Lucy said finally, rising from her chair. "If you're really staying, then I suppose we should make you as comfortable as we can." She moved to help Ellie with her travel bag. "Though I'm afraid comfort means something different here."

Ellie began unpacking her meagre possessions: a few dresses, some books, letters from Stuart tied with a ribbon. Each item seemed to belong to a different world. A life of propriety and certainty that she had left behind.

Lucy worked quietly beside her, spreading a patched blanket in the corner behind the faded sheet that the girls would be sharing as their sleeping space. Her movements were methodical, but the tight line of her mouth and the furrow between her brows betrayed her troubled thoughts.

"Stop blaming yourself," Ellie said softly. "This was my choice."

"A choice you never would have made if it hadn't been for me." Lucy smoothed down the blanket. "If I hadn't shown you that notebook, if I hadn't talked about my dreams—"

"Then I'd still be trapped in that awful academy, blind to half of London's reality. I don't want to be one of those people who ignores what's happening right outside their door, Lucy. Helping you make your dream come true is worth a few difficult nights on a hard floor to me."

The sounds of the rookery drifted through the thin walls: a baby crying somewhere above them, heavy boots on the stairs, the distant shouts of traders in the street below. All the noises of a world Ellie had only glimpsed before, but would now call home.

"You really mean to go through with this, don't you?" Jack asked.

"Yes." Ellie passed a hand over her skirts, ignoring how creased and dirty they had already become. "I know you all think I'm being naive. That I don't understand what I'm getting into."

"Because you don't," Lucy murmured.

"Then I'll learn." Squaring her shoulders, Ellie met their doubtful gazes. "Whatever it takes."

Percy studied her with those sharp, penetrating eyes of his, while Jack shook his head with a mixture of admiration and concern.

"There," Lucy said, surveying the result of her preparations in their private little corner of the room. "It isn't much though, I'm afraid."

"It's perfect," Ellie smiled.

"The nights get cold," Lucy continued gloomily. "And the rain comes in when the wind blows from the east."

"We'll manage," Ellie replied while her mind tried to block out the sight of the hard floor, the crumbling plaster and the stained ceiling.

Carefully, she slid the bundle of Stuart's letters beneath the makeshift pillow that Lucy had improvised for her. Would she ever be brave enough to tell her fiancé the truth of what she had done? Or where she now lived?

But those were questions for another day, she decided.

Today was for new beginnings.

Chapter Twenty-Six

"I'm going to sell my dresses," Ellie announced boldly the following day. "Every single one of them. Except for these two: they're the plainest I have."

The fine dresses she had laid out on the floor looked oddly out of place in Jack and Lucy's room, almost absurd even. Like exotic birds that had lost their way.

"Ellie," Lucy gasped in alarm. "You can't–"

"Of course I can. What use are fancy dresses here in Spitalfields? If I sell them, they'll serve a better purpose. The money can go straight into our new shop fund."

"Shop fund?" Jack asked.

"For Lucy's dressmaking shop." Ellie's eyes sparkled with enthusiasm as she gestured at the dresses. "These should fetch enough to make a good start. That blue silk alone cost–"

"You're not thinking clearly," Lucy interrupted. "Please don't get rid of your dresses just for my sake. You'll need them again someday. When you go home."

"I'm not going home, remember? Besides, this is my home now. And these dresses are going to help us make your dreams come true."

She bent down and lifted a dove-grey gown with a delicate lace trim. "I won't sell this one though. This one is for you."

"What?" Lucy took a step backward. "No, I couldn't possibly–"

"You'll need something nice to wear when we open your shop." Ellie held the dress against Lucy's thin frame. "Just feel the quality of the fabric. Someone with your talent should be wearing beautiful things."

Lucy's fingers moved automatically to touch the dress, her seamstress's hands recognising the fine material. For a moment, her professional appreciation overcame her hesitation.

"The stitching on this lace is exquisite," she said, before catching herself. "But Ellie, I can't accept–"

"Yes, you can." Ellie pressed the dress into Lucy's arms. "You'll wear it at the grand opening. I can picture it now. 'Lucy Mortimer's Dressmaking Establishment' in gold letters on the window. You'll stand in the doorway wearing this, and everyone who passes will see what a lady you are."

Lucy's arms tightened around the grey silk, but her face showed more worry than joy. "Ellie, a shop isn't just something you can–"

"We'll have to start small, obviously," Ellie continued, sorting her remaining dresses into piles. "But once people see what you can do, once they understand your talent…"

She trailed off, noticing the strained expressions on Jack and Lucy's faces. The siblings clearly didn't share her confidence in her plan.

But Ellie chose to ignore their doubts. Instead, she smoothed the skirt of a rose-coloured day dress, imagining how many pounds it might bring.

In her mind, each dress was already transforming into window glass and wooden shelves, into spools of thread and bolts of fabric.

Into Lucy's dreams made real.

The sound of Jack clearing his throat brought her back to the present.

"Since there's clearly no talking you out of this mad scheme of yours," he said, "at least let me show you where to go. There's a respectable wardrobe dealer on Commercial Street: Mrs Cooper. She's the third shop past the tobacconist."

"What about those other clothing shops I've seen during our walks? The busy ones with all the people outside? Would they be interested in buying my dresses, you think?"

"The rag shops?" Jack shook his head. "Those vultures would swindle you blind. They prey on desperate folk who don't know any better. Please don't go anywhere near them."

"I won't," Ellie promised. "So it's Mrs Cooper, you said? Past the tobacconist."

"She's stern, but fair." Jack gestured at Ellie's pile of dresses. "Mind you, even she won't give you anything close to what you think these are worth. But at least she won't outright cheat you."

"I'm sure I'll manage to negotiate a fair price. How hard can it be? Anyone can plainly see the quality of these dresses."

"It doesn't work that way, Ellie," Jack replied warily. "Some of these people are sharks. They'll offer you mere pennies for what cost you pounds."

"Pennies? That's preposterous. The lace on the fringes alone should be worth more."

Jack sighed and shook his head. "Look, why don't I come with you? I know how these people think, how they–"

"Thank you, Jack. But no. I need to learn to handle these things myself. If I'm going to live here, I can't always rely on you to protect me."

Lucy looked up from the grey silk dress she was still clutching. "At least let him walk you there."

"I know my way around these parts now." Ellie began gathering the dresses into a manageable bundle. "And I'm not some helpless child who needs an escort everywhere."

Jack threw his hands up in surrender, and then let them fall heavily to his sides.

"Just remember," he said. "Mrs Cooper. Third shop past the tobacconist. Don't bother with any of the others: they'll only try to trick you."

"I'll be perfectly fine." Ellie straightened, holding her bundle of dresses in her arms. The weight of them made her stagger slightly. "You'll see. I'll be back before you know it. And then we can start planning Lucy's shop properly."

Neither Jack nor Lucy replied as she headed for the door, her mind filled with visions of the coins these dresses would bring, and how they would transform Lucy's life.

Less than half an hour later however, her optimism had vanished entirely.

"Three shillings?" Ellie stared at Mrs Cooper in disbelief. "But this is silk. From Paris. The dress cost nearly fifteen pounds when it was new."

Mrs Cooper barely glanced up from examining the rose-coloured dress. "That were then, miss. This is now. And now it's second-hand goods, ain't it?"

"But surely..." Ellie's voice faltered as the woman began folding the dress.

"Look here." Mrs Cooper's tone softened slightly. "Silk don't keep well. Gets water-stained easy. And this one's already starting to wear thin at the seams." Her work-roughened fingers found a spot near the hem. "See? Beginning to fray."

Ellie gathered her remaining dresses closer, suddenly protective. "Thank you, but I believe I'll try elsewhere."

Unfortunately, 'elsewhere' proved even worse. The next dealer offered only half of what Mrs Cooper had, barely looking at the dresses before naming his price.

The third shopkeeper actually laughed when Ellie mentioned the original cost of her blue silk afternoon dress.

"Might as well tell me it's made of fairy wings, Miss," he said, wiping tears of mirth from his eyes. "Won't make it worth more than two shillings to me."

The fourth shop smelled of mildew, and the woman behind the counter handled Ellie's precious dresses with tobacco-stained fingers.

"Nine," she said in a bored tone.

"Pounds?" Ellie asked hopefully.

"Shillings," the woman replied, dropping Ellie's delicate muslin day dress onto the dirty counter. "For the lot."

"The lot?" Ellie's voice rose. "But there are half a dozen dresses here."

"And every one of 'em at least two years out of fashion." The woman shrugged. "Take it or leave it, dearie. Makes no difference to me."

Ellie gathered her dresses and fled, her earlier confidence thoroughly shaken. Despite the humiliating disappointment, she tried not to cry as she made her way back to Mrs Cooper's shop.

The older woman didn't look surprised to see her again. "Changed your mind, have you?"

Ellie nodded, not trusting herself to speak.

"Tell you what." Mrs Cooper studied Ellie's face for a moment. "Four shillings for the silk one, and two each for them others. That's the best I can do."

It was still far less than Ellie had hoped. But at least Mrs Cooper handled the dresses with something approaching respect after she had counted out the coins.

Walking back through Spitalfields' crowded streets, Ellie began to despair. At this rate, they would never have enough money to rent even the smallest of shop premises. Or to buy basic sewing supplies.

She thought of Lucy's promising designs, and of all the expensive materials they would need. And then of course there was also coal, lighting, and heaven knew what else they would have to pay for. Simple things she had taken for granted in her old life that seemed as distant as the moon now.

Suddenly, those few coins in her reticule felt frightfully light, hardly enough to notice they were there at all. Such a small return for such fine things.

A passing cart splashed brown, foul-smelling water across her skirts. Ellie jumped back with a startled cry, but the damage was already done. The carter didn't even glance her way: one more insult to add to the day's disappointments.

She stared down at her ruined hem, where the filthy water had left a stain that would likely never come out. Another reminder of how quickly things could be ruined in this harsh place.

"Spare a penny, Miss?"

The children seemed to materialise out of nowhere. One moment Ellie was alone with her thoughts, the next she found herself surrounded by a pack of ragged figures barely taller than her waist.

A boy with a cap two sizes too big for his head stepped forward, his hand outstretched. "We're really hungry, Miss," he begged.

"I haven't got much to spare, I'm afraid. But if it's food you want, why don't you go to St Mary's? They hand out decent meals for free every day."

A smaller boy darted past her right side, quick and nimble as a fox. Before she could turn, another one slipped behind her.

"What are you doing?" She turned her head, trying to keep her eyes on all of them at once.

A sharp tug at her reticule startled her. She clutched at it instinctively, but small hands were already pulling it away with practiced speed.

"Stop that. Please." Her voice cracked with fear as she desperately tried not to let go. "You don't have to–"

Something hit the back of her knees: another child diving low while she was distracted. Ellie staggered, her grip on the reticule failing.

"No! My money."

Thrown off balance, she toppled backwards and hit the ground hard. Her reticule was torn from her grasp in the same instant.

By the time she pushed herself upright again, the children had already disappeared into the warren of alleyways, taking her precious coins with them.

The entire attack had probably lasted less than a minute.

Ellie stared at her dirty, empty hands, and then at the mouth of the alley where the children had run into. Her skirts were ruined, and her hands stung.

But it was the shock that kept her frozen in place.

The boy with the big cap couldn't have been more than eight. The one who had struck her knees, even younger. In her mind, their faces began to blur with those of the many children she had seen playing in the gutters.

They weren't hardened criminals, she told herself. Just a bunch of street urchins with empty stomachs. Those precious few coins they took from her wouldn't last them very long.

And then they would need to steal again.

Because manners, education and fine words meant nothing here. Useless luxuries none of these people could afford. All that mattered in the rookery was getting through another day, by whatever means necessary.

A woman hurried past, averting her eyes from Ellie's muddied form. No one stopped to help. No one even seemed surprised. Spitalfields continued its daily business, indifferent to her small tragedy.

"What a fool I've been," she muttered as she tried to brush the worst of the mud from her dress.

What would she tell Lucy and Jack? That her grand plan to help them had ended with her being robbed by children half her size? The humiliation burned worse than the scrapes on her hands and knees.

Jack had tried to warn her. He had even offered to come with her. But Ellie had stubbornly insisted on her independence.

And this was the result.

With nothing left to show for her efforts but dirty clothes and a bruised dignity, Ellie turned toward the tenement, dreading the moment when she would have to admit to her friends how miserably she had failed.

Chapter Twenty-Seven

Each step up the tenement stairs felt like lifting a block of iron. Ellie paused on the landing, flexing her aching fingers. The tiny puncture wounds from her clumsy attempts at piecework had stopped bleeding, but they still stung.

Two weeks of pricked fingertips had taught her that a childhood of embroidery lessons hadn't prepared her for the brutal speed required by the rag trade.

The muscles in her legs protested as she forced herself up the final flight. She had walked for miles today, going from one dressmaker's shop to another. Each time she had been turned away before she could even show them Lucy's work.

Arriving at the closed door to their shared room, Ellie turned the doorknob and stepped inside. Jack was lounging by the table, his legs stretched out in front of him while he playfully tossed an apple core from hand to hand.

Over by the grimy window with its broken panes, Lucy sat hunched over her sewing as usual. Her needle darted swiftly through endless rows of precise stitches on a half-finished shirt.

Percy was nowhere to be seen.

The contrast between brother and sister struck Ellie with fresh force. Lucy's narrow shoulders were bent with exhaustion, while Jack relaxed with the careless ease of a wealthy gentleman at his club.

"You're back." Jack caught the apple core one final time before throwing it away. "I was starting to wonder if maybe you'd got lost out there. Any luck today?"

Ellie sank onto the room's other chair, too tired to straighten her wrinkled skirts. "They wouldn't even look at our work," she said, her voice flat with defeat. "Said they don't hire girls from the rookery."

"What else did you expect?" Jack stretched leisurely. "I told you them fancy shops won't touch anyone from Spitalfields, didn't I?"

A grin spread across his face as he propped his boots on the table's edge. "Better off sticking to the rag trade like our Lucy here. At least then you know you're meant to be miserable."

Lucy's needle never paused in its endless journey through the fabric, but Ellie saw the girl's shoulders tense at her brother's words.

Two weeks of watching Lucy work from dawn until late at night, when her eyes could no longer see the stitches. Two weeks of pricked fingers and aching backs and endless rejections. And now Jack sat there making jokes about it all.

It was too much for her.

"How dare you jest about this?" Ellie pushed herself up from her chair, pent-up frustration finally boiling over. "While Lucy works herself half-blind, you sit there horsing around. Like a fool without a care in the world."

She clenched her hands into angry fists.

"You have a gift, Jack Mortimer. I heard how those people listened when you sang at The Dog and Duck. Even the roughest men there fell silent."

Jack's lazy grin faded. "That was different."

"Why? Because you weren't being paid?" Ellie's voice grew sharp with scorn. "I could play the piano while you sing. We could go round the better public houses, pass a hat afterward–"

"No." Lucy's needle stopped for the first time. "The pubs aren't what you think, Ellie. You've only seen them early in the evening, before the real drinking starts." She rested her sewing in her lap. "Things can turn ugly fast once the beer and the gin start flowing."

"But surely if the music is good enough–"

"Music doesn't matter." Lucy's voice held the weary knowledge of someone who had seen too much. "One wrong word, one spilled drink, and suddenly there's blood on the floor."

Jack shifted in his chair, no longer looking quite so relaxed. "Lucy's right. Those two times you came with us, they were different. Special occasions, like."

"So you'd rather just sit here, watching your sister work herself to death?" Ellie demanded. "At least I'm trying to find a way out of this place. What are you doing besides making jokes about other people's misery?"

A muscle tightened in Jack's jaw. His casual humour had vanished now. "You don't understand," he began.

"No, it's you who doesn't understand." Ellie's voice shook with emotion. "Lucy has real talent. She could make something of herself, if only–" Frustrated, she gestured at the piles of mending. "But instead she's trapped here, doing endless piecework, while you waste your gift because you're too lazy to even try."

Jack shot to his feet, his eyes flashing thunder. But before he could speak, Lucy's quiet voice cut between them.

"Ellie, please. Jack does help, in his own way. He–"

"Fine." Jack's word silenced his sister. "You want me to sing in pubs? To risk getting my head bashed in by some drunken lout who doesn't like my voice?"

He snatched his coat from its peg by the door. "Then let's go find ourselves a public house. Right now."

"Jack–" Lucy rose from her chair.

"No, our fine lady here wants to see how the real world works." He yanked the door open.

"Coming then, Miss Dubois? Or was that just pretty words and fancy ideas?"

Ellie lifted her chin. "I'll fetch my shawl."

"This is madness," Lucy said. "You don't know what you're walking into."

But Ellie was already wrapping her shawl around her shoulders, while Jack waited with brooding stillness by the open door.

Neither of them seemed to hear Lucy's quiet words of warning, too caught up in their own storm of pride and anger to heed the voice of reason.

The Dog and Duck was already half-full when they arrived, the air thick with tobacco smoke and the sharp smell of cheap gin.

The old piano stood exactly as Ellie remembered it. Her fingers trembled slightly as she took her place at the keys, remembering how easily the music had flowed that first time.

But tonight was different. Tonight they weren't just playing for pleasure.

Jack stood beside her, his earlier anger seemingly forgotten as he gazed out at the crowd. "What shall we start with then?"

"Something they'll know," Ellie said softly. "Something to touch their hearts."

He nodded, drew in a breath, and began to sing.

The pure, clear notes of 'Come Into the Garden, Maud' floated above the pub's din. A few heads turned. Ellie's fingers found the harmony, weaving a gentle accompaniment beneath Jack's voice.

By the second verse, the usual cacophony of shouted conversations had begun to fade. Mugs were set down quietly instead of being slammed against tables. Even the barman paused in his work, cloth hanging forgotten in his hand.

A burly worker with coal-stained hands joined in the chorus, his rough voice harmonising naturally with Jack's smoother tones. Others followed, until the old song filled every corner of the pub like a warm embrace.

When the final note faded, there was a moment of perfect silence before the applause began. Jack's eyes met Ellie's, bright with surprised pleasure.

"Another," someone called from the back. "Give us 'The Dicky Bird and the Owl'."

Ellie's heart soared as her fingers moved to the opening notes. This was what she had imagined: music transforming this rough place, lifting them all above their daily struggles. Even the air seemed cleaner somehow, the faces around them softened by something more powerful than alcohol.

We can do this, she thought as Jack's voice rose again, strong and true. *We could actually make this work.*

Already she was calculating what they might earn if they performed every evening. Enough to help Lucy with her shop?

Perhaps not quickly, but it was a start. A real chance at something better.

The crowd was joining in again, feet tapping, voices raised in harmony. For this one shining moment, the dingy pub walls seemed to fade away, leaving only the music and the happy spell it cast over all of them.

But Ellie should have known it was too perfect to last.

The first crash barely registered over the music. Then came the shout. "Watch where you're going, you drunken fool."

Ellie's fingers faltered on the keys as she saw someone stumbling by the bar, spilling beer down another man's coat. The second man's face twisted with rage.

"This is my best–"

The shove sent the drunken man flying backwards into a table where three dock workers sat nursing their mugs. Their drinks toppled, shattering against the floorboards.

Everything happened at once after that.

The dock workers surged to their feet. A chair flew across the room. Someone threw a punch, missing their target and striking a complete stranger instead. That man's friends jumped into the fray, and suddenly the pub erupted into chaos.

Ellie's hands froze above the piano keys. The beautiful harmony they had created dissolved into a symphony of breaking glass and angry shouts.

A table overturned with a splintering crack. Men who had been singing together moments ago now grappled like animals, faces twisted with savage fury.

"You're dead, Jones," someone roared. "Dead!"

A bottle arced through the air, missing its target and smashing the huge mirror behind the bar. Glass rained down in a deadly shower, sending the barman diving for cover.

"Ellie," Jack's shouted through the madness. "Move!"

His hand seized her arm, yanking her away from the piano just as a heavy chair crashed onto the keys. The painful sound of breaking piano strings mixed with the general chaos.

Jack pulled her toward a door behind the bar, shoving her through ahead of him. They found themselves in the pub's kitchen, nearly colliding with a terrified pot boy who was crouched behind a barrel.

"This way!" Jack grabbed her hand again.

They ran past shelves of unwashed glasses, ducking under rows of hanging pots. Behind them, the sounds of combat grew louder. The fight was spreading.

Something large hit the kitchen door just as they reached the back entrance. Jack wrenched open the heavy back door and they burst out into the alley. The cold air stung her nose and stabbed at her lungs.

The sounds of breaking furniture and angry shouts followed them into the darkness, but Jack didn't stop. He pulled her further down the alley, away from the pub's warm lights and the violence that had shattered their brief moment of harmony.

They didn't stop running until they reached the end of the alley. Ellie leaned against the brick wall, her chest heaving as she tried to catch her breath. The sounds of chaos from the pub seemed more distant now, but no less savage.

Pressing a hand against her racing heart, she felt Stuart's locket underneath her dress. But tonight even that beloved token offered little solace as the truth of what she had witnessed sank in.

Lucy had tried to warn her. The violence hadn't come out of the blue. It had been there all along, lurking beneath the surface like a serpent waiting to strike.

Their music had merely papered over it for a few precious moments, creating an illusion of civilised peacefulness as fragile as a soap bubble.

"Now you understand?" Jack's voice was rough with emotion. When she turned to look at him, his face was half-hidden in shadow, but she could see he was trembling. Not with fear, but with anger.

"Jack, I–"

"No." He cut her off. "You wanted to see how things really work here? Well, now you know." He gestured back toward the pub. "It's just like Lucy told you. One wrong look, one careless shove: that's all it takes. Been that way since before either of us was born, and it'll be that way long after we're dead."

Ellie swallowed hard. "But your voice. And the way they listened–"

"For five minutes, aye. Five minutes of pretty songs, and you thought you could change everything? Thought you could lift us all out of the gutter with a bit of music?"

The bitterness in his voice made her flinch. "I only wanted to help," she protested meekly.

"Help?" Jack stepped closer. "Then stop trying to make this place into something it's not. Stop filling Lucy's head with dreams about fancy shops and better lives. You can't fix this with songs and pretty music, Ellie. The sooner you understand that, the better off we'll all be."

He turned away, leaving her alone with the distant sounds of the brawl that still raged in the pub.

Chapter Twenty-Eight

A frosty wind blew outside, every gust causing a draught in the room that made Ellie shiver. She wrapped her hands around her cup of weak tea, but it did little to warm her up.

Her meagre breakfast stood before her, untouched: a crust of bread with a scraping of dripping that had congealed in the cold morning air.

Across from her, Jack and Percy were finishing off their own breakfast, while Lucy sat by the window, already bent over her sewing work.

"That was delicious," Jack said as he used his finger to wipe off the last smears of dripping on his plate. Then, with evident satisfaction, he stuck his finger in his mouth and closed his eyes, to better savour the taste.

"Simple," he said after licking his finger clean. "But delicious nonetheless."

"It's nice to see people appreciating the simple things in life," Percy said with a sideways glance at Ellie's plate.

Jack looked at her untouched breakfast as well. "You should eat that," he smiled encouragingly. "Before the mice come and steal it right from under your nose."

"Bread's dear these days," Percy muttered. "Sixpence a loaf the bakers are charging now. Highway robbery, if you ask me." He leaned back, rubbing his leg. "But still, even in hard times like these, every mouth needs feeding, doesn't it?"

He didn't look at Ellie as he said it, but she knew what he meant. She was nothing but another mouth to feed. Another burden on their strained resources.

"I'm not very hungry this morning," Ellie replied by way of an apology, pushing the plate away slightly. "Perhaps later."

Lucy glanced up from her sewing, frowning. "Ellie, you really ought to–"

"Remarkable, isn't it?" Percy interrupted, his voice taking on a philosophical tone. "How quickly things change? One day you're eating exquisite food off fine china with silver forks, and then the next you're wondering if you'll eat at all."

He gave a dry chuckle. "But that's London for you. Brings us all down to the same level in the end."

"And that's why you and I have got business to attend to," Jack replied. He pushed himself away from the table and rose to his feet. "We should be off."

Percy nodded and stood up as well, wincing when he tried to put some of his weight on his bad leg.

"What sort of business?" Ellie asked. She dreaded the answer, but Jack's smile was quick and disarming.

"The profitable sort, with any luck," he said. "Might even bring back something nice for supper, if all goes well. Bit of mutton perhaps."

He winked at his sister. "Or who knows, one of those steak and kidney pies the ladies of this house like so much."

"We'd better buy some coal first," Percy said. "So we can finally afford to light a small fire and chase this blasted cold from my old, weary bones. Instead of splurging all our money on extravagant delicacies."

"We'll manage," Lucy intervened quietly. "We always do."

"Indeed, we do," Percy agreed, his tone softer when addressing Lucy. Slowly, he buttoned up his coat as his gaze drifted back to Ellie. "Although it seems to have become harder lately."

"Right then," Jack said, clapping his hands together. "We're off. Don't wait up for us if we're late though, ladies."

The door closed behind them with a dull thud, and then the room fell silent. Ellie remained motionless and alone by the table, while Lucy's needle resumed its busy rhythm.

"It's nice like this sometimes," Lucy said after a short while. "Just us two girls." She glanced up with a warm smile that didn't quite hide the worry in her eyes. "Though it would be nicer still if you'd eat your breakfast."

Ellie pushed her plate to the middle of the table. "I should come and help you with the sewing instead." She stood carefully, steadying herself against the table's edge. "Then at least I'd make myself useful."

"The sewing can wait." Lucy set aside her work. "Breakfast is important, too."

"I'm not hungry." The words came automatically, practiced from days of repeating them.

"You've been saying that rather a lot lately." Lucy paused to study Ellie's face. "And I don't think it's true."

"It's just the weather affecting my appetite," Ellie lied as she moved to join her friend by the window. "All this London fog. I don't think I'll ever get used to it."

"The weather? Ellie, you're barely eating enough to keep a sparrow alive."

"Don't fuss. Please." Ellie sank onto the chair she had brought over from the table, relieved to be sitting again. "This way, we'll save on bread. You heard what Percy said about the prices."

Her stomach chose that particular moment to betray her with a loud growl. Lucy's eyes narrowed at the sound.

"I'm worried about you," her friend said. "We all are."

"There's nothing to worry about. Honestly." But even as she said it, Ellie felt the gnawing hunger that had become her constant companion.

I fear you will learn that lesson soon enough.

Unbidden, Mrs Bennett's parting words resurfaced in Ellie's mind. Shaking her head, she pushed the thought away with the same determination she used to ignore her hunger.

She decided to take a few deep breaths, and instinctively, her hand went up to her chest, where it found Stuart's locket.

Perhaps...

Ellie unclasped the silver chain and looked at the locket she now held in her hand.

"Perhaps I ought to pawn this," she said. "It would feed us for weeks."

Lucy let out a horrified gasp. "Don't you dare. That locket stays right where it belongs: round your neck."

The fierceness in Lucy's voice took Ellie by surprise.

"But–"

"No, I won't hear of it. Some things aren't meant to be sold, no matter how hard times get."

Ellie nodded and opened the locket to look at the miniature portrait of Stuart inside.

'My heart is yours, always,' the inscription read.

Lucy was right, she thought. Pawning this would be nothing short of betrayal.

And yet...

She had betrayed so many of her principles already. What difference would one more make at this point?

"I'll make us some tea," Ellie said, trying to dispel the awkward moment. She put the locket down and pushed herself to her feet.

The room tilted sharply.

Black spots danced at the edges of her vision as she tried to take a step. She heard Lucy cry out, and felt hands trying to catch her. But her legs had turned to jelly beneath her.

"Ellie!"

She crashed to the floor, vaguely aware of dragging Lucy down with her.

When she opened her eyes again, slowly blinking in confusion, Lucy's worried face swam above her, blurring in and out of focus.

"Ellie, can you hear me?"

"I'm fine," she tried to say, but the words came out slurred and distant. "Just lost my balance."

The lie sounded weak even to her own ears.

"That's it." Lucy's voice had taken on a quiet steel that Ellie had never heard before. "We're going to St Mary's Mission right now."

"No, please." Ellie pushed herself up, her arms trembling with the effort. "I don't want them to see me like this."

"You're in desperate need of decent food, and you can barely stand." Lucy's arm slipped around her waist, supporting her with surprising strength for someone so slight. "I won't hear any more arguments from you."

Ellie started to protest, but Lucy's determination proved stronger. Together they struggled down the tenement stairs, Ellie clutching the bannister while Lucy steadied her from behind.

The journey to St Mary's passed in a fog of weakness and shame. Ellie leaned heavily against Lucy as they made their slow progress through Spitalfields' narrow streets. Each step required conscious effort, and on more than one occasion her legs threatened to buckle beneath her.

When Lucy pushed the mission's doors open, the rush of warm air that greeted them carried the smell of boiled vegetables and greasy mutton.

Inside, the hall was filled with the usual crowd: tired-looking women with crying babies, old men with hollow cheeks, and children watching hopefully as volunteers ladled out the stew.

Ellie remembered how proud she had once been to work here. And how virtuous she had felt for helping the poor. But now she stood on the other side of that invisible line.

It made her feel deeply ashamed of herself.

"Miss Dubois?" a startled voice asked. Ellie turned in the direction of the sound, and saw Mrs Collins hurrying over to them.

"Goodness me, it really is you," the older woman said. "I hardly recognised you. My poor child, you look terrible."

Gently, she took Ellie by the arm and led her to the front of the queue. "Come, we must feed you at once."

Mrs Collins got one of her volunteers to give her two generous bowls of stew: one for Ellie and one for Lucy.

"Because you look like you need it too, dear," she told Lucy. "Now sit down and eat, both of you. And if you want any more, you need only ask."

The two girls found seats at one of the long tables, sliding onto the wooden bench to sit side by side. Mrs Collins stood watching them from a short distance, her eyes brimming with pity. Then the matron shook her head sadly and returned to her duties.

Slowly, Ellie began to eat her stew. And with every careful spoonful, she felt a little bit of her old strength seeping back into her limbs.

"You can't go on like this," Lucy said. "Wasting away in the rookery, hardly eating anything, working yourself to exhaustion. And what for? To prove something to yourself?"

"I'm trying to help you," Ellie replied weakly.

"By destroying yourself in the process?" Lucy leaned in closer. "That's not helping, Ellie. That's pride."

"But your shop? Your dreams."

"They're meaningless to me if it's going to cost you your health. You need to go home, Ellie. Before it's too late."

"I can't," Ellie croaked, fighting the urge to cry. "Not after everything I've done, and all the rules I've broken."

"Nonsense. Your family will understand. They love you, don't they?"

Ellie nodded.

"Then they'll forgive you," Lucy said.

The mission doors creaked open, letting in a gust of chilly air. Ellie lifted her spoon for another mouthful of stew.

"But what if they don't?" she asked, not quite daring to believe forgiveness would come that easily.

"Ellie," a man called out from across the mission hall.

Her spoon clattered against her bowl. That voice. She knew that voice.

She turned, and there, by the doorway stood her beloved Stuart, his kind face lined with worry and relief. And beside him–

"Pierre?"

Her stepfather's expression was unreadable as he took in her worn dress, her pale face, the mission's humble surroundings.

Ellie gripped the edge of the table, unsure whether to run or faint. And no longer certain which would be worse.

Chapter Twenty-Nine

Stuart came rushing over. In an instant he was by Ellie's side, where he dropped to his knees and took her hands in his.

"Ellie," he sighed before planting a long kiss on the back of her hands. "Thank God." He said it as if all his prayers had finally been heard.

His eyes travelled over her face, taking in every detail: her gaunt cheeks, the dark shadows beneath her eyes, the pale colour of her skin.

"You're so thin," he whispered.

She could hear the pain in his voice and she tried to turn away from him, ashamed of her appearance and unable to bear the emotion in his eyes.

"Ellie, please look at me." Stuart's voice sounded soft, even though the slight tremor beneath his gentle words was plain to hear.

She turned back to him, but she found it impossible to hold his gaze. He was so pure, so innocent, compared to the despicable lows she had fallen to.

Her eyes darted nervously to her stepfather, who stood silently behind Stuart. "How did you find me?" she asked with an unsteady voice.

"We've been searching for you," Pierre answered, stepping closer. "Your mother is beside herself with worry. And Charlotte has locked herself up in her room, refusing all food, *la pauvre.*"

Hearing how her own poor choices had affected the people she loved most gave Ellie a painful jolt.

"The school wrote to us," Stuart explained. "They returned the letters I sent you, with a note saying you were no longer a student at the academy."

"Naturally, we travelled to London immediately," Pierre said. "We met with Mrs Bennett, and she told us everything."

Everything.

The word echoed tauntingly in Ellie's mind.

All her lies, her thefts, her disgraceful departure in the middle of the night. The shameful secrets she had tried to leave behind when she fled to Spitalfields.

"We talked to Phoebe as well," Stuart said. "She told us about your volunteer work here. So we decided that's where we needed to look first."

Ellie stared down at their joined hands: his strong and capable, hers thin and marked with tiny scars from her clumsy attempts at piecework.

"And now," she asked, "I suppose you'll want to drag me back to Sheffield? To punish me for my utter foolishness?"

She hated how bitter the words sounded, and how the hardness she had acquired clung to her voice like the grime of London's streets.

"We came to bring you home, yes," Pierre replied kindly. "Your mother has barely slept since we received word of your disappearance."

"But no one has said anything about punishment, my love," Stuart added.

"Why wouldn't you want to punish me?" Ellie shot back, more fiercely than she had intended. "I've done some truly terrible things after all. I don't deserve anyone's forgiveness. Or anyone's love."

"Calm down, *ma petite*," Pierre soothed, placing a tender hand on her shoulder. "You may have made some mistakes. But all we want now is to take you home again. Where you will be safe."

"And no matter what you think you've done wrong," Stuart said, "I will always love you, Ellie."

The gentleness in his voice nearly undid her. A single tear escaped, running down her cheek before she could stop it. Stuart reached up to brush it away, his fingers lingering against her skin.

"You don't understand," she whispered. "I'm not the same girl who left Sheffield."

"Wasn't that the whole idea behind your coming to London?" He smiled affectionately. "For you to change, and grow?"

She shook her head. "Not in this way. The things I've done... There's simply no excuse for them."

"Life is not always a straight path, Ellie," Pierre said. "We all wander from time to time. We think we are heading toward the light, when we are merely chasing shadows."

He glanced at Stuart, then back to Ellie. "The important thing is not that we stumble, but that we find our way back to those who love us."

"And we do love you, my darling angel," Stuart said. "So please, come home with us."

"They're right, Ellie." Lucy had kept silent throughout the reunion so far. But now she spoke up. "You need to go home with them."

"I can't just desert you like this," Ellie objected. "What sort of friend would I be if I did that?"

"A sensible one," Lucy replied firmly. "I never asked you to sacrifice yourself for me. I never wanted that."

"But I only–"

"No, please. Look at yourself, Ellie. You're half-starved. I've seen you grow weaker by the day. And that worries me more than you can imagine. Because this place? It takes everything eventually."

Ellie hesitated. She wanted to stay and fight. For Lucy and her dreams. But she knew she likely didn't have the strength for it any more.

"Believe me, your kindness won't be forgotten," Lucy said. "But your real life is with them." She nodded toward Stuart and Pierre. "Not here with me and Jack in this miserable hell."

Ellie looked from face to face. Stuart's eyes were pleading and full of devotion. Pierre stood watching her, patient and steady, like a tower of compassion.

Finally, she looked at Lucy. Dear Lucy, whose friendship might have been the only thing that had saved Ellie from complete collapse.

"All right," she whispered. "I'll go home."

The tension broke. Stuart smiled and pressed her hands against his lips. Pierre closed his eyes briefly and mouthed a silent word of thanks to the heavens. While Lucy merely gave a short nod before turning away and casting down her eyes.

"We have rooms at the Great Northern Hotel," Pierre said. "We can leave for Sheffield tomorrow, after you've had a proper night's rest."

Ellie tried to rise from the bench, but the blood seemed to drain from her head all at once. The room swam before her eyes, faces and shapes blurring into indistinct patches of colour.

"Steady there," Stuart said as he gripped her elbow to stop her from falling. "Are you all right?"

"Yes," she murmured. "Stood up too quickly, that's all. I just need a moment."

She closed her eyes, waiting for the dizziness to recede. Her hand touched her cold and damp forehead, and then she lowered it towards her chest that was rising and falling with shallow breaths.

But as she did so, her eyes snapped open instantly.

"My locket," she gasped. "I left it–" She turned to Lucy. "It's still in the room. I need to get it."

"I can fetch it for you," Lucy offered quickly. "There's no need for you to go back."

"No, I have to collect my other things as well." Ellie straightened her shoulders, trying to summon what little strength remained. "And I should say goodbye to Jack. I owe him that much."

Lucy's face clouded. "Jack isn't there. Out on business, remember? He might not be back until evening. Why don't I bring your things to the hotel later?"

Ellie looked at Stuart. *No*, she decided. She couldn't leave his locket behind in Spitalfields, not even for a little while. It simply didn't feel right.

"I'll come with you anyhow," she told Lucy. "It's only a short walk back."

"But–"

"Eleanor is probably right, *mademoiselle*," Pierre said. "It'll be quicker and more convenient if we all go together to collect her belongings. Saves you the trip to our hotel later."

"It's no bother," Lucy protested. "Really. I wouldn't want you gentlemen to get your clothes dirty by walking through the filthy streets of Spitalfields."

"Lucy," Ellie cut in. "Are you ashamed for them to see where you live?"

"It's not that. It's just–"

"They won't judge you," Ellie assured her. "Stuart and Pierre aren't like that. They understand what it means to work for a living."

Stuart nodded earnestly. "We've seen how people live in Sheffield's poorest quarters, Miss. We don't look down on anyone for circumstances beyond their control."

Lucy's hands twisted frantically in her apron.

"Please, Lucy," Ellie said. "I need to get my locket. And I want to say a proper goodbye. After everything we've been through together, I owe you and Jack that much."

For a long moment, Lucy stood frozen, her expression torn. Then her shoulders sagged in defeat.

"Very well," she conceded, though the reluctance was plain in her voice. "But we should go now, while it's still early. Before–" She stopped herself. "Before it gets too late."

Pierre gestured toward the door with a slight bow. "Let's be on our way then."

Stuart offered Ellie his arm for support, which she gratefully accepted as her legs still felt wobbly beneath her.

When she glanced at Lucy, Ellie noticed her friend biting her lip, a shadow of worry crossing her face. But the moment their eyes met, Lucy quickly masked it with a nervous smile.

Chapter Thirty

The walk back to their shared room seemed endless. Each cobblestone felt like a mountain to climb, each corner an impossible distance away. Ellie leaned heavily on Stuart's arm, grateful for his solid presence as her own strength continued to let her down.

"I can manage," she protested weakly when he adjusted his grip to support her better.

"I know you can," he replied gently. "But I'm here now, and I won't leave your side again. You can lean on me as much as you need."

Heat crept into her cheeks. This wasn't how she had imagined their reunion: her shuffling along like an invalid, with him practically carrying her through London's dirty streets.

She had left Sheffield as a proud and headstrong Northern girl. Now she would return as a mere shadow of her former self.

"I hate that you're seeing me like this," she said, so quietly that only he could hear.

Stuart glanced at her and smiled, "I'd rather see you like this than not see you at all."

Pierre walked ahead with Lucy, their conversation a distant murmur that Ellie could barely follow. She was too consumed by the struggle to keep moving forward, one step at a time.

"We can rest if you want to," Stuart offered when she stumbled slightly.

"No." She squared her shoulders, fighting against the weakness in her limbs. "We're almost there. I can manage a few more steps."

When they finally reached the tenement building, Ellie felt Stuart's slight hesitation as they entered the dim hallway with its damp walls and pervasive smell of human waste and mildew. The sudden tenseness in his arm told her he was trying hard not to betray how he felt about the squalor that was evident all around them.

The climb up the narrow stairs was the worst part. Twice she had to stop, leaning against the wall while spots danced before her eyes. Each time, Stuart waited patiently, his hand steady on her arm, never rushing her despite the obvious concern on his face.

By the time they reached the door to the room, Ellie was trembling with exhaustion.

Lucy had hurried ahead up the final flight. "Let me check for rats first," she called back over her shoulder. She quickly unlocked the door and peered inside before opening it fully.

"All clear," she announced with a sigh, ushering them in. "Jack's not back yet."

The room looked smaller somehow, with Stuart and Pierre's tall figures filling the cramped space. Ellie watched their faces as they took in the broken furniture, the cracked window stuffed with rags to keep out the draft, the makeshift sleeping corner separated from the rest of the room by nothing but a faded sheet.

Though they tried to hide it, she could see the shock in their eyes. Pierre's gaze lingered on the ceiling, where water stains marked the path of countless leaks. Stuart stared at the tiny fireplace, cold and empty despite the chill in the air.

A wave of shame washed over Ellie. This was the life she had chosen over the comfort and safety they offered: this squalid room with its rickety chairs and mouldy corners.

"I'll help you pack," Lucy said a little too brightly. "It'll be quicker with the two of us, and then you can be on your way. The sooner the better, right?"

Without further ado, she moved to the small pile of Ellie's remaining possessions, tucked away beside the patched blanket that had served as Ellie's bed.

As Lucy began gathering Ellie's meagre belongings, Stuart approached the spot by the window where Ellie had left her locket. It still lay there, the silver chain in a small heap, its shiny gleam looking out of place among the shabbiness of their quarters.

"I almost pawned it," Ellie confessed to Stuart as he picked it up and held it up in front of him. "We had so little and I–"

She sighed hopelessly and gestured at the room. "I thought I could help."

Stuart didn't say anything. He merely watched the locket as it slowly dangled and spun on its chain before his eyes.

"Lucy stopped me," Ellie went on. "She wouldn't let me sell it. She said some things shouldn't be sold, no matter how desperate the times."

"She was right," Stuart replied. Then he unclasped the delicate chain. "May I?"

Stepping behind her, he gently put the locket around her neck again. His fingers brushed against her skin as he fastened the clasp, sending a shiver down her spine.

"Back where it belongs," he whispered close to her ear.

She turned to face him, her hand closing around the locket. "After everything I've done, how can you still–"

"Because I know you," he interrupted, his voice steady and sure. "The girl who left Sheffield might have made mistakes, Ellie. But your heart was in the right place. It always has been. And always will be."

His simple faith in her goodness made tears spring to her eyes. She had no words to answer such grace, such forgiveness freely given when she had done nothing to earn it.

Behind them, Lucy was working frantically, stuffing Ellie's remaining clothes into her travel bag with uncharacteristic haste.

"You should all hurry," she said. "These streets aren't safe after it gets dark."

Pierre looked puzzled. "It's barely past midday, *mademoiselle*."

Lucy gave a nervous titter. "Yes, but the main roads will be so awfully busy later in the day. All those carts and hansoms. Much better to travel now while the streets are clearer."

She thrust the last of Ellie's belongings into the bag and fastened it with trembling fingers. "There. All packed." Her smile was brittle. "You should go straight to your hotel now. Rest properly. Doctor's orders."

"What doctor?" Ellie asked.

Lucy flushed. "Well, if there had been a doctor, that's what he would say, wouldn't he?" She moved toward the door, reaching for the handle. "Let's not dally."

A floorboard creaked on the landing outside, and Lucy froze. Her eyes darted to Pierre, then back to the door.

"Probably just Mrs Finlay," she said, her voice pitched slightly too high. "She's always poking about, that one."

The sound faded, and Lucy released a breath. "Let's get you on your way then. Mustn't linger too long."

"But I still need to say goodbye to Jack," Ellie objected, frowning at her friend's nervous behaviour.

"I think it's better if you don't wait." Lucy wiped down her hands on the front of her apron. "Jack will understand. He knows you belong with your family."

Stuart lifted Ellie's bag. "Are you ready?"

She nodded, taking a final look around the small room. Strange how a place so wretched could still tug at her heart. She had come with such grand intentions, only to discover how little she truly understood about the world.

"Let me carry that." Pierre took the bag from Stuart. "You focus on helping Ellie."

More footsteps sounded on the stairs, heavier this time. Lucy's face turned deathly pale. "You need to go," she whispered urgently. "Now."

But it was too late. The doorknob turned and Lucy backed away from the door as it swung open.

"You'll never believe our good fortune today," Jack announced cheerfully as he strode in. "We've managed to–"

He stopped short, his eyes darting between the unfamiliar faces in the room and Ellie's travel bag in Pierre's hand.

"Jack," Ellie smiled. "I'd like to introduce you to Stuart Wainwright, from Sheffield. And this is my stepfather, Pierre Dubois."

"Ah, the famous Stuart," Jack grinned before turning to Pierre. "And Mr Dubois, what a pleasant surprise."

"They've come to take me home, Jack. But I wanted to wait and say–"

"What a pleasant surprise indeed," a sneering voice interrupted from beyond the open doorway.

Percy Yates came limping into the room slowly, his cane tapping a deliberate rhythm against the warped floorboards.

"A family reunion," he smirked. "How lovely."

His gaze travelled over the assembled group and then came to rest on Pierre. Percy's thin lips curved upward, transforming his smile into something predatory.

"Hello, my old friend," he said. "So nice to see you again."

Chapter Thirty-One

The blood drained from Pierre's face, leaving it as pale as freshly fallen snow. "Percy?" Ellie's stepfather croaked. His voice sounded strange, as if it belonged to someone else. "*Mon Dieu*, I hardly recognised you."

"Not quite the man you remember, am I?" Percy sneered. "But then again, it has been a few years, hasn't it?"

Pierre gaped at Percy's hunched form. "You look... older. Much older than you should."

"Russian prison camps will do that to a man, I suppose." Percy flexed his shoulders before leaning on his cane again. "Not to mention a year at the mercy of Her Majesty's secret service. Quite the education, I must say."

He tilted his head, studying Pierre with an unsettling intensity. "But you, on the other hand, you seem to have landed on your feet. Bagged yourself a wealthy widow, I heard?"

The casual cruelty in his voice made Ellie flinch. She looked from Percy to her stepfather, struggling to make sense of this unexpected connection between them.

"You know each other?" she asked.

Percy's eyes gleamed with malicious delight. "Oh, we know each other very well indeed. Don't we, Pierre? Old friends, one might say."

Savouring the moment, his cynical gaze briefly flicked to Ellie before darting back to Pierre.

"Do you want to tell her, or shall I?" he grinned. "Or haven't you told your new family about your darkest secrets yet?"

Pierre straightened his shoulders, regaining some of his usual dignity. "Madeleine knows everything about my past. And Ellie is aware that I haven't always been an honest man."

"That's putting it rather mildly, wouldn't you say?" Percy let out a short, harsh laugh as he turned to Ellie. "Your stepfather was an experienced and clever swindler once, my dear. One of the best Paris has ever seen."

"As were you, Percy," Pierre replied evenly. "Though you preferred crueler methods."

Ellie's mind reeled, trying to absorb this revelation. Her stepfather and Percy had once been partners?

The kind and gentle man who had helped her mother to save the factory after her father's death: that same man had known this bitter, twisted creature?

Jack stood by the door, watching the exchange with a silent and gloomy expression. Lucy had backed away until she stood pressed against the wall, hugging herself tightly while her hands stroked up and down her arms.

"So you know each other from your time in France?" Ellie asked her stepfather.

Pierre nodded. "Before I met your mother, yes. Before I decided to change my ways."

"And Mr Yates?" she went on. "He was your... your partner in crime?"

Percy barked out a mocking laugh. "Business associates, yes. And our relationship was a very profitable one, too." His smile vanished. "Until we fell out with each other rather brutally."

Pierre finally set down Ellie's travel bag. "How did you come to be in London, Percy? I thought you were–"

"Rotting away in some faraway prison?" Percy finished, his voice dripping with bitterness. "Dying of fever in a Siberian wasteland? You would have loved that, wouldn't you?"

"Whatever hardships you suffered, you only have yourself to blame."

"Is that so?" Percy's face contorted into a mask of hatred. "After you helped that prissy Miss Lee turn me over to the authorities, my life became a living nightmare."

His knuckles whitened around the handle of his cane. "Thanks to your dirty little trick, British intelligence mistook me for a Russian spy. Now, who could have put that insane notion into their foolish heads, I wonder?"

"Not I," Pierre shrugged. "It was Inspector Woodcock who thought you might be the mysterious Russian agent he and his colleagues had been chasing for so long. Miss Lee and I, we simply decided to use that to our advantage."

"How convenient," Percy scoffed. "After Paris, they took me to some godforsaken castle in the English countryside. Kept me there for a year. No trial, no legal recourse. Only endless questions and interrogations."

Stuart moved closer to Ellie, his hand steadying her elbow as she trembled. The venom in Percy's voice seemed to chill the very air.

"And when they finally gave up, do you know what they did with me?" Percy's eyes burned with fury. "They shipped me off to Russia. Traded me away and handed me over to the Tsar's men without a second thought."

"But surely the Russians must have realised fairly quickly that you were not one of their agents?" Pierre asked.

"The Russians were just as confused as the British," Percy replied. "They couldn't decide if I was a British spy or a traitor to the Tsar. So they sent me to a penal colony in Siberia. Two years I spent in that frozen hell."

He took a limping step forward. "Have you ever seen a man's fingers turn black with frostbite, Pierre? Have you watched prisoners fight over scraps of bread like wild dogs? Because I have. I've seen it all."

"I am sorry to hear about your plight," Pierre said. "But your scheme had gone too far. You needed to be stopped."

"Save me your sympathy," Percy hissed. "You destroyed me."

"And yet here you are, alive and well," Pierre replied. "Did the Russians let you go, eventually?"

"No, I escaped." A gleam of pride broke through Percy's bitterness. "There was a blizzard that killed two of the guards. I walked for days through snow up to my knees. Nearly died of fever afterward."

He tapped his bad leg with his cane. "Lost the proper use of this one along the way."

"And so you came back to London," Pierre said, his voice neutral.

Percy gave a harsh laugh. "Where else was I to go? Paris had more or less soured on me, as you may well have guessed. London seemed the better option. Familiar territory, and full of gullible fools ready to be relieved of their money."

His gaze shifted to Ellie, and a slow, terrible smile spread across his face. "Then one day this bleeding-heart little do-gooder appears at St Mary's Mission. Some spoiled rich girl playing at charity."

His grin widened. "Imagine my delight when I discovered the silly little saviour of the poor was none other than Pierre Dubois' precious stepdaughter."

Ellie's stomach twisted into a knot. All those questions about her family. His particular interest in her stepfather's name.

"I couldn't sleep that night," Percy continued, his voice now almost dreamy. "Consumed by the possibilities. By the perfect justice of it all." He pointed a crooked finger at Pierre. "You took everything from me. My freedom. My health. My very life."

His eyes shone with madness. "So I decided to take something from you. I knew the stupid girl's disappearance would bring you running to London eventually."

"You used me," Ellie whispered, horrified. "All this time."

Percy's cold eyes found hers. "You were all too eager to be used, my dear. So desperate to prove your goodness by saving the poor unfortunates of Spitalfields."

He gave a mocking bow. "And I? I was more than happy to provide you with the opportunity to destroy yourself."

Pierre shook his head, his expression sad. "You're even more deranged than before, Percy," he said quietly. "Whatever happened to you was regrettable. But it doesn't justify this twisted game you've been playing."

"Game?" Percy's voice rose to a shrill pitch. "Is that what you think this is?"

"What I think," Pierre said while taking a cautious step forward, "is that you need help. This path you're on, it won't bring you peace."

Percy's face hardened. "I don't want peace. I don't want your help. And I don't want your pity either."

"Then what do you want?"

"Justice."

"Justice?" Pierre asked, his eyes never leaving Percy's face. "I wonder what that looks like to you."

"Oh, it's very simple, my dear old friend," Percy grinned. "You and I are going to have some fun."

He nodded once in Jack's direction.

A flicker of movement caught Ellie's eye as Jack lunged forward. His arm arced through the air, and with a sickening crack he swung a billy club against the back of Pierre's head.

Ellie's stepfather went down instantly, sprawling motionless on the floor.

"No," Ellie gasped.

Stuart threw himself at Jack. "Why, you wretched—"

Another swing, another horrible crack. Stuart staggered, his eyes rolling back into his head before he too collapsed.

Ellie's scream caught in her throat. She fell to her knees beside Stuart, trembling fingers searching for a pulse as Percy laughed above them.

"They're not dead, you silly girl," he said. "Although I can't promise you that won't change at some point later today."

Lucy stood frozen against the wall, her face ash-white with horror. "Jack," she whispered. "What have you done?"

Jack avoided his sister's eyes as he tucked the billy club into his belt. "What needed doing," he muttered. "You knew what was coming."

"Tie him up," Percy ordered, pointing to Pierre with his cane. "Securely, mind you. He's more resourceful than he looks."

Jack dragged one of the rickety chairs to the centre of the room and hauled Pierre's limp form onto it. With practiced efficiency, he began binding Pierre's wrists to the back of the chair.

"Stop it," Ellie pleaded, her voice breaking. "Please, whatever quarrel you have with my stepfather–"

"Quarrel?" Percy laughed. "My dear girl, this goes far beyond a mere quarrel. This is about retribution. Justice. The scales finally being balanced."

He gestured toward Stuart, who lay still on the floor beside Ellie, unconscious. "Take that one and the girl down to Murphy's shed in the courtyard. The old man won't be needing it any more, seeing as he died last week."

Jack finished binding Pierre to the chair and turned to Ellie. "Come on then," he said gruffly. "And don't argue."

"I'm not leaving him," Ellie said, her arms tightening around Stuart's shoulders. "I won't let you–"

Percy's cane slammed against the floor with a sharp crack. "This isn't a debate, my dear. Either you walk to the shed on your own two feet, or Jack drags you there. The choice is yours."

Chapter Thirty-Two

The shed door slammed shut with a bang. From outside came the harsh scrape of a key turning in a rusty lock, followed by Jack's retreating footsteps.

Darkness enveloped Ellie while Stuart's unconscious form lay beside her. Only a shimmer of daylight filtered through a few gaps between the weathered boards, casting thin lines across the dirt floor.

"Stuart?" Ellie whispered, her hands trembling as she touched his cheek. "Please, wake up."

The shed smelled of damp earth and rotting wood. Something scurried in the corner. A rat perhaps, disturbed by their sudden arrival.

Ellie ignored it, leaning closer to Stuart, desperately searching for signs of life in his pale face. A sticky wetness matted his hair where Jack's club had struck him.

"Stuart, please," she pleaded, her voice breaking as she pressed her ear to his chest. The steady thump of his heart gave her a moment's relief. But the gash on his head looked frighteningly severe in the dim light.

Ellie tore a strip from her petticoat. She folded it carefully and pressed it against Stuart's wound, trying to clean up the worst of it as tears blurred her vision.

"What have I done?" she whispered. "This is all my fault."

The walls seemed to close in around her as she thought of Pierre, bound to that chair upstairs. The vivid memory of Percy's vengeful eyes haunted her. But it had been her own foolish choices that had led everyone to this dreadful moment.

Gently she dabbed at the blood on Stuart's head, willing him to open his eyes. "Please, Stuart. I need you. I can't face this alone."

Her fingers brushed back his hair, when suddenly a soft groan escaped his lips.

"Stuart?"

His eyelids fluttered, then opened. Confusion clouded his gaze as he tried to focus on her face.

"Ellie?" His voice was hoarse.

"Yes, I'm here." She took his hand, squeezing it. "Don't try to move too quickly."

Stuart blinked several times, wincing as awareness brought pain. "What happened? Where are we?"

"In a shed. Jack knocked you unconscious." She wiped away the tear that rolled down her cheek. "And Pierre too. Percy has him upstairs."

Stuart struggled to sit up, hissing through clenched teeth as he touched the wound on his head. "I remember now." He glanced around the dingy space, taking in their prison. "We need to get out of here. Pierre–"

"I know." Ellie helped him into a sitting position, steadying him when he swayed. "But the door's locked."

Stuart's hand found hers in the gloom, fingers interlacing with a gentle pressure that sent warmth coursing through her veins.

Ellie felt a flicker of strength returning. Not enough to dispel her fear, but sufficient to hold back the crushing weight of despair.

"We'll find a way," Stuart murmured. "Together."

He tried to stand but immediately fell back, his face blanching with pain.

"Don't," Ellie urged. "You're hurt. You need to rest."

"Pierre doesn't have that luxury." Stuart's jaw tightened as he forced himself to his knees, gripping Ellie's shoulder for support. "We need to–"

A sharp rap on the door interrupted him. There was a narrow gap between two boards of the door, and Jack pressed his face to it, peering in at them.

"Don't bother trying to break out," he said. "The shed's more solid than it looks. And I've been told to do whatever's necessary if you cause trouble."

"Jack," Ellie moved toward the door. "Please don't do this. You know this is wrong."

There was a pause. Through the crack, she could see Jack's eye shift away.

"It doesn't matter what I think," he replied, the hard edge in his tone undermined by a slight tremor. "Percy has his score to settle, and I've no choice but to help him."

"There's always a choice," Stuart said, his voice steady despite his weakened state.

Jack's laugh was hollow. "Maybe for people who have plenty of options in life. Like you."

His eye appeared at the crack again. "Just keep quiet and stay put. It'll be easier for everyone."

"What's Percy going to do to my stepfather?" Ellie demanded. "Jack, please."

The silence stretched for so long that Ellie thought he might have left. Then his voice came again, softer this time.

"You shouldn't have brought them here, Ellie. You should have gone back to Sheffield when you had the chance."

"Jack–"

"Just be still," he interrupted, and now she could clearly hear the conflict in his voice. "Don't make me do something we'll both regret."

A sliver of daylight reappeared when Jack pulled his face away from the gap. His footsteps faded, leaving Ellie and Stuart alone once more in the dusty half-darkness, with only the distant sounds of Spitalfields as a reminder of the world beyond their prison.

Stuart struggled to his feet, using the rough wall for support.

"What are you doing?" Ellie asked, alarmed by the determined set of his jaw despite his obvious pain.

"Getting us out of here." His voice was tight with effort as he limped toward the door, examining its hinges and frame with careful fingers. "We can't just wait for whatever Percy has planned."

"You're hurt," Ellie protested. "You can barely stand."

Stuart ignored her concern, bracing himself against the wall before ramming his shoulder into the door with all his strength. The impact sent him staggering backward with a grunt of pain, but the door remained firmly in place.

"Stuart, please," Ellie begged as he prepared for another attempt. "You'll only injure yourself further."

"I have to try." He slammed against the door again, harder this time. The wood creaked but held fast. Stuart's face had gone deathly pale, sweat beading on his forehead.

"What do you think you're doing in there?" Jack's voice came sharp and angry. "Are you fools trying to break down that door?"

"Jack, please," Ellie began, but he cut her off.

"I warned you to keep quiet." His voice dropped lower, more threatening. "Do you want Percy to come down here himself? Because he will, and he won't be as patient as I am."

Wincing in pain, Stuart leaned against the wall and lowered himself to the floor. "If you're going to hurt us, then at least have the courage to look us in the eye when you do it."

There was a long pause. Then Jack's face appeared at the crack again.

"I've no intention of hurting either of you," he said. "But if you keep making noise, you'll have worse than me to deal with. The things Percy would do to you–"

"We demand to be released," Stuart said. "Along with Pierre."

Jack gave a short, bitter laugh. "That's not going to happen, I'm afraid. So unless you want to make things worse for everyone, I suggest you sit down and shut up. Or else..."

"Or else what?" Stuart challenged.

"Or else Percy might decide that keeping you alive isn't worth the trouble." Jack's voice hardened. "Don't test him. You've no idea what he's capable of."

Ellie squatted down by Stuart's side. "Hush now," she whispered while stroking his shoulder. "Let's save our strength. For Pierre's sake."

The murmur of another voice came drifting into the shed. It was soft and hesitant, but Ellie recognised it at once.

Lucy!

Ellie moved to the door and pressed her ear to the weathered wood. It sounded as if the two siblings were having an argument.

"I don't care what Percy said. This has gone too far, Jack."

"Keep your voice down," Jack hissed at his sister. "What do you think Percy will do if he hears you talking like this?"

"I can't just sit by while he–" Lucy's words dissolved into a choked whisper Ellie couldn't quite hear.

"This doesn't concern you, Lucy," Jack said. "Stay out of it."

"No. I want to speak with her."

A tense silence followed. A moment later, Lucy's face appeared at the crack in the door.

"Ellie?" she whispered. "Are you all right?"

Ellie's heart leapt at the sight of her friend's face. "Lucy, please, you have to help us. Percy is going to kill Pierre."

Lucy's eye darted away. "I'm so sorry," she said. "I didn't want any of this to happen."

"Then help us," Ellie pleaded. "Unlock the door."

"I can't." Lucy's voice broke. "Jack has the key, and even if I could... There's just no stopping Percy."

Behind Ellie, Stuart stirred, pushing himself up with visible effort. "Then go for help," he suggested. "Find a constable."

"And tell him what?" Lucy's voice turned bitter. "That my brother and I helped a criminal to kidnap innocent people? We'd be arrested alongside Percy."

"Lucy," Ellie said. "Whatever happens to you or Jack would be nothing compared to murder. Do you want to have that on your conscience? To be part of killing an innocent man?"

"You don't understand. Jack is all I have." Her voice was barely audible now. "If I betray him, I lose everything."

"And if you don't, you lose yourself," Ellie countered softly.

Lucy remained silent for a long moment. When she spoke again, there was shame and sorrow in her voice.

"I tried to keep you away, you know. And when your stepfather and Stuart found you at St Mary's, I tried to make you leave without coming here." A ragged breath escaped her. "I knew what Percy was planning, but Jack said no one would get hurt. He promised it was just about getting money from your stepfather."

"Money?" Stuart asked, coming to stand beside Ellie at the door.

"For what happened after that nasty business in Paris," Lucy explained. "Jack said Percy just wanted to be compensated for all the hardship he went through. I never thought–" Her voice faltered for a heartbeat. "I never imagined he was after a very different kind of revenge."

"But you knew enough to try to keep us away," Ellie said. There was no accusation in her tone, only sadness.

"Yes." Lucy's confession was a whisper. "But I was too much of a coward to stand up against Jack."

"Lucy, listen to me," Ellie said urgently. "I know you care about your brother. But this isn't about him any more, or about you. Or even about me. This is about an innocent man's life."

"I truly came to care for you, Ellie," Lucy said. "You're the first real friend I've ever had. When you brought us food, and when you listened to my dreams about the shop..." She trailed off. "I'm sorry I lied to you. About being sick that time. About so many things."

"None of that matters now," Ellie assured her. "What matters is what you choose to do next. Not for me, but for Pierre."

Lucy went silent, and Ellie could almost feel her friend's inner struggle.

"Pierre has done nothing to deserve this," Ellie continued, pressing her advantage. "He's made mistakes in his past, that's true. But haven't we all? If you let Percy hurt him, you'll never forgive yourself."

"He seemed like a nice man," Lucy said. "You care for him, don't you? Even though he's only your stepfather."

"Yes, I do," Ellie replied. "He came into our lives when my mother and I were at our lowest point after my father died. He helped us save the factory when everyone else had written it off as a lost cause."

She swallowed hard, as memories of the fire that nearly destroyed everything came back to her.

"Pierre never tried to replace my father. But he became family all the same."

"I wish I had a stepfather like that. But I never even knew my real dad. He died when I was a baby."

"Please, Lucy. I'm not asking this for myself. I'm asking for a man who deserves a chance to grow old with my mother. And to see the life Stuart and I will build together."

Even through the crack, Ellie could see Lucy was crying.

"Remember you told me that some things should never be sold?" Ellie said. "You were right. Some things are worth more than money."

"Like honour, you mean?" Lucy whispered. "Like doing what's right, even when it costs everything."

A sparkle of hope lit up in Ellie's chest.

"Yes," she said. "Exactly like that."

"That's enough talk," Jack's voice broke in, reminding Ellie that he had been there all along, hovering somewhere in the background. "Get away from the door, Lucy."

"This isn't right, Jack," Lucy replied, sounding stronger. "You know it isn't."

"Keep your voice down," Jack hissed.

"No," Lucy shot back. "I won't whisper about murder as if it's just another job. Percy means to kill him, doesn't he?"

Ellie and Stuart exchanged glances in the dimness. Stuart moved closer to the door, his face intent as he listened to the siblings argue just beyond the thick wooden barrier.

"What did you think was going to happen?" Jack's voice turned defensive. "Percy's obsessed with revenge. You've heard him talking about it."

"I thought he wanted money," Lucy insisted. "Not blood."

"It's too late now. We're in this too deep. If Percy gets arrested for murder, what do you think happens to us? We helped him. We'd hang right alongside him."

"And if we do nothing?" Lucy challenged. "If we just stand by while he tortures that man to death? What happens to us then, Jack? Not to our bodies, but to our souls?"

"Souls don't fill empty bellies, Lucy. They don't pay the rent."

"Are you willing to gamble with your soul now, Jack? Imagine Mother were here. Or our Nan – may the Lord bless them and keep them both. What would they say if they heard you talking like that?"

The heavy silence that followed told Ellie that Lucy's words had found their mark. She held her breath, afraid that even the slightest sound might break the spell Lucy appeared to have cast.

When Jack spoke again, his voice had changed, uncertainty replacing bravado.

"What would you have me do? It's too late to stop Percy."

"It's never too late to do what's right," Lucy answered. "Never."

Another long silence followed. Ellie pressed her ear closer to the door, straining to hear what was happening.

"Percy will kill us," Jack muttered.

"Perhaps," Lucy admitted. "But at least we'll die as honest people. Not as cruel monsters."

The yard beyond the shed fell quiet. Ellie glanced at Stuart, whose face showed the same anxious hope she felt.

Had Lucy's words reached her brother? Or had he simply walked away, unwilling to risk Percy's wrath?

The silence stretched until Ellie's nerves felt ready to snap.

Then, a key slid into the lock.

Chapter Thirty-Three

With a rusty groan the key turned in the lock. The shed door swung open, revealing Jack with Lucy standing by his side. Jack quickly lowered his eyes and stared at the ground in shame. But Lucy's face was streaked with tears.

For a moment, no one moved or spoke.

But as soon as Ellie stepped out of the shed, Lucy rushed forward with a strangled sob. She flung herself into Ellie's arms with such force that both girls nearly toppled backward.

"I'm so sorry," Lucy cried. "I should have warned you. I should have stopped this from the beginning."

Ellie held her friend tightly, speechless. Coming from Lucy, who always kept her emotions so tightly under control, this outpouring was like watching a dam break.

"It's all right," Ellie murmured. "You're helping us now. That's what matters."

Stuart had emerged from the shed as well. "Why the change of heart?" he asked Jack, his voice quiet but direct.

"This wasn't what I agreed to," Jack said. "Percy told me he wanted money from Ellie's stepfather. Compensation, he called it. For what happened in Paris. He never said anything about–" He paused and cleared his throat. "About hurting anyone. I didn't sign up for murder."

"But you knew he was using Ellie," Stuart said with a hint of anger. "You knew she was just bait to lure Pierre to London."

Jack didn't flinch from the accusation. "Yes. I knew."

Ellie released Lucy to stare at Jack. "Right from the start? Even when we first met?"

"Aye," Jack nodded. "When Percy caught your name at St Mary's, and heard that you were Pierre Dubois' stepdaughter... He couldn't believe his luck, could he? The perfect way to make your stepfather pay, delivered right into his hands."

"And you went along with it," Stuart said.

"Because Percy offered to share whatever he could squeeze out of Pierre. It would've been enough to get Lucy her shop. And for us to leave Spitalfields for good." He glanced at his sister. "But not like this. Never like this."

Lucy reached out to touch her brother's arm. "You did right in letting Ellie and Stuart go, Jack. I'm proud of you."

"Don't be too proud of me yet," he muttered. "We still need to deal with Percy. And he won't be pleased about this little rebellion of ours."

"We have to save Pierre," Ellie said. "Before it's too late."

Stuart nodded grimly. "I'll go up there right now."

"Not alone, you won't," Jack replied. "Percy may be an old cripple, but that doesn't make him harmless." He adjusted his cap with a determined tug. "I helped get Ellie's stepfather into this mess. I'll help get him out."

"I'm coming too," Ellie said.

"And me," Lucy added immediately.

"Absolutely not," Stuart objected. "It's too dangerous."

"Percy's unpredictable," Jack agreed. "No telling what he might do. He's mean and he's vicious."

Ellie shook her head stubbornly. "I want to talk to him first. Before anyone does anything rash." She laid a hand on Stuart's chest. "Let me try to reason with him."

"Reason?" Stuart replied. "With a madman bent on revenge?"

"Stuart's right, Ellie," Jack said. "Percy's past listening to sense. Has been for many years if you ask me."

"Maybe," Ellie conceded. "But I need to try."

"We don't have time to stand here arguing," Lucy said. "Every minute we waste puts Pierre in more danger."

Stuart and Jack exchanged frustrated glances.

"Fine," Stuart relented. "But you stay behind us." He stared into Ellie's eyes and took hold of her hand. "Promise me."

"I promise," she replied.

"There's something else you should know," Lucy said. "Percy's cane: it's not just for walking. There's a blade hidden inside."

"It's true," Jack said. "I've seen him draw it once, when a man tried to cheat him at cards. Fellow nearly lost an eye."

Stuart's jaw tightened. "Then we'll need to disarm him. Before he can use it."

Together, they entered the tenement building and went up the stairs. All Ellie could think about was her stepfather, alone with that twisted man lusting for blood.

Hold on just a little longer, Pierre, she prayed silently. *We're coming.*

When they reached the door to the room, Jack held up his hand, signalling them to wait. He pressed his ear against the wood, listening intently before nodding once.

"Ready?" he whispered.

Stuart positioned himself directly behind Jack, while Ellie and Lucy stood further back. Then Jack took a deep breath and pushed the door open.

Rushing into the room after the two young men, Ellie let out a short shriek when she saw Pierre.

Her stepfather sat bound to the chair, his head hanging forward, his elegant suit torn. Blood trickled from a cut on his cheek, and his left eye had begun to swell shut. Percy stood before him, cane in hand, ready to deliver another blow.

"Enough," Stuart ordered.

Percy whirled around, surprise registering on his face before transforming into a grotesque smile. "Ah, it would appear that the cavalry has arrived."

His eyes narrowed when he spotted Jack. "You disappoint me, lad. I thought we had an understanding."

"It's over, Percy," Jack replied. "Let him go."

"Over? My dear boy, nothing is over until I say it is." With surprising swiftness, he twisted the handle of his cane and pulled out a slender, gleaming blade.

Before anyone could react, he pressed the cold steel to Pierre's throat. "One false move," he threatened, "and the French frog bleeds to death right before your eyes."

"Don't be a fool," Stuart said. "There's four of us and only one of you. You don't stand a chance."

"Four of you?" Percy sneered. "Two half-starved girls and a pair of pups who think they're wolves? Against a man who survived the Siberian wastes?"

A single, mocking laugh escaped him. "You know nothing of real hardship. Nothing of what it means to fight when all hope is lost."

"Mr Yates, please," Ellie said, stepping forward. "This won't undo what happened to you."

"It might not," he admitted. "But justice demands balance, my dear. An eye for an eye. A life for a life."

"The life you lost wasn't Pierre's doing. It was your own choices that led you to being arrested."

"My choices?" Percy's voice rose sharply. "He betrayed me. Left me to rot while he built himself a new life with your mother's money."

"But hasn't there been enough suffering already?" she pleaded. "I've certainly seen plenty of it here in Spitalfields. And I think I understand now what drives people to desperate acts: hunger, hopelessness, the need to survive."

Something flickered in Percy's eyes, a momentary uncertainty.

"You survived the prison camps," Ellie continued, her voice gentle. "You escaped. You made your way back to England against impossible odds. That took courage, Mr Yates. Real courage."

She extended her hands, palms up, as if offering something precious. "Don't throw away that strength now. Not for revenge. Not when you could still build something better."

For a breathless moment, Percy's grip on the blade seemed to loosen. His gaze drifted from Ellie's face to her outstretched hand, then to Pierre.

"Something... better?" he whispered, his voice suddenly small, almost childlike.

Pierre, sensing the shift, spoke for the first time. "She's right, Percy. It is not too late to–"

"Shut up," Percy screamed. His face contorted with rage, making him look barely human. "You don't get to speak. Not after what you did to me."

Percy raised his blade, preparing to strike. "I'll silence you forever, you treacherous–"

Stuart lunged forward with unexpected speed, crashing into Percy's arm. The blade flew from the older man's grasp, clattering to the floor.

Jack rushed to help Stuart, and together they forced Percy away from Pierre, pinning him against the wall.

"The blade," Stuart shouted. "Get the blade."

Lucy darted forward and snatched up the fallen weapon, retreating quickly to the far corner of the room with it.

Ellie hurried over to Pierre, her fingers fumbling with the ropes that bound his wrists.

"Are you all right?" she asked, tears of relief flowing freely as she worked at the knots.

"Better now," Pierre replied, his voice hoarse. A strained smile crossed his battered face. "You came back for me, *ma petite*."

After the ropes gave way, Ellie helped her stepfather to his feet as he swayed unsteadily. She wrapped her arms around him, careful to avoid the worst of his injuries, and felt his gentle embrace in return.

"I was afraid I would never see you again," she whispered against his chest.

A sudden crash from across the room made Ellie turn.

Percy had broken free from Stuart and Jack's grip. With unexpected strength, he shoved Jack into Stuart, sending both men stumbling backward.

"This isn't over," Percy snarled, his eyes wild with hatred. He lunged for the door, his movements awkward without the support of his cane.

"Stop him," Stuart shouted.

But Percy was already through the doorway and onto the landing. He gripped the bannister, casting one final glance of pure venom back at the room.

"I'll have my revenge," he spat. "One way or another, I'll see you all suffer as I have suffered."

He turned to hurry down the stairs, but his bad leg buckled beneath him. For a terrible moment, Percy's arms flailed wildly as he tried to regain his balance.

Then he fell.

The sickening sound of his body tumbling down the steep staircase echoed through the building. A final, horrible crack ended his descent, followed by an eerie silence.

Jack was the first to reach the landing. He took the stairs two at a time, with Stuart close behind him. When they reached the bottom, Jack dropped to his knees beside Percy's crumpled form.

"Is he...?" Stuart's question hung in the air.

Jack gently turned Percy's head, then looked up with a solemn nod. "His neck's broken. He's gone."

A door creaked open across the landing. Mrs Finlay peered out at the scene, a threadbare shawl clutched around her bony shoulders.

"What's all this noise then?" she demanded, stepping closer to look at Percy's body. "Oh, it's him. Fell down the stairs, did he?"

She sniffed dismissively. "Good riddance, I say. Nasty piece of work, that one. Always creeping about, looking down his nose at decent folk."

She crossed herself perfunctorily. "May the Lord have mercy on his soul. Though I doubt whether even He has enough to spare for the likes of him."

By now, Ellie, Pierre, and Lucy had made their way down the stairs. Ellie's hand flew to her mouth at the sight of Percy's broken body.

"Such a waste," she whispered. "It didn't have to end this way."

Pierre leaned heavily against the wall. "Death is seldom fair or timely, *ma petite*."

"I know," Ellie replied. "But even after everything he did... I can't help thinking of how different things might have been for him. If life had been kinder. If he'd found forgiveness instead of nursing his hatred."

The others fell silent, struck by the compassion in her words.

"I hope his soul finds peace," she added quietly. "Wherever it may be now."

Pierre placed a gentle hand on her shoulder. "You're right. And I will see that he receives a proper burial. It is the least I can do for... an old acquaintance."

"You need to see a doctor first," Ellie insisted, eyeing his injuries with concern. "And Stuart too."

"Yes, we will return to our hotel," Pierre agreed. "The doctor can attend to us there."

He surveyed the small group gathered in the dim hallway, his gaze lingering on Jack and Lucy. Despite their part in his captivity, his expression held no malice.

"Perhaps you would both care to join us?" he suggested. "After such an ordeal, I believe we could all benefit from a decent meal and a warm place to rest."

"You'd sit and eat with us?" Jack asked in disbelief. "After what we did?"

Pierre's smile was tired but genuine. "In my experience, *mon ami*, holding onto grudges benefits no one." He glanced meaningfully at Percy's dead body. "As we have all just witnessed."

"We would be honoured to come with you, sir," Lucy replied hesitantly. "If you're certain, that is."

"I am," Pierre nodded. "Now, come. And let us leave this sad place behind us."

When they stepped out into the street, the late afternoon sun broke through London's perpetual haze. Ellie breathed deeply, filling her lungs with air that somehow seemed fresher, cleaner than before.

The darkness had lifted. It was time to go home.

Chapter Thirty-Four

"Well, blow me down," Jack said as they stepped into the grand lobby of the Great Northern Hotel. His wide eyes darted from the polished marble floors to the crystal chandeliers overhead.

"Never thought I'd set foot in a place like this. Feels like we've walked straight into some sort of bloomin' palace."

Lucy elbowed him sharply. "Mind your language," she whispered, though her own face betrayed equal wonder at the rich opulence surrounding them.

"Come along, you two," Ellie chuckled. "It's just a building where people come to eat and sleep, you know."

"Everyone's staring at us," Lucy mumbled, clutching her shawl a little tighter around her shoulders.

It was true. Several hotel guests had turned to look at their unusual party: Pierre leaning heavily on Stuart's arm, his elegant suit torn and bloodied; Stuart with dried blood still visible in his hair; and Jack and Lucy in their patched clothes, looking as misplaced as muddy work boots at a royal ball.

"Let them stare," Ellie said. "None of us have anything to be ashamed of."

Pierre approached the front desk with as much dignity as his battered appearance would allow. Despite his bruised face and torn clothing, he carried himself with the confidence of a man accustomed to such establishments.

The clerk's eyebrows rose slightly at their dishevelled group. But when he recognised Pierre, he quickly adopted a deferential tone.

"Welcome back, Mr Dubois. Will you be needing any help at all, sir?"

"Thank you," Pierre replied. "And yes, we shall require the services of a physician as soon as possible."

"Of course, sir. Right away."

He rang a small bell, summoning a young bellboy. "Please escort Mr Dubois and his party to their suite. And ask Jenkins to fetch Dr Howard immediately."

As they followed the bellboy up a sweeping staircase, Lucy whispered to Ellie, "I've never walked on carpet this thick before. It's like treading on clouds."

Jack remained silent, his hand brushing the leg of a statue that stood at the top of the stairs, as if testing whether it was real.

"Must cost a fortune to stay in a place like this," he said.

When they reached the suite, the bellboy threw open the double doors with a flourish. "Your rooms, sir."

Pierre handed a coin to the young man, who then departed with a bow. They had barely stepped over the threshold when a familiar voice boomed from within.

"Eleanor! Thank heavens you're safe."

Mrs Pemberton-Thorpe rose from a plush armchair by the window, her imposing figure silhouetted against the afternoon light. And beside her–

"Phoebe," Ellie cried out in joy.

The girl jumped to her feet with a little shriek of delight and came running over. "We were all so worried about you," she said, tears of relief and happiness streaming down her face.

"Good heavens, child," Mrs Pemberton-Thorpe remarked when she took in Ellie's appearance. "You look as if you've been dragged through a hedge backwards. And Pierre! Stuart! What on earth happened to you both?"

Pierre sank into the nearest chair. "It's been quite an eventful day, Constance."

"So I see." Mrs Pemberton-Thorpe's gaze shifted to Jack and Lucy. "And who might these two young people be?"

"Lucy and Jack Mortimer," Ellie said. "They saved our lives today."

Jack shifted uncomfortably under Mrs Pemberton-Thorpe's scrutiny. "I wouldn't quite put it that way, I should think."

"I absolutely would," Ellie insisted.

A knock at the door announced the arrival of the physician, a balding man with spectacles and grey whiskers. He wasted no time in attending to Pierre and Stuart, directing them to an adjoining bedroom where he could examine and treat their injuries.

Ellie sank onto a sofa with Phoebe, suddenly aware of how bone-tired she felt. But Lucy and Jack stood lingering by the door, gaping uncomfortably at their surroundings.

"Please, sit down," Ellie said, gesturing to a set of nearby chairs. "You must be exhausted too."

Jack scratched the back of his head, eyeing the pristine upholstery. "We're not exactly clean, Ellie."

"Nonsense," Mrs Pemberton-Thorpe said. "It's only furniture. Easily cleaned. Besides, any friends of Ellie's are welcome here."

Cautiously, the siblings perched on the edge of their seats.

"Now," Mrs Pemberton-Thorpe said, settling herself opposite Ellie. "Perhaps someone would care to explain why Pierre and Stuart look as though they've been in a street brawl? And why you, my dear, resemble a waif from the workhouse?"

Ellie swallowed hard. The entire story seemed too fantastic, too shameful to relate. But then the events of the past weeks all came pouring out in a confused rush.

Her first visit to St Mary's Mission, meeting Percy and the Mortimer siblings, her escalating thefts at the academy, ending in her expulsion and her foolish decision to live in Spitalfields.

As she described Percy's revenge plot and their harrowing escape, Phoebe's hand tightened around hers.

"And then Percy fell down the stairs," Ellie concluded. "He died instantly." She looked up at Mrs Pemberton-Thorpe, expecting to see judgement or disappointment on the older woman's face.

Instead, she found only compassion mingled with the widow's characteristic frankness.

"My oh my, what a tale," Mrs Pemberton-Thorpe said. "I know I told you to have some fun in London, but I didn't quite have life-threatening adventures in mind."

Then she chuckled. "Much more exciting than dance cards and music recitals though, I'm sure."

Leaning in closer, she patted Ellie's knee. "I'm relieved to see you safe, my dear. We were all beside ourselves with worry, when your mother received that letter from the academy."

"Is that why you came to London?" Ellie asked. "Because of me?"

"Naturally. When Madeleine and Pierre learned of your disappearance, it caused quite the uproar. Pierre and Stuart set off immediately, and I decided to accompany them. I thought that perhaps a woman's touch might be needed."

"And Phoebe," Ellie asked, turning to her friend. "Why are you here? Shouldn't you be at the academy?"

Mrs Pemberton-Thorpe sniffed disapprovingly. "After speaking to that Bennett woman, I decided on the spot to remove Phoebe from the academy. That place is not fit for any girl with a spark of spirit or intelligence."

"You should've seen Mrs Bennett's face," Phoebe giggled.

"I'm sorry, Phoebe," Ellie sighed. "Your father sent you to that school, and now I've ruined everything for you."

"Are you mad?" Phoebe said. "I'm positively over the moon to be out of that dreadful place. All those horrible girls constantly looking down their noses at us."

She pulled a haughty face, imitating the fancy airs some of the other students liked to put up.

"And those silly classes," she went on. "Earlier this week, Mrs Bennett made us balance a book on our heads while reciting from 'The

Matrimonial Companion: A Lady's Guide to Domestic Felicity and Wifely Devotion'. We looked absolutely ridiculous."

Jack let out a derisive snort. Phoebe glanced his way with curious interest, then looked back at Ellie with a meaningful nod toward the siblings.

"Of course," Ellie said. "Where are my manners? I haven't introduced you properly yet. Phoebe, please meet Jack and Lucy Mortimer. Lucy, Jack, this is my dearest friend, Phoebe Greenwood."

Phoebe smiled warmly at the siblings. "I'm pleased to finally meet you both in person. Ellie has told me so much about you."

"Can't have been very flattering things," Jack replied. "Considering what we put her through."

"On the contrary," Phoebe said. "She spoke very highly of you."

Jack looked down, clearly uncomfortable with the praise. "We've got a lot to apologise for," he mumbled.

"No more apologies," Ellie said. "I understand better now. I was a stranger from another world, barging into your lives with my foolish notions. Of course you were wary."

"Still doesn't excuse what we did," Lucy said softly.

"Perhaps not," Ellie conceded. "But I'd like to think we've become friends, despite it all." She smiled at the siblings. "Real friends, this time. Without any deceptions between us."

Lucy's eyes shone as she nodded. "I'd like that very much."

The door to one of the bedrooms opened, and Dr Howard emerged with Pierre, whose face was now cleaned and bandaged. Stuart followed right behind them.

"Nothing too serious," the doctor announced. "Rest and proper nutrition should see them fully recovered within a week or two." He packed his bag and departed with a polite bow.

"You heard the good doctor," Pierre smiled. "We need nourishment. We all do. That's why I've taken the liberty of ordering dinner to be served here in the suite."

Soon the hotel staff began to arrive, bearing covered silver trays that they arranged on a large table. Mouth-watering aromas of roast beef and fresh bread filled the air, making Ellie's stomach growl in anticipation.

Pierre gestured to the table. "Please, everyone. Be seated."

Jack hesitated, looking uncertain until Pierre personally guided him to a chair. "You've earned your place at this table, young man," he said. "No matter how complicated the journey that brought you here."

As they ate, the atmosphere grew warmer and cordial. Mrs Pemberton-Thorpe even took a real liking to the Mortimer siblings, especially after Lucy shyly mentioned her dream of opening a dressmaking shop.

"A respectable ambition," the older woman nodded approvingly. "The world always needs skilled seamstresses."

After dinner, the group began to disperse. And Ellie soon found herself alone with her stepfather by the fireplace.

"Thank you for coming to save me," she said. "I don't deserve such kindness after everything I did."

Pierre smiled. "I believe, *ma petite*, that it was you who saved me today."

"But if I hadn't run away in the first place–"

"Then Percy might never have found his peace." Pierre's eyes grew distant. "Death came for him, but perhaps it was a mercy. His soul was so consumed by hatred, there was little left of the man I once knew."

Ellie bit her lip nervously. "Do you think Mother will be very angry with me?"

"Your mother will be overjoyed to see you safe," Pierre assured her. "The rest can be sorted out in time."

A gentle knock interrupted them. Stuart stood in the doorway, with a serious face and blushing cheeks. "Mr Dubois," he said, "I was wondering if I might have a word with Ellie. Privately?"

Pierre's eyes twinkled as he rose from his chair. "But of course." He squeezed Ellie's shoulder as he passed. "I shall see you in the morning."

After her stepfather had left, Stuart crossed to where Ellie sat and took her hands in his. "Would you care to step onto the balcony with me? The night air is quite pleasant."

Heart suddenly racing, Ellie allowed him to lead her through the French doors to a small balcony overlooking the city. London spread before them, a sea of twinkling lights under a star-filled sky.

Stuart turned to face her, still holding her hands. In the soft glow from the room behind them, his face looked at ease, unburdened by the day's ordeal.

"It's beautiful," she murmured, leaning against the stone railing.

"Yes," Stuart agreed. But when she glanced at him, he wasn't looking at the view. His eyes were fixed on her face with such tenderness it made her blush.

"Ellie," he began. "Today I came close to losing you. Too close, in fact."

"Stuart—"

"Please, let me finish." He took a deep breath. "When I think of how differently things might have ended... But they didn't, thank heavens.

We're here, together. And I don't ever want to be parted from you again."

He reached into his pocket and withdrew a small velvet box. Opening it, he revealed a delicate golden ring adorned with a single pearl.

"Eleanor Dubois," he said, his voice steady despite his slightly trembling hands. "Will you do me the very great honour of becoming my wife?"

Tears spilled down Ellie's cheeks as she nodded, unable to speak. Stuart slipped the ring onto her finger, then gently wiped away her tears with his thumb.

"A pearl symbolises purity of heart," he said. "Something you've never lost, despite what you might think."

"Oh, Stuart," she finally managed.

"It's meant to complement the locket," he added. "My heart is yours, always."

"Always," she echoed, as his lips found hers in a kiss that sealed their devotion to one another.

Later that night, Ellie lay in her bed, listening to the gentle sounds of Phoebe's breathing from across the room. Her friend had been overjoyed at the news of the engagement, hugging Ellie so tightly she could barely breathe.

Now, Ellie's fingers played with the ring on her hand, still marvelling at the feel of it around her finger.

She thought of Jack and Lucy, of Percy Yates and his bitter end, and of Mrs Pemberton-Thorpe with her fierce yet compassionate personality. Each of them had taught her something, whether they had meant to or not.

Her eyelids grew heavy, the exhaustion of the day finally catching up with her. As she drifted off into sleep, Ellie felt a profound sense of peace settling over her.

Tomorrow they would go back home to Sheffield, to her mother and to good old Charlotte. But she would return changed, her heart fuller for having been broken and mended again.

And Stuart would be by her side, as her fiancé this time.

Slowly, and with a smile on her lips, Ellie fell asleep. The adventure that had begun with a reluctant journey to a London finishing school was ending with the promise of a new beginning. One that she would face not with fear, but with open arms and a happy heart.

Epilogue

Ellie stared out the carriage window, watching London's streets roll by. A year had passed since she'd left the city behind her, and now she returned as an entirely different person.

No longer Eleanor Dubois, it was Mrs Eleanor Wainwright now. The gold band on her finger caught the morning light as she adjusted her bonnet.

"Nervous?" Stuart asked, covering her hand with his.

"A little," she admitted. "It feels strange to be back. Like revisiting a dream."

Stuart squeezed her hand. "A rather turbulent dream, I should think."

"That's one way of putting it." Ellie laughed softly. "But it ended well, thankfully."

The carriage slowed, turning onto a modest but respectable street lined with neat storefronts. Nothing like the wretched alleyways of Spitalfields where she had once stayed with Lucy and Jack. This was a proper neighbourhood, where honest tradespeople earned their living.

"There it is," Stuart said, pointing to a freshly painted façade.

Ellie leaned forward and smiled when she saw the gleaming sign: 'Mortimer & Co. Fine Dressmaking'.

"It's perfect," she whispered proudly.

As the carriage came to a halt, the shop door flew open. Lucy emerged, her face radiant with happiness.

"You're here," she called out, rushing toward them.

Ellie barely had time to step down from the carriage before Lucy embraced her tightly.

"Look at you," Ellie said, holding her friend at arm's length.

Lucy twirled, showing off her dress: the same dove-grey gown with delicate lace trim that Ellie had given her all those months ago.

"You remembered," Ellie said.

"Of course I did." Lucy smoothed the fabric. "You gave it to me to wear on the day my shop opened. I've kept it safe all this time. Modified it here and there, to bring up to the latest fashion."

Stuart tipped his hat. "The shop looks impressive, Miss Mortimer."

"All thanks to your father-in-law and Mrs Pemberton-Thorpe," Lucy replied. "I'd still be doing piecework if not for them. Please, come inside. They've already arrived."

The shop's interior smelled of fresh paint and new fabric. Bolts of cotton, wool, and silk lined the walls in neat rows, their colours ranging from practical browns and navies to festive pinks and greens. A cutting table dominated the centre of the main room, while elegant mannequins displayed finished garments.

Mrs Pemberton-Thorpe stood near the window, directing a young maid who was arranging sweet pastries on a silver tray.

"No, no, no, girl. Not like that. The pink ones must alternate with the chocolate. We're not savages, for heaven's sake."

The imposing widow turned at the sound of the bell above the door. "Ah, Ellie and Stuart. At last. We were beginning to think your train had derailed."

"The traffic was dreadful," Stuart explained.

"It always is in this wretched city," Mrs Pemberton-Thorpe said, sweeping forward to embrace Ellie. "Though I must say, it has its charms. Particularly when one is investing in promising ventures."

Pierre emerged from a back room, a ledger tucked under his arm. His face brightened at the sight of his stepdaughter and son-in-law.

"*Ma petite.*" He kissed Ellie on both cheeks before shaking Stuart's hand vigorously. "The journey from Sheffield was comfortable, I hope?"

"Quite comfortable, thank you," Ellie replied. "But never mind that. How are things progressing here?"

Pierre and Mrs Pemberton-Thorpe exchanged satisfied glances.

"Remarkably well," Pierre said. "Our Miss Mortimer has a natural talent for business, it seems. Not just for needle and thread."

Lucy blushed under the praise. "I'm still learning. But we've already received commissions from several respectable families."

"Mostly for alterations thus far," Mrs Pemberton-Thorpe added. "But word is spreading. Quality workmanship always finds its audience."

The shop door flew open with a gust of wind, and Jack Mortimer strode in, his face flushed with excitement.

"Sorry I'm late," he announced, removing his cap. "Had to settle matters with Mr Marlowe."

Though still dressed modestly, Jack looked a world apart from the rough youth Ellie had known in Spitalfields. His clothes were clean and well-fitting, his hair neatly trimmed.

"And?" Lucy asked, her eyebrows raised expectantly.

Jack's face split into a wide grin. "It's settled. Next Saturday night. Opening act at the Alhambra."

Lucy squealed with delight and threw her arms around her brother's neck. "I knew it! I just knew it."

Ellie glanced at Stuart, puzzled by the exchange.

"Jack's been singing at some of the more respectable public houses," Lucy explained. "Building quite a name for himself in the process. And now the Alhambra Music Hall has engaged him to perform."

"That's wonderful news, Jack," Ellie said, genuinely pleased for him.

"Proper job, proper pay," Jack nodded, his eyes twinkling. "No more petty schemes for me. Turns out honest work suits me better."

The bell above the door chimed again, and everyone turned to see an elegantly dressed woman step inside. She glanced around curiously, clearly having arrived earlier than expected.

"Oh, I beg your pardon," she said, noting the gathering. "I saw the displays in the window and couldn't resist. But if you're not yet open..."

"Not at all," Lucy said quickly, stepping forward with professional composure. "You're most welcome. We're simply enjoying a small celebration before our official opening."

The woman smiled. "How lovely. I'm in need of a day dress, something suitable for garden parties. Your window display caught my eye. Such fine needlework."

"Thank you," Lucy replied. "I'd be happy to discuss designs with you. Perhaps you might like to view our pattern book?"

As Lucy guided the woman to a small table near the window, Ellie watched in amazement. Her friend moved with a newfound confidence, speaking knowledgeably about fabrics and fashions.

Jack sidled up beside Ellie. "Hard to believe she's the same girl who used to hide in the corner whenever strangers came around, isn't it?"

"She's flourishing," Ellie agreed.

"Come," Pierre said, gesturing toward a door at the back of the shop. "While Lucy attends to her first customer, let me show you the workroom."

They followed him into a bright space lined with shelves containing threads, ribbons, and various sewing supplies of every description. A large work table stood beneath a roof light, several half-finished garments draped across its surface.

"This is amazing," Ellie said. "I can see Lucy creating the most beautiful dresses here."

"And look here," Pierre added, opening another door. "A proper fitting room."

Ellie stepped into the small but elegant space, complete with a tall cheval mirror and a comfortable chair for waiting customers.

"It's perfect," she said. "Everything Lucy ever dreamed of."

"Not everything," Lucy said from the doorway. "Not yet. But it's a start."

Having settled her customer with some tea and pattern books, Lucy joined them.

"I have something special to show you," she told Ellie, retrieving a leather-bound book from a drawer. "I've been working on wedding gown designs, inspired by yours."

Ellie took the book, leafing through pages of exquisite sketches. "Lucy, these are beautiful."

"One day, I hope Mortimer & Co. will be known for our bridal creations," Lucy said, her eyes shining with ambition. "But that's for the future. First, we must establish ourselves with everyday dressmaking."

"A wise approach," Pierre nodded approvingly. "I was just discussing this with Constance. If the first six months prove successful, we might consider expanding."

"In business matters, as in life, one must strike while the iron is hot," Mrs Pemberton-Thorpe said.

Jack reappeared at the door. "Nearly eleven o'clock. Shouldn't we be preparing for the ribbon-cutting?"

Lucy's eyes widened. "Goodness, is it that time already? There's still so much to arrange."

"Everything is in order," Mrs Pemberton-Thorpe assured her. "The refreshments are laid out, the shop looks immaculate, and your first customer is already happily browsing patterns. What more could one ask for?"

Outside, a small crowd had begun to gather: neighbours, local shopkeepers, and a few curious passers-by attracted by the festive atmosphere.

Lucy stood in the doorway, pink-cheeked with excitement, as Pierre handed her a pair of scissors.

"Would you care to do the honours, Miss Mortimer?" he asked formally.

With trembling hands, Lucy took the scissors. A blue ribbon had been stretched across the doorway, held at either end by Jack and Stuart.

"I never thought this day would come," she said nervously. "There were times when it seemed impossible."

"Nothing is impossible," Jack replied. "Not when you have the courage to follow your dream, against all odds."

He looked out at the gathered crowd. "My sister started with nothing but her needle and her talent. Making do with scraps in a cold tenement room, working until her fingers bled sometimes."

His voice boomed with pride. "And now look at her: Miss Lucy Mortimer of Mortimer & Co. Fine Dressmaking."

A murmur of approval ran through the small crowd. Lucy blinked back tears as she raised the scissors.

"To new beginnings," she said, and cut the ribbon with a decisive snip.

Applause broke out as the shop officially opened its doors. People streamed in, eager to view the displays and sample the refreshments.

"Are you happy?" Ellie asked Lucy when the two of them had found a rare quiet moment.

Lucy's gaze swept over the busy shop: Mrs Pemberton-Thorpe charming potential customers, Pierre discussing business with a local banker, Jack entertaining a group of ladies with his easy wit and charm.

"More than I ever imagined possible," she replied. "But also terrified. What if I fail? What if I can't live up to everyone's expectations?"

"You won't fail," Ellie said firmly. "You're too talented, too determined."

Lucy squeezed Ellie's hand. "I would never have found the courage without you. Even when things went wrong, when we both made mistakes, you showed me that dreams could be more than just dreams."

"You must promise to write," Ellie said. "And when the shop is running smoothly, you must come visit us in Sheffield."

"I promise," Lucy replied. "Though I doubt I'll have much time for travel in the coming months. There's so much to learn, so much to do."

All too soon, it was time for Ellie and Stuart to depart. Their train back to Sheffield wouldn't wait, and Pierre had business meetings to attend later in the afternoon.

Goodbyes were exchanged with warm embraces and promises of future visits. Just before Ellie climbed into the waiting carriage, Lucy pressed a small package into her hands.

"A gift," she explained. "Nothing grand. Just a handkerchief I embroidered."

"I'll treasure it," Ellie said, blinking back tears while she embraced her friend one last time.

From the carriage window, Ellie and Stuart waved as the horse pulled away from the curb. Lucy stood in the doorway of her shop, Jack beside her, both waving back until the carriage turned the corner.

Ellie settled back against the seat, still clutching Lucy's gift.

"Happy, my darling?" Stuart asked.

"Very," she replied, resting her head against him. "It's strange to think that a journey that began so badly could end so wonderfully well."

"I wouldn't say it's an ending at all," Stuart mused. "More of a beginning."

Ellie smiled, watching London's streets give way to broader avenues as they headed toward the railway station and home. Yes, she thought. Not an ending, but a beginning. For all of them.

The handkerchief in her hands bore Lucy's initials and a single embroidered phrase: *'Dreams, stitched with courage'*.

Indeed, Ellie reflected as the carriage bowled onward. Dreams and courage: the two threads that had woven their lives together in patterns none of them could have predicted.

And who knew what designs still lay ahead, waiting to be revealed?

The End

Continue reading...

You have just read Book 5 of The Victorian Orphans Saga. Other titles in this series include:

Book 1 ~ The Courtesan's Maid
Book 2 ~ The Ragged Slum Princess
Book 3 ~ An English Governess in Paris
Book 4 ~ The Young Widow's Courage

Coming soon:
Book 6 ~ The Dressmaker's Dream

*For more details, updates,
and to claim your free book,
please visit Hope's website:*

www.hopedawson.com

Printed in Great Britain
by Amazon